Sugar Spinelli's
Little Instruction Book

Now, this **Rex Trowbridge** is a slick one! He's turned out real elegant, real lawyer-like! Sits on the board of directors for the ranch, drives a big ol' fancy car.... But I wouldn't be one bit surprised if he hasn't cooked up something with little Lindsay Duncan. If those two aren't in cahoots, I'll eat my shirt! She's biddin' on him now—I knew it! Those two are up to something, for sure! Of course, they've known each other for close to twenty years. Old friends, Lindsay always says. Hah! That look in Rex's eye when he glances her way is *not* friendship....

Dear Reader,

We just knew you wouldn't want to miss the news event that has all of Wyoming abuzz! There's a herd of eligible bachelors on their way to Lightning Creek—and they're all for sale!

Cowboy, park ranger, rancher, P.I.—they all grew up at Lost Springs Ranch, and every one of these mavericks has his price, so long as the money's going to help keep Lost Springs afloat.

The auction is about to begin! Young and old, every woman in the state wants in on the action, so pony up some cash and join the fun. The man of your dreams might just be up for grabs!

Marsha Zinberg
Editorial Coordinator, HEART OF THE WEST

Best Man in Wyoming
Margot Dalton

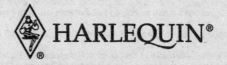

TORONTO • NEW YORK • LONDON
AMSTERDAM • PARIS • SYDNEY • HAMBURG
STOCKHOLM • ATHENS • TOKYO • MILAN • MADRID
PRAGUE • WARSAW • BUDAPEST • AUCKLAND

Margot Dalton is acknowledged as the author
of this work.

ISBN 0-373-82596-X

BEST MAN IN WYOMING

Visit us at www.romance.net

Printed in U.S.A.

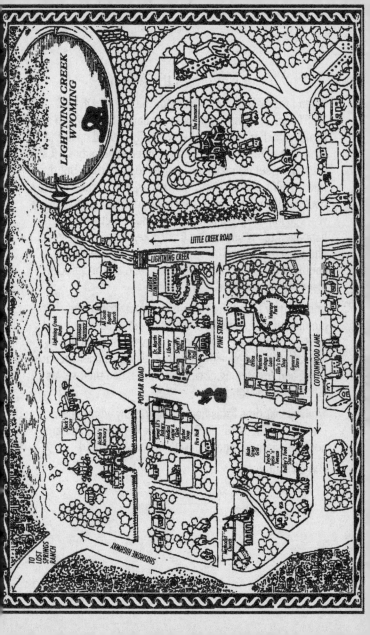

A Note from the Author

When I was asked to do a book for the HEART OF THE WEST series, I must confess to hesitating for a couple of heartbeats. For one thing, I was heavily booked up at the time with other projects. Also, a limited continuity series presents a set of unique challenges to any writer. But then I heard a little more about the stories, and learned that my book was going to involve childhood friends who take many years to fall deeply in love. Since this is exactly what happened to my husband and me, I began to get intrigued. And I discovered the series is set on a boys' ranch in southern Wyoming, one of the most wild and magnificent places in all the world.

Immediately I began to picture a camping trip in the mountains with some boys from the ranch, an outing that goes terribly wrong. I imagined a couple who go along to look after the boys—longtime friends who, under the most trying and frightening of circumstances, find themselves falling passionately in love.

Well, by that time I was hooked, just as my editor knew I would be. The result is *Best Man in Wyoming*. I sincerely hope you have as much fun with this story as I did.

Margot Dalton

For Marsha Zinberg—who's more fun to work with
than anyone I've ever met!

CHAPTER ONE

REX TROWBRIDGE'S new car was a Cadillac sedan, gun-metal gray with a black leather interior and every option he could think of. The big sleek vehicle was satisfying to him in a deep, almost visceral way. Not only did this new car announce his hard-won success with its quiet luxury and power, the Caddy also set him apart from most of his peers, who drove pretentious sport-utility vehicles.

Privately Rex was amused by these fellow lawyers and the doctors and accountants with their costly four-by-fours.

Sheer hypocrisy, he told himself.

All of them were trying to look like rugged outdoorsmen, when the truth was, they were too busy making money to take a vehicle off-road for any reason.

His new car announced its owner simply as a hard-hitting successful man who lived for his job and didn't pretend to be anything he wasn't.

Rex enjoyed the solid thunk of the door, the sparkle of setting sun on chrome and glass as he parked near the show ring at the Lost Springs Ranch for Boys, got out and ad-justed his dark glasses, then looked around.

The ranch was holding a bachelor auction fund-raiser and the place thronged with people. Booths and exhibits were set up in the yard, selling everything from lemonade to homemade quilts. It looked more like a county fair than a bachelor auction.

Not that he knew how such a bizarre event was supposed to look, Rex thought, checking out his immaculate white shirtfront, the black onyx studs, gray silk cummerbund and crisp tuxedo trousers.

Rex knew the monkey suit looked good on him. The two seamstresses who'd done the alterations had practically gone into raptures over the fit on his tall frame with its broad shoulders and lean waist.

Still, he felt deeply uncomfortable. In fact, he wished the whole event were over with.

Or better yet, he wished Lindsay could just have left him out of it altogether. But that was probably too much to ask, once his busy little friend got an idea in her head.... Besides, as owner of the ranch for troubled youths, she had a lot at stake here today.

He made his way to the arena and found a seat on the stage next to a tall, dark-haired man in the dress uniform of a U.S. Marine.

"Nick!" he said, doing a double take when he recognized the man's handsome features. "What brings you here? I thought you were out keeping the world safe for the rest of us."

Grinning, Nick Petrocelli shifted in his chair, stretching his long legs in the blue dress trousers. "I was supposed to be here for a little R and R," he said wryly.

Rex grinned and punched his friend lightly on the arm. "Lindsay got to you, too?" he asked.

Petrocelli nodded. "That cousin of mine could talk the birds down from the trees. But I can't believe I'm doing this."

"Why *are* you doing it?" Rex asked, puzzled. "You weren't in the catalog, were you?"

Nick shook his well-barbered head. "No, I was spared that embarrassment, at least. Lindsay was so excited about the response to this whole ridiculous idea, she bullied a few more of the guys into going along with it. I got tagged because I was out here for a visit. She even had this old uniform stored away in a closet, so she made me wear it.''

"Hey, you look great,'' Rex said. "With any luck at all, you'll be scooped up by some military groupie who wants to spend a weekend playing paintball in the woods.''

Nick lifted a dark brow. "You're awfully chipper for a penguin.''

Rex smiled amiably and watched as Lindsay rushed past in a bright-red dress, holding a clipboard and looking harried. Her short blond hair stood out around her head in a rumpled halo of curls and her pretty face was drawn with fatigue, contrasting sharply with the brightness of her outfit.

"She may be excited about all this,'' he told Nick, "but it's still been damned hard on her, getting it organized.''

"She's got a huge emotional investment in the whole thing. She can hardly eat or sleep, worrying about what's going to happen if it doesn't all work out the way she's hoping.''

Rex felt a jolt of sympathy as he watched Lindsay moving through the crowd. With her slim erect figure and the bright crown of hair, she looked like a glowing red candle.

Abruptly he turned aside and leafed through the auction catalog he'd been sent, searching for his own page.

A man stared back at him from within the glossy brochure, looking suave and relaxed in tux and horn-rimmed glasses, holding a file folder. His sandy hair was smoothly combed and the blue eyes were level and unrevealing, though his mouth lifted on one side in a crooked, sardonic grin.

Rex always found it strange and a little unsettling to look at photographs of himself. This man on paper in front of him, the face he showed the world were so utterly different from the real person who was never revealed to anybody.

It was like examining a picture of some handsome stranger.

"Rex Trowbridge," the idiotic text read. "A man who's terrific in briefs…and not just legal briefs! Rex is thirty-three years old and came to Lost Springs Ranch when he was twelve. He attended UCLA, where he obtained a law degree with distinction. Rex is now a junior partner with a Casper, Wyoming law firm and enjoys gourmet cooking, classical music and collecting first editions of nineteenth century English literature. Any gal with a taste for the finer things would dearly love a dream date with this luscious lawyer."

Nick was reading over his shoulder. "Luscious lawyer," he snorted. "God, that's rich."

"Lindsay's copywriters got a little carried away with this thing," Rex agreed. "Just be damn glad you aren't included."

He settled back in the chair, looking around at the familiar faces of his old schoolmates waiting to be auctioned off, while Nick watched the excited crowd of women, many of whom were turning surreptitiously to study him.

"All the ladies are attracted by your uniform," Rex told his companion. "God knows what kind of date you're going to wind up with."

Nick looked increasingly amused. "So what about you?" he said at last. "You don't seem very worried about all this."

"I'm not worried." Rex leaned back comfortably.

"Why not?"

"Don't tell anybody, but Lindsay and I have an understanding," Rex murmured, knowing that Nick Petrocelli was the most discreet guy in the world.

"What kind of an understanding?"

"She's going to buy me," Rex said, "and I'll reimburse her for whatever she has to pay. That way the ranch will get the money but I won't have to go on some ridiculous date."

Nick grinned. "You lucky dog. If I'd known she was open to bargains, I'd have done something like that myself."

"I doubt if she would have agreed to anything at this point."

"Yeah? So how did you manage to work out your deal with her?"

Rex shrugged. "Way back at the beginning when we first came up with the auction idea, Lindsay said she needed to have me in the catalog so she could talk the other guys into it. I told her those were my terms, take it or leave it."

"You always were a coldhearted son of a bitch," Nick said with grudging admiration. "No wonder Lindsay says you have ice water in your veins."

"She said that?" Rex asked. "When?"

But the bidding had commenced. The auctioneer's raucous patter rang out over the crowd as poor Rob Carter stood on the stage, looking for all the world like a steer being led to slaughter. A whole group of women seemed to be bidding on him, and the atmosphere in the building was growing increasingly frenzied.

Rex raised his eyebrows, astonished by the sum of money they'd already reached. This plan was apparently going to succeed beyond Lindsay's wildest dreams.

He glanced around the arena in search of her slim red figure, hoping to catch her eye and see if she'd smile at him.

Nobody else in the world had a smile like Lindsay Duncan's. Her mouth lifted at the corners, dimples flashed in her cheeks and her whole face shone with a luminous, childlike glow.

But the trim red-clad figure was nowhere to be seen. Rex craned his neck and scanned the crowd again, feeling a touch of alarm.

What if she didn't make it back in time to bid on him as they'd planned?

The thought of going on an enforced date with a stranger, having his neat, well-ordered life invaded by some woman he didn't even know, was totally repugnant to him. Rex was hugely relieved when a fat woman moved nearer the auction ring, and behind her he saw Lindsay seated on the bleachers.

She seemed a little more relaxed as the auction proceeded, and was chatting with her uncle, Sam Duncan, who looked lean and handsome in his western suit, string tie and pearl-gray Stetson.

Rex watched her surreptitiously, feeling that same troubling warmth the sight of her always aroused in him. She looked so pale and fragile, still tense enough that he wanted to take her in his arms and shield her from worry and harm.

"Something's wrong with her these days," Nick said at his elbow, following Rex's glance. "I noticed it right away."

Rex considered Petrocelli's words, still watching her. "You mean something more than all this worry over the ranch and its finances?"

"She's just not the happy-go-lucky girl she used to be." Nick's expression lightened for a moment. "Hey Rex, do you remember how much fun we had when we were kids?"

"I'll never forget those days," Rex said. "What do you think might be wrong?" he added, watching Lindsay's pale face.

Nick shrugged, his smile fading. "She won't talk about it. Keeps saying she's just fine. I assumed she had some kind of unhappy love affair."

Rex's jaw tensed. He hated to think of Lindsay having any kind of love affair, if the truth was known. But the idea of some jerk being cruel to her was more than he could bear.

He was still troubled when the cadence of the auctioneer's voice suddenly shifted. The crowd turned to look at him expectantly, and Petrocelli gave him a merciless grin.

"Well, off to the wars, old buddy," the Marine told him. "Knock 'em dead."

TO A CASUAL onlooker, Rex Trowbridge probably appeared suave and comfortable, even arrogant, as he paraded around and played to the crowd, aping the controlled swish and stiff-legged gait of male fashion models.

But in his heart, Rex was deeply, painfully uncomfortable.

Ever since the dreadful events of his early boyhood, he'd hated this feeling of being judged and weighed on outward merit alone. More than anything, he craved someone who could look into his soul, beyond the kind of easy confidence he showed the world, and take the time to understand what he was truly like.

Unfortunately, everybody in his life seemed content with the image. Rex Trowbridge looked and acted like their idea of a successful, high-powered lawyer, and that was enough for them.

But it hadn't always been this way.

For a while in their late teens, after they grew past the rough-and-tumble stage of their childhood, Rex had been certain Lindsay could see further into him than most people. He recalled her tenderness and warmth, her gentle probing questions, and that long-ago blissful feeling of being completely understood.

To his astonishment he felt a lump in his throat, even a brief mist of tears in his eyes.

Probably the glare of the hot sun overhead, he thought, blinking rapidly as he stared up past the top row of seats.

Besides, that gentle time with Lindsay had passed soon enough. He'd gone away to college in California and got wholly caught up in sports and the chase for academic distinction. By the time he came back, she could barely give him the time of day.

Whenever Rex called she seemed to be busy, until finally he'd gotten the hint and stopped calling altogether...

Resolutely, he shoved the memories out of his mind and concentrated on the auctioneer's patter, wondering if anybody was bidding against Lindsay.

To his alarm, he suddenly realized Lindsay wasn't bidding at all. She was just sitting next to her uncle Sam, tapping an auction brochure against her cheek with a thoughtful, bemused expression while two other women fought to purchase him.

Rex scanned the crowd and felt a rising panic. One of the bidders was Angelique Parrish, and she looked even more elegant than usual in some kind of white cape and broad-brimmed hat.

Three years ago Rex had handled Angelique's divorce and made sure she got a ton of money out of poor Buddy Parrish, her genial but unfaithful ex-husband.

As a result of the huge settlement, Buddy's contracting business had failed and the last Rex heard of him he was in Denver, working with a framing crew and trying to start over.

Rex had always felt guilty about that case. Angie had been so greedy, and both she and her lawyer made a fat meal off Buddy's broken dreams.

Near the end of the proceedings Angie had indicated to Rex a few times that she might be interested in more than his legal expertise, but he'd sidestepped her advances carefully.

Now she was back, and it looked as if she'd spent a good bit of Buddy's money on liposuction and plastic surgery. Her newly smoothed mask of a face seemed intent on acquiring Rex Trowbridge's services for, in the auctioneer's words, "whatever y'all want, ladies. A happy weekend of fun and frolic as unlimited as your little ol' imagination can devise...."

His panic deepened. Rex glared passionately at Lindsay, willing her to bid, but she gave him another of those sweet vacant smiles, then turned away to whisper something to Sam.

The other party bidding on him seemed to be a group effort. He recognized three grim-looking young women from Lightning Creek, all of whom, according to Sam Duncan's unfailing grapevine, were rumored to be having marital difficulties.

So this was a business arrangement, Rex surmised. The women figured they could buy a lawyer for a weekend, pump him for his legal knowledge and split the costs among the three of them.

Not such a bad idea. Rex brightened a little. In essence it was the same thing as donating his legal services or fees directly to the ranch.

But then he remembered the law firm in Casper where he'd just been named partner, and how they frowned on any kind of non-fee-paying clients or quid pro quo legal work.

"Absolutely no way," the senior partner had stated at Rex's orientation meeting, "do we want to open ourselves to any sleazy charge of professional misconduct, tax evasion or mail fraud. If you tie a shoelace for somebody, Rex, then you're gonna bill it and charge it as a legal service. No freebies for your old Auntie Elma, and no legal advice for your dentist in exchange for a root canal. You got all that?"

"Yes," Rex had assured his boss. "Believe me, I've got it."

So if those three women intended to buy his time with

the hope of spending a weekend exploiting his legal knowledge, they were going to be sorely disappointed.

Angelique raised the bid aggressively. Two red spots burned in her pale cheeks.

Again Rex cast an urgent, furious glance at Lindsay. She gave him the smile of maddening innocence that he remembered from childhood, a bright, teasing look that said she knew exactly how much he was suffering but had no intention of helping him.

Rex fought the urge to stride across the ring and shake her. Lindsay beamed up at him, her blue eyes sparkling with laughter. At last she relented and entered a languid bid just a few dollars higher than Angelique's, electrifying the crowd.

With the arrival of this new bidder, the three young wives soon dropped out, looking disappointed. Bidding continued between Lindsay and Angie, but the older woman finally gave up as well, waving her hand with a gesture of disgust. She gathered her huge leather bag, tossed her brochure on the floor and went stalking out, her white cape quivering with indignation.

It was over. Rex escaped the showring and made way for Nick Petrocelli, whose uniform and rigid military bearing created a fresh stir of interest. Nick was already being bid up aggressively by a middle-aged woman sitting with some stern-looking matriarch.

Nick would probably have to spend a weekend cleaning gutters and raking leaves at these rich women's country homes, Rex thought with a private grin.

But then, all things considered, the ex-Marine could have done a lot worse.

Rex winked at his friend and left the ring, going over to sit by Lindsay and Sam.

The old cowboy leaned forward to clap a firm hand on

Rex's shoulder, then jerked his thumb in the direction that Angelique Parrish had just stalked off.

"Looks like Linnie saved you from a fate worse than death, son," Sam murmured. "You better be real grateful to her."

Rex chuckled and reached into the breast pocket of his tuxedo, looking for a checkbook, but Lindsay put a hand on his arm.

"Not now," she murmured, bending close enough that he could smell the scent of her hair.

For as long as Rex could remember she'd used the same kind of shampoo, something that smelled faintly like sage and wild roses. Nowadays, even catching a whiff of it was enough to unsettle him and make him forget what he'd been planning to say.

"No? Why not?" he asked, his hand still on the checkbook.

"Angie Parrish was so upset," Lindsay murmured, "and she certainly knows I can't afford to pay that much for a few days of your company. I don't want her to start spreading nasty rumors about something underhanded in the auction."

"If I loan you the money to pay the fee," Rex argued, "how could that be underhanded?"

"I'll bet Angie could think of some way to make trouble."

Lindsay frowned, an expression Rex enjoyed almost as much as her smile. Her brow furrowed and her blue eyes looked so troubled and intent that he wanted to laugh out loud and hug her.

But he was never casual with Lindsay anymore, not the way they used to be when they were kids. Briefly he recalled Nick's troubling assertion that something was wrong with her besides the constant worries over finances at Lost Springs Ranch.

Rex leaned back, stretching an arm along the back of her seat and extending his tuxedo-clad legs. The sun light almost glistened on his polished handmade shoes. He noticed Lindsay staring down at them with an unfathomable expression, but when he caught her eye, she looked away without speaking.

Rex watched her more closely, concerned by the hollow curve of her pale cheek and the dark-blue shadows around her eyes.

"Are you okay?" he asked, leaning over to whisper beneath the auctioneer's patter.

She glanced at him in surprise. "Of course I am. This is going really well, Rex. If the rest of the bids are even half so generous, I'm pretty sure all our worries are over."

As she spoke, Lindsay was briefly animated and her eyes sparkled with a bit of the old fire. Still, Rex could see what Nick had been talking about. There was an underlying air of fatigue and unhappiness that didn't seem to be touched by her present optimism.

"All your worries, Lin?" Rex studied her closely, aware of old Sam Duncan nearby, who listened with sudden intentness.

She looked down again to avoid meeting his eyes, turning a brochure aimlessly in her hands. "Of course," she murmured. "What are you talking about? You sound just like Nick."

"Maybe you've been working too hard, and I know this whole thing has been really stressful." Rex hesitated, wondering why he felt so awkward. "Anyhow," he went on with sudden inspiration, "why don't you take advantage of this weekend you just bought?"

"What weekend?" Her cheeks turned pink. "Look, I didn't buy anything, and you know it. This is all your money, Rex."

"But the world thinks you just purchased a bachelor,"

he argued, "so why not take advantage of it? Come on, Linnie," he continued, warming to the idea. "Pick a nice place for a holiday and I'll take you there. I'll look after all the details so you can just rest."

"Yeah, right," she scoffed, kicking his ankle. "I can just see that happening, all right. You and me on a romantic weekend."

She was so scornful that Rex felt vaguely hurt. But he could sense Sam's silent approval on his other side, so he decided to try again.

"We'd have separate rooms, of course," he assured her. "And you wouldn't have to do anything but lie on the beach, soak in the sun and have a long, long rest. Why not just think about it, Linnie?"

"Because," she said with some asperity, "it's the silliest thing I ever heard of, that's why."

"Silly?" Rex felt, stung. "To spend a holiday weekend in my company would be *silly?*"

"If I'm going to take a holiday with anyone," she said, "I can tell you, Rex Trowbridge, it won't be some high-powered corporate animal with a shiny Cadillac and a pair of five-hundred-dollar shoes."

Her glance flicked over him again.

"So who would be your dream man, Lindsay?" he asked. "A sweaty mechanic, or maybe a high-rigger with a hard hat? Or how about a cowboy in dusty chaps, smelling like manure?"

She pretended to consider, her dimples flashing with another touch of the old mischief. "Well now, those all sound really good. I guess the smelly cowboy would be my first choice, though. Now, if you two will excuse me, I have a whole lot of money to collect."

With that, she got up and whirled away from the auction ring, her bright hair sparkling, and left Sam and Rex to look at each other in thoughtful silence.

CHAPTER TWO

One year later

WHEN SUMMER came again, the Wyoming sun shone on a much different world, at least for Lindsay Duncan and the other residents of Lost Springs Ranch for Boys.

The bachelor auction a year earlier had been a much greater success than anyone had anticipated. Long after the actual event, a groundswell of momentum kept building. By now the media publicity had generated a flood of spin-off income they could never have imagined when she and Rex first came up with the idea during a casual brainstorming session down at her uncle Sam's house.

The auction had been covered by both print media and state television, and was later picked up by a national feed. When reporters discovered that a number of the bachelor weekends had ended in romance and even marriage, the media was ecstatic at this human interest angle. Pictures of Lost Springs and success stories about its work with troubled boys were flashed around the nation.

Camera crews became a regular occurrence at the ranch, at least for the first few months after the auction, and some of the boys developed considerable skill at posing for photos and answering reporters' questions.

And the money kept rolling in.

In addition to thousands of outright cash donations, a number of scholarships and several generous endowments had been established. This allowed Lindsay to raise wages, organize staff pensions, hire some additional help. She even began looking at long-held dreams like a fully equipped gymnasium and boxing ring, and a music room with good instruments and qualified instructors.

Her father would have been so happy, she thought wistfully, sitting at her desk in the office and gazing at the drift of sunshine on a field of waving grass beyond the window.

The Duncan family had always visualized this place not just as a haven for the abandoned, but as a training ground where underprivileged boys could learn the arts and graces of life, where they could not only survive but triumph. Robert Duncan had firmly believed these lost boys needed self-esteem almost as much as they needed food, and that music lessons were valuable even if a boy planned to be a carpenter when he grew up.

Remembering, Lindsay smiled as she riffled through stacks of contractors' bids for the new gymnasium.

The floods of money had been a blessing, no doubt about it, but they also caused a lot of extra work. A happy responsibility, of course, but a pressing one, nonetheless.

She sighed and pushed a lock of hair back from her forehead, then froze.

The morning newspaper lay under one of the contractors' bids. Lindsay jumped, pulling her hand away as if she'd just touched a snake, then shuddered and buried her face in her hands.

But hiding her eyes couldn't erase the image of that small article on the lower right-hand corner of the front page. The words were burned into her memory.

The same thing had happened a year ago, just before the auction, and it had upset her terribly back then as well.

Now, after all these months, she'd begun to hope the nightmare was finally going away. But Lindsay knew she was only kidding herself.

She alone held the key. This thing was never going away until she acted, yet it had left her too afraid to do anything.

A coward, she told herself in the stillness of her office. She was such a coward. And because of her, other people would keep being hurt…

The smell of fresh-cut grass wafted through the window along with a strong scent of roses. The ranch seemed pastoral and safe, far removed from the kind of dark horror that gripped her mind.

Lindsay wiped her eyes with a tissue, blew her nose and dropped the folded newspaper into a wastebasket at her desk.

Briefly she had an urge to talk to somebody about what happened four years ago, and relieve herself of this terrible, humiliating secret.

But she couldn't think of anyone who could really help except for Rex Trowbridge, and the thought of telling him was simply unbearable.

Maybe if Rex were still the man he used to be, hard-fisted, impulsive and sympathetic, quick to throw a punch and just as ready to laugh…

Maybe then Lindsay could talk to him.

But Rex had changed so completely in the course of pursuing his dreams. Nowadays he seemed more like a handsome clotheshorse than a man. His chief concerns appeared to be keeping his car shiny and his bank account padded.

How could a woman ever confide her deepest secret to a man like that? Especially the kind of story Lindsay needed to tell.

She forced herself back to work. The numbers swam in front of her eyes at first, but after a while she settled down and became engrossed in designing a computer spreadsheet to weigh the elements of the various bids, trying to decide which contractor would make best use of the ranch's newly acquired funds.

Suddenly she looked up, startled. Four dandelions and a tattered wild rose had appeared magically at the edge of her desk and were rising slowly into her line of vision. Next a small hand appeared, dirty and marred by a couple of scratches. The hand was quickly lowered again, making the flowers wobble.

"My goodness," Lindsay said loudly, addressing the window. "What on earth is going on here? Some beautiful flowers seem to be growing on my desk, and I have no idea where they came from."

A muffled giggle and the scuffling of boots sounded below the front of her desk.

Lindsay grinned but kept her voice sober and thoughtful. "I'll bet these flowers need watering, since they seem to be growing so fast."

She took a pitcher of water and tipped it gently over the edge of the desk, sprinkling a few careful drops onto the tight clump of wildflowers.

A howl of protest sounded and a small boy scrambled into view, still clutching the flowers, droplets of water glistening on his curly red hair.

"My goodness," Lindsay said, pretending alarm. "Now there's a *boy* growing out of my floor, too. What on earth is going on here?"

"It's me," the child protested with a throaty giggle. "I picked you some flowers and sneaked in here to give them to you, and you never even saw me."

"I certainly didn't." Lindsay wiped the drops of moisture from his hair and took the bedraggled clump of flowers, which felt hot and limp. She smiled, wondering how long Danny had been clutching them in his dirty freckled hands.

Lindsay crossed the room to fill a coffee mug with water,

then inserted the clump of flowers and arranged them a little more gracefully before she set them back on her desk.

"There," she said, smiling at the little boy as she returned to her swivel chair. "Aren't they pretty?"

Danny nodded and studied the flowers in deep satisfaction, then came past the desk to lean against her chair.

Lindsay put an arm around his small frame, hugging him, and frowned when she felt the way he nestled close to her.

Poor little mite, she thought.

Danny Graves was only eight, a sensitive, complex little boy who'd lost both his parents in the crash of their light plane two years earlier. He was the youngest child at the ranch and the older boys were generally protective of him, but Lindsay knew they could also be rough, like most adolescent males.

Danny still missed and needed a woman's touch, and Lindsay tried to supply it whenever she could. She also had stern private chats with some of the older boys who teased Danny for sleeping with his teddy bear or needing a light near his bed.

"He's much smaller than the rest of you," she told the other youthful residents at Lost Springs. "It's our responsibility to understand that, and keep him from being scared or miserable."

But lately it seemed they hadn't been all that successful looking after their youngest resident. Divested of his bouquet, Danny left her chair and lingered by the door with a sad, pinched expression that tore at her heart.

"So," she said, setting down her pen and folding her hands on top of the papers, "what's up, kiddo? Are you having fun on your holiday?"

"Not much." Danny looked down, kicking at the edge of the Navajo rug.

"Not much?" Lindsay echoed, pretending disbelief.

"Why, Danny Jefferson Graves, you're eight years old and it's summertime! How could you not be having fun?"

He glanced up, his freckled face so twisted with misery that Lindsay's heart was wrung.

"The other guys don't want me around much." He swallowed hard and dashed a grubby hand across his eyes. "They do lots of stuff like going to the swimming hole and playing rodeo, but I'm not big enough. They think I'd just be in the way."

Lindsay nodded thoughtfully.

It was true, a lot of the activities at Lost Springs weren't geared to such a small child. Especially when the ranks of boys were so greatly thinned during the summer. Almost all the kids had somewhere to go when the school term ended. Even the parentless boys spent the summer months with relatives or other benefactors.

Only a few like Danny had nowhere to go and were forced to cool their heels at Lost Springs, filling the long summer days as best they could until the student body returned and comforting routines started up again.

Danny took hold of the door handle and turned it experimentally a few times, his customary procedure as he prepared to leave the office.

"Maybe..." Lindsay said, clearing her throat, "maybe soon there's going to be something exciting for you to do, Danny."

The little boy's face lit up with sudden hope. "Something really neat?"

Lindsay nodded soberly. "Oh yes," she promised, "it will be really neat. All the boys who are gone now will be jealous when they get back and hear about this wonderful thing you got to do."

"What?" he shouted, running back across the room to jump up and down near her desk. "What is it, Lindsay? Tell me, tell me!"

What indeed, she thought gloomily, staring at the wilted flowers.

She'd made this rash promise, and judging from Danny's shining face there was no doubt she needed to come up with something.

"This special treat is a big secret," she told him, trying to sound solemn. "I can't tell you about it just yet, and you have to be a very good boy and keep it to yourself for a while until I can...get things organized. All right?"

"Okay," he breathed, eyes sparkling.

"Don't tell a soul," she cautioned. "Not a soul, do you hear, Danny?"

He bobbed his head in abrupt jerky nods and used a pudgy forefinger to cross his heart. "Not a soul," he whispered.

"Good. Now you run off and play. I'll let you know as soon as the treat is going to happen."

Feeling both amused and despairing, she watched through the window as his small figure whirled and dipped joyously across the meadow, arms outspread, looking more like a bird in flight than a little boy in khaki shorts and T-shirt.

Lindsay looked down ruefully at her desk full of papers, wondering what on earth she could do for Danny that would make him feel special.

Perhaps a trip to Casper and a day on the water slides? No, that was already scheduled for the younger boys in the coming autumn term.

Possibly a whole day alone with her at the Cheyenne rodeo? Or maybe a...

Her thoughts were interrupted by the arrival of a van bearing the logo of a television station. Almost grateful for the distraction, Lindsay shoved the papers aside and smiled as a couple of young newswomen entered the ranch office. But she tensed again when they displayed their press cards. The two women represented a station in Los Angeles that had been to the ranch before. They worked for a program that fancied itself as a kind of West Coast "60 Minutes," doing hard news and exposés, turning rocks over and searching tirelessly for any whiff of scandal.

Lindsay had been upset by the tone of a feature they'd done on the bachelor auction the previous autumn. Rex had actually discussed launching a suit over some of the veiled allegations about fraud and misappropriation of charity funds at Lost Springs Ranch. Finally the board had chosen to let it pass rather than stir up the kind of publicity the show's producers obviously craved.

She forced herself to give the two women a casual smile as they settled into the visitor chairs opposite her desk.

"What can I do for you today?" she asked.

The spokeswoman was also one of the on-camera personalities, a tall woman with clipped black hair and a pugnacious manner.

"We're still interested in your bachelor auction fund-raiser," she said. "The station is considering a small follow-up piece. You know, just some light human interest stuff."

I'll bet, Lindsay thought.

"Well, that sounds fine," she said aloud. "Most of the boys are away for the summer, but you're welcome to wander around and get any kind of footage you want."

The other woman, a heavyset blonde with a clipboard, consulted her notes. "Actually, we're more interested in the bachelor auction couples," she said. "Who bought each of the men and how their weekends turned out, that sort of thing."

"There's already been a lot of coverage on that," Lindsay said mildly. "In fact, I think every single bachelor has had a camera shoved in his face at some point during the past year."

"All but one of them," the anchorwoman said, her eyes suddenly hard and watchful.

Lindsay tensed again, sensing danger. "What do you mean?"

The woman glanced at her partner, who consulted a report affixed to the clipboard.

"According to our notes, Ms. Duncan," the blonde said, "you personally purchased Rex Trowbridge, the director of the board of Lost Springs Ranch. That transaction occurred near the beginning of the auction and set the tone for some very high bidding throughout the event."

Lindsay's heart began to thud uneasily, but she kept her face calm. "Yes," she agreed, "that's true, I bid on Rex. It was…kind of a joke. He was so reluctant to be a personal part of the auction."

Neither of her visitors seemed amused. "We have no record of what you did with the bachelor you purchased, Ms. Duncan," the blond woman said. "It does seem like a rather expensive joke."

Two pairs of eyes watched her closely.

"What do you mean?" Lindsay said. "Are you implying some kind of wrongdoing?"

The dark-haired woman shrugged. "Considering all the money you've raised and the huge coverage this thing has received, your purchase of Mr. Trowbridge really doesn't look good, does it?"

"It would appear," the blonde chimed in, "there was some kind of collusion between you and the ranch director to inflate the auction prices. We wondered if that isn't a little fraudulent."

"But the money I bid for Rex was paid in full!" Lindsay protested. "There was no fraud, nothing like that at all."

"Still, it appears you never did anything with Mr. Trowbridge after going to the considerable expense of purchasing his company," the woman persisted with maddening calm. "We have records of all these other transactions, Ms. Duncan. The Lost Springs bachelors did things like escort women to school reunions, hunt down lost family members and help solve all kinds of other problems for their purchasers."

"Yes," Lindsay said. "I know they did."

"So what did Mr. Trowbridge do for you in return for all that money you spent?"

"We…" Lindsay picked up a ballpoint pen and began to make some aimless doodles on a notebook. "This past year has been a really busy time for us," she said. "The auction gave me a ton of administrative headaches."

"No doubt." The brunette newswoman favored her with a dazzling, insincere smile. "But now that a whole year has passed, you must be ready to take advantage of having spent so much money to acquire Rex Trowbridge. Because, you know, we'd really hate to think…"

The woman's smile vanished abruptly and her eyes glittered.

"We'd hate to think," she continued, "that your purchase of the board director was just a setup to inflame the other buyers to high bids. That wouldn't sound good at all, Ms. Duncan. Would it?"

"No," Lindsay said, taking a deep breath. "It wouldn't. But the fact is—" she crossed her fingers under the desk "—I have…something in mind that I want Rex to do for me. Actually, we're planning to spend a few days together before the school term starts."

"You're quite sure about that?" the blonde asked sharply, her pen poised above the clipboard.

"Of course I am. It's going to be happening very soon."

"How soon?"

"I told you, before school starts again. Within the next couple of weeks."

Two false promises in the same morning, Lindsay

thought in despair, and she had no idea how to fulfil either of them.

Danny's sad little face appeared in her mind, accompanied by an image of Rex in his sunglasses and handmade shoes.

Suddenly she had an idea.

Crazy, she thought slowly. It was a totally crazy plan, but it just might work.

At least it would get these women off her back, and it would certainly be a thrill for Danny.

The only one who wouldn't be happy was poor Rex. His choice for their enforced weekend would probably be some luxury resort in Acapulco where they could go their separate ways. Lindsay would suntan on the beach while Rex went scuba diving and conducted discreet flirtations with beautiful girls in bikinis.

There was no doubt, Rex preferred the glamorous life.

Well, who cares what he prefers, Lindsay thought recklessly. *I bought him. He'll be mine for a few days, anyhow, and totally under my control....*

"You're smiling, Ms. Duncan," the blonde woman said, startling Lindsay out of her reverie. "This must be a pleasant weekend you've got planned."

"Yes, it is." Again Lindsay crossed her fingers. "We're all going to enjoy it."

"All?" the other woman asked. She still looked alert but also mildly regretful, as if sorry to see Lindsay wriggling off the hook.

"What I'm planning," Lindsay said, for all the world as if this had been in her mind for months, "is to have Rex help me take a few of the boys on a trail ride and camping trip."

The blond woman began to write again. "How many boys?"

"We have half a dozen boys who spend the summer here

at the ranch because they have nowhere else to go during the holidays. They get pretty bored and restless, so I thought this would be a nice treat for them."

"And is Mr. Trowbridge also looking forward to your camping trip?"

"He doesn't know about it yet," Lindsay said, relieved to be giving a truthful answer for once. "But he can hardly object, right?" she added with a cheery grin. "After all, the man's bought and paid for."

Her guests didn't smile back. "How long will you be gone?"

"About a week." Lindsay calculated rapidly. "We'll haul our horses over to some of the rough country in the mountain ranges just west of here, and then ride in with a couple of pack animals to carry our camping gear. It's going to be a real adventure."

Danny would be out of his mind with excitement, she thought. Even the older boys were going to be thrilled by this plan.

But Rex...

"Is Mr. Trowbridge an accomplished outdoorsman?" the blond woman asked, as if reading her mind.

"He used to be," Lindsay said. "Years ago when we were growing up together, Rex was the best rider and wilderness survivalist at the ranch. But his interests have... changed in recent years."

Well, that was certainly putting it mildly.

The truth was, she didn't know if he'd even been on a horse in more than a decade, and he wasn't going to be the least bit happy about spending days on end in the mountain wilderness.

Maybe he couldn't even ride anymore. Rex had never been the kind of man who was anxious to revisit his childhood.

Lindsay felt a brief pang of guilty concern for him, but

it passed immediately when the two newswomen got to their feet and the tall brunette gave her another penetrating glance.

"We look forward to hearing about your adventure, Ms. Duncan," the woman said. "In fact, maybe we'll drop around in a few weeks to see how it went, and bring a camera crew with us."

The warning in her tone was unmistakable.

"That's just fine, " Lindsay said calmly. "I'm sure we'll have some exciting stories to tell."

She got up and escorted them to the door, then watched as they drove off, vanishing into the dazzle of sunlight beyond the ranch gates.

After they were gone, Lindsay went back to her desk and sat down, twirling a curl of hair nervously around her finger.

She frowned, wondering exactly how to break the news to elegant Rex Trowbridge that he was about to spend the better part of a week riding horseback, eating beans from a frying pan and sleeping under the stars with his childhood friend and a half dozen high-spirited boys.

CHAPTER THREE

WHILE LINDSAY was brooding about Rex's probable reaction to the bombshell she was about to spring on him, the object of her concern was much nearer than she suspected.

Instead of being in Casper, as Lindsay assumed, seeing clients or lunching downtown at the elegant Mesquite Club, Rex Trowbridge was actually within the confines of Lost Springs Ranch. In fact, the man was only a couple of miles away from her.

He drove his Cadillac carefully down a rutted trail bordering an old fence line, then eased it into a stand of birch trees, being careful not to scratch the gleaming surface.

When he decided the car had been sufficiently concealed, Rex parked and got out, took off his designer sunglasses and tossed them onto the seat. First checking to make sure nobody else was around, he reached into the back seat for a crisp new cowboy hat, which he fitted on his head.

Then he paused, a little sheepishly, to admire his image in the reflective surface of the big car's side window.

Keys in hand, Rex strode to the rear of the Cadillac and opened the trunk, taking out a duffel bag and a round metal can about two feet in diameter, designed for transporting nylon lariats.

He carried the bag and the rope can down a leafy trail to an old set of corrals, enjoying the warmth of the summer day. Magpies chattered raucously in the trees overhead, and a black squirrel scampered across the trail in front of him.

Near the corrals an older man waited, sitting patiently on

horseback near one of the sagging fences. At the man's side was another saddle horse, a big sorrel standing hip-cocked and silent against the fence, swishing his tail lazily at flies.

"Hi." Rex approached and tossed his gear down near the fence. "Beautiful day, isn't it?"

Sam Duncan grinned and coiled a rope in his gloved hands.

"That's a nice hat," he commented with approval. "Now you look like a real hand, not some fancy drugstore cowboy."

"Well, that was the general idea," Rex said, feeling another touch of embarrassment.

"So you're ready for this?" Sam asked. "Not too sore from last time?"

Rex rubbed his shoulder and grimaced. "I took a pretty nasty tumble. Who'd have thought team roping could be so dangerous?"

"When you've got two horses weighing half a ton each, and a five-hundred-pound steer with a mind of his own, and two nylon ropes in the hands of two cowboys, and one of those cowboys doesn't know what the hell he's doing," Sam said mildly, "then team roping can be a real dangerous sport."

"Sorry," Rex muttered, knowing that his carelessness during their last practise session had come perilously close to causing his partner a serious injury, too. "I won't make the same mistake again."

"Damn right you won't," Sam agreed.

He watched as Rex gathered the reins, fitted his boot in the stirrup and mounted the tall sorrel gelding, who danced and sidestepped nervously when he felt the sudden weight on his back.

"Let the reins off easy," Sam cautioned. "Don't saw at

him, he's got a nice tender mouth. All right, now pull him in gently, let him know who's boss...."

Rex obeyed the curt instructions. He felt tense and cautious, every nerve alert to danger. But as he did what Sam told him, the big horse settled down, ears twitching, and fell into a placid walk around the outside of the corral.

"Nice touch," Sam called behind him.

Rex felt warmed and happy, as if he were thirteen years old again with Sam teaching him to ride for the first time.

Sam Duncan's praise had always been sweet to the boys at Lost Springs, because it was hard-won and given only sparingly.

Over the years, everybody else had changed except Sam, Rex thought as the older man's horse fell into step beside his, circling the corral.

Though he must be seventy now, Sam looked practically the same as he always had, with his lean, craggy face and gentle smile, his big rangy body and the bald head concealed by a characteristic pearl-gray Stetson.

Sam did his own laundry and was always immaculately clean, his blue jeans neatly pressed, his plaid western shirts crisp and bright.

Rex loved the old man deeply, although he could never recall saying the words out loud.

"Well," Sam said at last, reining his horse toward the open gate, "let's try some roping. You ready for this, son?"

"Ready as I'll ever be." Rex dismounted and opened the metal can to take out a couple of stiff nylon ropes, which he slung over his saddle horn, and a pair of leather gloves to protect his hands.

From the back of his horse, Sam watched these preparations with an unfathomable look on his face. "I still don't rightly understand why you're doing all this," he said.

"I told you." Rex concentrated on attaching the spare

rope. "I want to enter the team roping with you at the Lightning Creek Rodeo next month, and I intend for us to win."

"That's a real tough roping," Sam said mildly. "It's hard to win even for guys who've been cowboying all their lives. And you..." He paused tactfully, picking at a rawhide strap on his glove.

"I'm a lawyer," Rex said with a rueful grin. "Haven't even been on a horse for years. That doesn't mean I can't learn if I want to, Sam."

"I reckon not." Sam cleared his throat. "But I'm still not sure why you want to. You know, Lindsay always says..."

Rex looked up so abruptly that the sorrel horse rolled his eyes in alarm and danced backward a few steps.

"Look, you haven't said anything about this to Lindsay, have you?"

Sam looked amused. "Don't bite my head off, son. I told you it would be our secret, and I'm a man of my word. As far as Lindsay knows, you haven't even been near the ranch since the last board meeting."

"Good." Rex gathered the reins and hauled himself into the saddle again. "That's how I want it to stay, right until the day of the rodeo."

"And then you're planning to ride out, win the roping and knock her socks off," Sam observed.

Rex rode beside him into the practice ring. "Yes, that's exactly what I plan to do. I've been thinking about it all winter."

The two men dismounted, looped their reins over a fence rail and went inside the barn to run a few long-horned steers up the alley and into a roping chute.

"Seems to me," Sam grunted, heaving on the gate while Rex held the final steer in position, "that it'd be a whole lot easier to send her flowers or chocolates like normal guys do.''

''Come on, Sam, I'm not trying to win her hand or anything.'' Rex frowned and adjusted his roping glove. ''It just annoys the hell out of me that she thinks I'm some kind of hopeless city slicker.''

The humorous creases deepened around Sam's eyes as he jerked his Stetson in the direction of the hidden Cadillac down the trail.

''Son, you *are* just a city slicker. It's been a long time since you were any kind of cowboy. I figure this is all a big waste of time, pretending to be something you're not.''

''But I'm not doing it just for that,'' Rex said, hauling himself into the saddle again. ''I mean, not just to make Lindsay see me in a different light. I'm doing it for myself, too. I want to find out…what I really am,'' he concluded, feeling a little awkward at the turn their conversation was taking.

Sam rode alongside, eyeing him thoughtfully. ''Seems to me a man should know what he is. I reckon that's what being a man is all about.''

''It always sounded simple when you said it back it in the old days,'' Rex told his friend and mentor. ''But nowadays things aren't as cut-and-dried as they used to be, Sam. Life can get really complicated.''

Sam shook out his loop and gave it a few experimental swings. ''So that's what made you decide to waste a whole lot of my time taking team-roping lessons?''

Rex grinned. Despite the brusque tone, he knew how much the old man was enjoying their secret afternoons at the corral. But the smile faded as he considered his answer.

''I guess,'' he said slowly, ''it started last year during the bachelor auction. Lindsay made it so clear she had no desire to spend any time with me, even though she was supposed to have bought a weekend of my time and we used to be good friends. It made me wonder, if she feels that strongly, just what's been happening to me these past few years."

"Maybe the real question is what's happened to her." Sam urged his horse forward in a sudden burst of speed to practise swinging the loop, then reined in and came back to Rex's side.

"To Lindsay?" Rex watched his friend, startled. "Has something happened to her?"

"Seems like it," Sam said. "You haven't been around enough to notice, but I see her every day. That's a different girl from the one she used to be."

"In what way?"

"She seems sad," the old man said after a moment's thought. "It's like something's hurting her, real deep down."

"Since when?" Rex recalled suddenly that her cousin, Nick Petrocelli, had said much the same thing last summer at the bachelor auction.

Sam shrugged. "I'd say three, maybe four years ago. Quite some time, anyhow."

"Did she—" Rex's gloved hands tensed on the rope. "Do you think somebody hurt Lindsay? I mean, did she have a boyfriend who broke her heart, or something like that?"

"Not as I recall." Sam squinted at the row of long-horned steers waiting patiently in the roping chute. "It just seemed to me one day she was different, but when I tried to find out why, she'd never talk about it. After a while I quit pestering the girl."

"And now…"

"Nowadays she seems like her old self most of the time," Sam said, "but she's stayed sort of…sad. Like there's some kind of big unhappiness at the back of her eyes."

Rex nodded, frowning.

"Well, come on, boy," Sam said at last. "We can't waste the whole day gossiping. Let's see if you can learn to lay a decent figure-eight loop in front of that steer's heels. Now, take the rope in your right hand..."

With an effort, Rex put aside his worries about Lindsay, shook out a loop and tried to concentrate on the things Sam was telling him.

Soon he was caught up in the intricacies of team roping and his dream of riding out into the arena at the Lightning Creek Rodeo next month while Lindsay watched in stunned amazement.

THE TWO MEN finished their roping practise, turned the steers out and sat for a while on a fence rail in the sun, chatting amiably about trivial things while their horses cooled down.

Sam could see how much Rex enjoyed the drowsy summer stillness, the chatter of insects and the smell of dust and horse, the feeling of the sun on their faces. It was probably like traveling back to his boyhood, no doubt a pleasant change of scene for a city lawyer.

Finally Rex got up, coiled his ropes into the metal can and headed off down the leafy trail to the grove where he'd hidden his Cadillac, pausing to wave before he vanished into the trees.

Sam waved back, then mounted his horse and gathered up the rein of the sorrel gelding, heading in the opposite direction toward the main ranch. It was a considerable distance because Rex, in his obsession with secrecy over this project, had chosen a practise area as far removed from the ranch buildings as possible.

But it was a beautiful summer day and Sam had nothing pressing to do. He liked the placid ride, the gentle creak of saddle leather and the clopping of hooves on baked earth.

As he rode he thought about Rex and his surprising decision to become a team roper just so he could impress Lindsay Duncan.

"That poor boy's in love and he doesn't even know it yet," Sam told his horse. "You'd think such a smart fellow would have a better handle on a thing like that, wouldn't you?"

The horse's ears twitched as he jerked his head at a passing fly, looking as if he nodded agreement.

Sam grinned. "Not that I know enough about being in love to criticize anybody," he ruminated aloud. "Seventy years old and never had much to do with women. I'm just a crusty old bachelor, but I can still tell when a man is smitten."

Maybe it was harder for Rex, he mused, because he and Lindsay had been such good friends all during their growing-up years. They'd had a rough-and-tumble relationship, full of adventure and fun, but that probably made it even more awkward when the time came to turn things around and start being romantic.

Sam patted the horse's arching neck and thought wistfully about romance.

Oddly enough, it was something he missed more all the time as he grew older.

He'd had a good life, and with the procession of boys passing through Lost Springs over the years, he'd raised hundreds of "sons." Many still kept in touch with him. But there were times nowadays, though he wouldn't admit it to a soul, that Sam Duncan was terribly lonely.

He hungered for a kind of relationship he'd never really known, except for a few shy, awkward love affairs back in his youth.

In his early twenties, just when other men were settling down and starting families, Sam had gone off to fight in Korea. When he came back, the girls he'd known were all married and raising babies, and his brother was starting the ranch at Lost Springs and needed his help. Sam had settled in to teach horsemanship to a whole lot of troubled boys, and the years had flown by with dizzying speed.

Nowadays he didn't regret most of his choices, but he cursed the youthful shyness that had kept him from going out and finding a lifetime partner.

It would be so nice, he thought wistfully, to have somebody who cared about him, who knew all his secrets and liked to be with him, somebody who'd sit next to him while he watched television in the evening, and travel with him to all the places he'd never seen.

Finally he forced his thoughts back to his niece, who worried him these days by apparently following in his footsteps and choosing a solitary life.

Sam frowned, thinking about Lindsay's luminous smile, her generous warmth and absorption in the boys at the ranch, and the troubled sadness he often detected in her face.

He wondered if she felt the same about Rex as the lawyer did about her, and it was only shyness or stubbornness keeping them apart.

Probably not, he decided.

Lindsay didn't seem the least bit interested in finding a husband or starting a family of her own. Whenever Sam teased her gently about the subject, she brushed him off by saying there'd be plenty of time for that kind of thing once the ranch was running smoothly and the work was caught up.

But there wasn't plenty of time, Sam thought sadly, looking back at his own life. The years went by so fast and the work never got caught up. Before you knew it, you were old and alone.

His gloomy turn of thought was interrupted by a sudden

change in his horse's gait, a tensing of the ears and a quick jerk on the bit.

Sam followed the horse's gaze and saw a patch of color in the brush next to the road. It was bright-red, probably some boy's lost coat or sweater.

But then along with the color he sensed some rhythmic movement, almost as if somebody was crouching in the tall grass, rocking back and forth.

Frowning, Sam reined in, dismounted and looped the reins over a fence post, then made his way into the brush with an awkward, bowlegged gait. He parted the tall grass and found somebody huddled on a big flat rock, curled up in obvious misery.

He hesitated, looking down in confusion, unsure what to do.

The person crouched in the brush was a woman, and she was clearly in distress. At his approach she raised a panicky, ravaged face and wrapped her arms tightly around herself, shuddering and gulping.

"Are you hurt, ma'am?" Sam asked, touching her shoulder.

She jerked away from him and lowered her head, beginning to cry again.

It was, he now realized, the older woman who lived with Rob Carter and his new wife. Rob and Twyla had got together because of that bachelor auction last summer. This woman was Twyla's mother, he recalled, dimly remembering the woman from a few social events in Lightning Creek over the past year.

He searched his memory, trying to come up with her name.

"Mrs. McCabe?" he ventured at last, hoping he had it right. "Can you tell me what's the matter?"

She gulped and shook her head, keeping her face hidden while Sam watched her uncertainly.

Though she looked terrible at the moment, he now recalled seeing her at Rob's wedding and thinking what an attractive woman she was. Gwen McCabe was probably in her sixties, with nicely styled white hair and pretty blue eyes.

At the wedding she'd smiled pleasantly when anybody approached but kept to herself mostly, sitting at the back of the hall with Twyla's young son. Sam even remembered wanting to go and ask her to dance, but he'd refrained because she looked so self-contained and he was certain she'd refuse.

Now, completely at a loss, he sank onto the rock beside her and put a hand on her shoulder again, patting her the same way he soothed a nervous horse.

"Easy now," he murmured. "There, there. It's all right. Easy now. Just take it easy."

He was relieved to see that her panic appeared to subside a little, and she was no longer violently rocking back and forth. But she couldn't look at him, and Sam still had no idea what the problem was.

"There, there," he said again, still patting her. "Easy now."

Gwen McCabe wore jeans, a checked shirt under the red jacket and a pair of businesslike-looking sneakers. She smelled pleasantly of some kind of woodsy fragrance that Sam liked.

At last she was still, huddled next to him on the rock, though she shivered occasionally and gulped aloud like a child recovering from a sobbing fit.

"Did something scare you?" Sam asked when he thought she might be able to talk.

The woman shook her head and muttered something inaudible.

"Beg pardon?" Sam leaned forward. "I didn't catch what you said."

"I'm such a mess," she whispered. "Sorry."

"No need to apologize." Sam lifted his face to the sun. "This is a real nice place to sit, this big rock. You know," he added in a casual, conversational tone, trying to set her at ease, "I've ridden down this same road probably a thousand times, and I never knew this rock was even here. How did you happen to find it?"

"I was running and I fell on top of it," she said, her voice still so muffled that he had to strain to catch her words.

"Why were you running?" he asked.

"Because I'm crazy," she told him in obvious despair. "Completely out of my mind."

Sam leaned back and extended his boots, digging the spurs idly into the soft grass at the base of the rock.

"You know," he said, "I've seen you around town a time or two, and last fall at Rob's wedding, and I sure never thought of you like that. You always seemed to me like a lady who had her life together."

"I did?" Gwen looked up at him in bleary surprise. Her eyes were red-rimmed, her face still pale with strain, but again Sam was astonished by her prettiness.

"You sure did. I especially liked that dress you wore at the wedding," he continued. "It was a real soft yellow, like sunshine. I remember thinking you looked as pretty as a buttercup."

He paused abruptly, hot with embarrassment. Sam had been rambling just to set her at ease, but she must think he was some kind of idiot, blathering on about sunshine and buttercups.

No doubt she'd start to panic again, finding herself alone in the woods with such a fool of a man.

But she didn't seem frightened. In fact, she turned to him with a twisted expression that he recognized as a gallant attempt at a smile.

"What a lovely thing to say," she murmured. "Thank you, Sam."

He relaxed a little and felt the flush of embarrassment slowly fading from his cheeks. There was a long, awkward silence while both of them stared down at the grass.

"Now," he said at last, "do you think you can tell me what scared you?"

"It was an owl." She shuddered again, gripping her hands between her knees. "A big gray owl. It kept flying back and forth over my head like a ghost, sweeping down closer and closer. I just…panicked."

It seemed like a strange thing to be frightened of, especially for a woman who'd lived any length of time in the country, but there had been no doubt of her terror. Sam looked down at her thoughtfully.

"That owl probably has nestlings somewhere nearby," he commented. "She was looking out for her babies, not trying to hurt you."

Gwen nodded in an abrupt, jerky fashion, looking away from him toward the road.

"Were you just out for a walk?" Sam asked.

Another brief nod. "I've been trying…" she whispered, then swallowed hard and forced herself to continue. "I try to go for a walk every day, and make it a little farther from home each time. But today the sunshine felt so lovely, and I got…too ambitious."

She shivered again and shifted nervously on the rock, then got to her feet. Sam watched her, wondering how it could be so difficult to go for a walk in the country. Maybe she had some kind of physical illness he didn't know about.

"Well," she said without looking at him, "I'd better… start heading back. Sorry to have been such a bother."

But he could see the pallor of her cheeks, and the way her hands shook before she jammed them into her jacket pockets. The woman was in no condition to walk a mile or two down a deserted country road, Sam decided.

"Can you ride?" he asked.

She glanced up, clearly startled. "Well…yes, I can. I used to ride a lot."

Sam jerked at thumb toward the two horses. "Then I'll put you up on my bay. He's a gentle old fellow, and I can ride the sorrel. We'll have you home in no time."

Her blue eyes widened in alarm. "But I couldn't possibly. It's so far out of your way."

"No problem, this is a real nice day for a ride," Sam said comfortably. "Come on, let's mount up."

She followed him, looking timid, and allowed Sam to help boost her into the saddle. Her body when he lifted her was firm and light, and Sam's hand tingled like fire as it brushed against hers.

"Well now," he said with false heartiness to hide his embarrassment. "You sure do look fine up there, Mrs. McCabe."

And in fact she did sit a horse well, he thought as he busied himself adjusting the stirrups. Her crown of silvery-white hair glistened in the sunlight, and a touch of pink even appeared in her cheeks. Sam had an urge to tell her how pretty she was, but resisted firmly, knowing he'd already made a big enough fool of himself for one day.

The poor woman would probably never speak to him again.

In fact, they didn't exchange a word as he led her slowly down the trail, then across the meadow to Twyla and Rob's place. But he had the sense she was actually enjoying the ride. A couple of times when he glanced back at her, Gwen met his eyes with a touch of alarm, but her body swayed easily in rhythm with the horse, and her hands on the reins seemed calmer, almost relaxed.

At the old house he helped her down from the saddle,

hoping wistfully for another smile, maybe even an invitation to drop in for coffee.

But Gwen trembled and ducked her head with a return of the painful uneasiness Sam had witnessed earlier. She whispered a few embarrassed words of thanks and bolted for the house, leaving Sam watching with his two horses.

Finally, after the door closed behind her, he mounted the bay horse and turned to ride off, feeling strangely bereft.

CHAPTER FOUR

THAT SAME EVENING, wholly unaware of Rex's secret rodeo practise or her uncle's curious meeting with one of their neighbors, Lindsay Duncan was in her bedroom at Lost Springs Ranch, preparing for an upsetting encounter of her own.

After the television van left at noon, she'd tried to call Rex but his secretary kept saying he was out and they had no idea when to expect him back. Lindsay was on the verge of giving up when he finally returned her call late in the afternoon.

"I wondered..." She'd hesitated, twisting the phone cord. "Rex, I hoped we might be able to get together this evening and talk about something."

"Talk about what?" His tone sounded wary, almost evasive.

"Just...something." Lindsay took a deep breath. "Could I buy you dinner, Rex?"

The long silence had shown how startled he was. But when he spoke, his voice once again held all of the smooth professional charm she'd grown to dislike so much.

"Well, that's the best offer I've had all day. How about the Beefeater at eight o'clock?"

"Good. I'll see you there."

Lindsay had hung up quickly before he could ask any more questions. Now she was rummaging through her closet, wondering what to wear for her long drive to Casper and the awkward meal that was certain to follow.

Maybe he wouldn't be all that upset, she told herself bravely, holding up a long denim skirt with a silver belt, then casting it aside.

After all, Rex must have known they wouldn't get off scot-free when he'd allowed himself to be offered for sale at a bachelor auction. And they'd already discussed going through with some kind of a charade for the sake of appearances.

She put on a coppery silk blouse and searched her jewel case for the earrings that matched, tipping her head critically to study the effect.

Then, barefooted, wearing only the blouse and a pair of cotton panties, Lindsay continued to burrow through her closet.

The problem was that she and Rex had turned into such completely different people. He wanted to go off for some luxurious weekend at a resort, the kind of place where men like him gathered to lie around the pool and talk about their investment portfolios.

But Lindsay scorned such self-indulgent behavior. She was actually looking forward to the trail ride and a camping trip with a group of her boys, though she couldn't take them out for that long without some additional adult supervision, and Sam was supposed to be on vacation for the summer.

She drew out a pair of black pleated slacks, pulled them on and added a coppertone belt and loafers, then ran a brush through her short blond hair and dabbed on some makeup.

Rex probably wouldn't be thrilled by her appearance, Lindsay thought, looking at herself in the mirror. The few times she'd seen him with a date in recent years, he'd invariably been escorting gorgeous creatures who looked as if they spent their whole lives going from the tanning salon to the hairdresser and manicurist.

Well, sorry to disappoint you, Rex, but that's not my style.

Lindsay tugged impatiently at an unruly lock of hair next to her ear.

Nevertheless, she took the time to remove a smear of mascara from her right eyelid and reapplied it more carefully, then blotted her lips and headed downstairs to her car.

As she pulled out of the ranch yard she noticed Sam sitting on a fence rail in the sunset, looking forlorn. She waved but her uncle didn't see her. He just kept chewing on a long stalk of grass and gazing moodily into the distance.

Lindsay would have liked to scramble onto the fence and perch next to him, chatting for a while in the mellow twilight. But she glanced at her watch and dismissed the wistful idea.

Rex, who was obsessively punctual, would probably be waiting for her long before she arrived at the restaurant.

As SHE'D EXPECTED, he was already in the leather booth when she arrived, sipping a martini from its shallow flared glass. He wore a sport jacket over a black turtleneck, and she had to admit he looked more handsome than ever in his studied, sophisticated manner.

"The lady is exceptionally gorgeous tonight." He raised his glass in an admiring salute while Lindsay slid onto the opposite bench.

"I'm not gorgeous," she said with a flash of annoyance. "Don't start giving me that suave crap, Rex. You know I can't stand it."

He raised an eyebrow. "So I'm not even allowed to pay you a compliment?"

"Not when it's insincere."

"Come on, Lindsay, what makes you so certain I'm insincere?"

"Because my nose is peeling, my hair is getting all dry

and bleached from too much sunlight, and I have this paint under my fingernails that won't come out no matter how hard I scrub.''

She extended her small, callused hands to show him the residue of green paint from a stable she and the boys were painting.

Rex smiled at her stained fingers, then called the waiter over, casting Lindsay a questioning glance.

''I'll just have a glass of white wine, please,'' she said.

''The martinis are good here,'' Rex told her. ''You really should try one.''

''I think martinis always smell just like paint thinner,'' Lindsay said curtly, hating his air of sophistication. She had an almost uncontrollable urge to reach out and punch him, just to ruffle that smooth composure.

He was watching her with a maddening smile that tugged at her heart, reminding her vividly of the boyish crooked grin she'd loved so much when they were young.

Lindsay felt a brief flood of sadness and a crazy impulse to ask him why her old friend had disappeared, leaving behind this elegant shell of a man.

''Well, I'm fairly certain it's not just the pleasure of my company you're after,'' he was saying. ''So you must have something on your mind to have asked me out for dinner, right?''

Lindsay took a deep breath to steady herself, and smiled gratefully when the waiter delivered her wine. She took a long sip, then began to tell Rex about the two women from the L.A. station and their veiled reference to fraud in the bachelor auction.

''They can't be serious,'' he said in genuine surprise. ''After a whole year? I'd assumed that whole thing was a dead issue by now.''

''Apparently not. These media people never let something die while there's still a bit of scandal or human interest to be squeezed out of it.''

"So which are we?" he asked. "Scandal or human interest?"

"It all depends.'' Out of sight beneath the table, she twisted her hands together nervously in her lap. "I think we need to do something together, Rex, just to satisfy them the auction was all aboveboard. If we don't they'll keep hounding me, and maybe even publish some kind of documentary about fraud."

"There was no fraud,'' he said calmly. "You made the highest bid on me, and you paid the money."

"But they suspect we colluded to get the bids artificially inflated, and you had no intention of honoring the purchase. I think,'' she added reluctantly, "that Angelique Parrish might be putting them up to it, just out of spite."

"It sounds like Angie's style, all right.'' He raised a sardonic eyebrow. "But, Lindsay, you have to admit it's the truth, don't you?"

Again Lindsay had an urge to punch him. "Of *course* it's true. But you know we can't have that kind of shadow over us or all our new funds could start drying up again. I want to avoid the slightest appearance of impropriety."

Rex shrugged and accepted another martini from the waiter. He removed the olive, shook it and placed it carefully on a napkin, lining it up beside the first with tidy precision.

"I don't see any problem,'' he said. "I'd be happy to take you away for a holiday. In fact—'' his eyes flitted over Lindsay, making her feel hot and unkempt "—you really look like you could use a break and some pampering. So where shall we go?"

"I was thinking…"

"We could fly to Greece,'' he mused. "I know somebody who owns a villa on one of the islands. It's really beautiful, Lin. And there's even a world-class spa nearby where you could spend a day or two. If we get it booked soon enough, that is."

"Greece?" She stared at him in disbelief. "But, Rex, I've already…"

"Or Ireland, if you want something a little cooler. Two years ago I found this nice bed-and-breakfast in Connemara, not much more than a thatched cottage, really, but with comfortable beds and marvellous food. It looks out over the ocean, and on Saturday evenings some of the locals come up and…"

"Rex," she interrupted in growing despair, "please just *listen* to me for a minute! We're not going to a villa in Greece, or a seaside resort in Cabo San Lucas, or some charming little cottage in Ireland. I already told those television people where we'll be spending our weekend together."

"You did?" His eyes brightened with a flash of the old teasing sparkle. "Lindsay, don't tell me you've been making plans without consulting me."

"Yes, I guess I have," she said without an answering smile. "Look, I purchased your services, remember? And according to the auction rules, you have very little input."

"So tell me, where are we going for this romantic holiday?"

"To the mountains," she said bluntly. "With six boys from the ranch, fourteen horses and a ton of camping equipment."

"You're kidding, of course."

"Come on, Rex. Do I look like I'm kidding?"

"Unfortunately, no," he said after a brief study of her face, then returned to his drink.

At least he wasn't taking it quite as badly as she'd feared. Lindsay twisted her napkin and glanced at him cautiously.

"Can you ride at all anymore? It must be years since you've been on a horse."

"It's been a while," he said. "But I assume it's like riding a bicycle. Or making love," he added, looking directly into her eyes. "Some things you don't forget no matter how long it's been."

She flushed and turned away, grateful for the brief distraction when the waitress arrived with their soup. Rex watched the woman set out the steaming bowls.

He picked up his spoon and poked at a crouton. "What's the matter, Lin?" he asked suddenly when the waitress was gone.

"What do you mean?"

"I get the feeling there's been something bothering you for a long time. Look," he added, "even if you don't like me much anymore, we used to be pretty good friends. It might help to talk about it."

Lindsay's stomach tightened in alarm and fear as she stared down at the soup bowl. "There's nothing to talk about," she said. "Except this camping trip and all the supplies we're going to need. I'd like to go next week, Rex. It'll take a lot of planning and hard work to be ready on such short notice."

"I'll talk about the camping trip if you'll tell me what your problem is."

"My problems are none of your business," she said, more curtly than she'd intended.

His hand tightened on the soup spoon, and she felt a pang of regret for her sharpness. It seemed perhaps Rex Trowbridge still had a few cracks in his veneer of sophistication.

"Look, I'm sorry." Lindsay reached over to touch his arm. "I don't mean to be rude, but I really have no interest in heart-to-heart talks about my private life, with you or anybody else."

He shrugged, his sardonic mask once again firmly in place. "Well, I guess that's your choice, isn't it? I just thought you might make a small concession to twenty years of friendship."

"But those years are long gone. We were both completely different people in our teens than we are now, Rex."

He studied her with disconcerting steadiness. "How were we different? I don't see that you've changed much, Lindsay, except that you're a little more quiet and withdrawn than you used to be."

She toyed with the saltshaker. "Maybe I am. And you're a whole lot more sophisticated," she said. "So I guess that makes us even."

"Sophisticated?" He raised an eyebrow. "What does that mean, exactly?"

"Come on, Rex," she said, unsettled by the turn of the conversation. "Let's not discuss our differences right now, okay?"

"What should we talk about? The prospect of spending a fun-filled week sleeping under the stars?"

Lindsay grinned suddenly. "Remember that story Sam used to tell, about the cowboy who woke at dawn and found a big rattlesnake curled up on his chest inside his sleeping bag?"

She had the satisfaction of seeing Rex's handsome face turn a little pale. But immediately Lindsay felt a pang of guilt, remembering how this man had always abhorred snakes of any kind, even back in his tough-guy youth when nothing had scared him much.

"Sorry," she said impulsively, laying a hand on his arm again. "That was mean of me, Rex. Especially when you're being so nice about this camping trip."

"I'm not being nice." He finished his soup and pushed the bowl aside. "I'm just hoping I'll be there to watch when that snake winds up inside *your* sleeping bag. It'd serve you right, you coldhearted woman."

She laughed. For a brief moment it felt almost like old times being with him, so warm and pleasant that she realized just how much she'd missed his friendship in recent years.

But then another lawyer stopped by their table and Rex was immediately absorbed in a conversation about torts and writs, topics so abstruse that she couldn't even understand what they were saying.

Lindsay watched him covertly as she sipped her wine, thinking how much he'd changed and how completely this new life suited him.

At least, she thought with a moment of private satisfaction, he wouldn't be quite so much in his element out there in the Wyoming mountains.

THE NEXT MORNING, Gwen McCabe woke to a warm flood of sunshine that lay across her quilted bedspread.

White muslin curtains lifted in the breeze and a chorus of birdsong trilled beyond the window. Inside the house she could hear the comforting sounds of morning, the bubble of her coffeepot from the next room and her grandson's boyish shouts down in the other kitchen.

She smiled drowsily, then remembered the previous day and stiffened in alarm.

It all came back to her in a humiliating rush. Gwen rolled over, whimpering, and buried her face in the pillow.

Her eyes filled with hot tears of shame.

She'd been out for one of her cautious, timid walks, and she'd ventured too far from the house. It was her own stupid fault, all of it.

Gwen lay rigidly in the bed, trying to get a grip on her emotions.

Ever since the tragic death of her husband eight years

earlier, under circumstances that had forced her and Twyla to leave their old home town and search for another place to live, Gwen's fears had become more and more overwhelming.

In time she'd become totally agoraphobic, unable to leave the house for any reason. But then Rob Carter had come along. He was a breath of fresh air, the perfect man for Twyla. With his arrival, all their lives had changed, including Gwen's.

As her daughter's love blossomed and Brian became more happy and secure with his new stepfather, Gwen had determined to overcome her phobias so she wouldn't be a burden to them. She tried every day to go out for a walk or accompany Twyla into town on shopping trips and errands. For a while these efforts had gone well, making her happy and optimistic.

Then winter had closed in on southern Wyoming. With the freezing temperatures and deep snow it was often hard to get out, so Gwen decided to settle in the house and wait for spring.

But even when the weather moderated, somehow Gwen couldn't summon the energy to begin her recovery again in earnest.

Twyla and Rob were absorbed in each other and their new marriage, while Brian was growing up and getting more involved in activities at school. Nobody seemed to notice that Gwen's walks became shorter, and her forays away from the house less frequent.

She knew there was a real danger of sinking back into the self-imposed prison that had been her life for so many years, and she was resolved not to let that happen. Lately she'd begun forcing herself to venture a bit farther afield, even though the open skies and empty roads were terrifying to her.

And she'd been getting a little better with each summer day that passed.

Until yesterday...

Gwen shuddered and gripped the pillow, remembering the sheer, gut-wrenching terror of that owl flying silently above her like some malignant sprit, hovering nearer and nearer until its shadow chilled her and its wings felt close enough to brush her head.

She'd been so far away from the house, on an unfamiliar stretch of road with nowhere to run, no place to hide.

Her resulting panic attack had been one of the worst she'd ever experienced, so visceral and terrifying that she could still remember the blind horror and resulting nausea in the pit of her stomach.

And worst of all...

Gwen shuddered again, rolling her head on the pillow. Tears spilled from her eyes and ran down her cheeks.

That nice man had come along and helped her. Sam Duncan, his name was. She'd seen him around town a few times and admired his long, spare body, his broad shoulders and faded blue eyes set in weathered creases, his courtly manners and gentleness with the boys who lived at Lost Springs.

Sam was such a kind man, he hadn't given any hint that she was behaving like a fool. But of course he must think her a complete idiot. A grown woman, sobbing like a child, frightened out of her wits by an *owl*, of all things.

Gwen was overcome by self-loathing. It was even worse when she remembered the man's consideration, his thoughtful insistence on escorting her right to her door.

But what had been in his mind as he cantered off, sitting so comfortably erect in the saddle and leading his other horse back to Lost Springs Ranch?

She felt another hot flood of shame. Maybe at this very moment he was telling the story to his friends at the ranch, and they were all laughing about the crazy woman who'd been reduced to a shuddering mess by an owl flying overhead.

Gwen shook her head and sat up, running a hand through her tousled curls.

Sam Duncan hadn't seemed like that kind of man. She was certain that he wouldn't tell anybody about the humiliating incident.

But she was equally sure of something else as she climbed out of bed and shrugged dispiritedly into a dressing gown.

In spite of her determination to fight this illness and win, her longing for independence and her hatred of the phobias that kept her trapped within these walls, it was going to be a long, long time before Gwen McCabe could summon enough courage to leave the house again.

CHAPTER FIVE

THE DAY AFTER she had dinner with Rex, Lindsay called a meeting for the six boys who were year-round residents. They gathered in her office with a good deal of noisy shuffling and jostling, then waited a little nervously for her to speak.

Danny Graves sat cross-legged on the floor near her chair, holding a jar containing a live garter snake. Clint Kraft also refused to take a chair. Instead he lounged near the door, arms crossed, looking bored and sulky. The other four boys, Jason and Tim Bernstein, Lonnie Schneider and Allan Larkin, all sat in front of Lindsay's desk and seemed increasingly tense about this unexpected summons.

Lindsay smiled at their anxious expressions.

The Bernstein brothers were thirteen, still teetering on the edge of puberty. They were slender and delicately blond, identical in appearance but with widely varying characters. Tim, who suffered cruelly from asthma, was shy and easily upset. But Jason Bernstein was cocky to the point of belligerence, and very protective of his fragile twin.

Lonnie Schneider at fourteen was a plump boy, affable and lovable as a clumsy puppy, though lazy and often careless with his work. In one of those odd, mismatched friendships that Lindsay often observed among the boys, Lonnie had chosen a completely opposite personality for his best friend. Allan Larkin, also fourteen, was thin, bespectacled and full of energy, obsessively neat, a perfectionist almost to the point of compulsiveness.

Lindsay loved the whole group of them, quirks and all, and knew most of their secrets, their fears and shy boyish hopes. Besides little Danny, the only one who caused her much concern was Clint Kraft, their newest resident. Clint was sixteen, with a voice that had already deepened and the beginnings of a moustache sprouting on his upper lip. He was tall, dark and lean, with a coldly withdrawn manner.

Clint had been sent to the ranch on remand by the Colorado Juvenile Court after being involved in a gang-related robbery in Denver. The court felt the boy had some potential and would benefit more from the supportive environment at Lost Springs than a dreary stay in some detention facility. But during the three months since Clint's arrival, Lindsay hadn't observed much progress.

The dark-haired boy talked as little as possible to anybody. The only thing he seemed to enjoy at the ranch was working with the horses, so Sam had assigned him to the stables, where he spent the day currying, grooming and exercising dozens of horses while the other boys were gone for the summer.

Lindsay watched as Clint cast her a restless glance, then began edging toward the door.

"Is this gonna take long?" he asked in his deep young voice. "Because I got things to do."

"Not very long, Clint. Besides, you can afford to take a little break from work." She gave the tall boy a warm smile, which he ignored, staring down at his boot toe as he kicked the floor.

Lindsay raised Danny to stand next to her, and slipped an arm around him.

"I'm going to keep my snake until it has babies," the little boy told her, squinting into his jar, "and then I'm going to name every one of them and have them all for pets."

"Not much chance of that snake having babies unless she gets a boyfriend." Lonnie snickered, nudging Allan, who sat next to him.

"Why not?" Danny said.

All the boys guffawed except for Clint, who scowled and looked out the window again.

"Looks like somebody has to tell Danny where babies come from," Jason Bernstein said, setting off another round of chuckles.

"I'll tell him," Lonnie volunteered.

"Oh, no you won't," Lindsay said firmly. "*I* will tell Danny all about his snake and its babies, thank you very much."

"What about them?" Danny asked, while the older boys watched Lindsay with expectant grins.

"Tonight, after supper," she told the little boy, "we'll go for walk by the creek and have a long talk about snakes. Right now," she added, anxious to divert the group's attention from snakes and sex, "there's something else I want to tell all of you."

Danny looked up at her alertly, gipping the jar in his arms. "Is this about the big secret?"

Lindsay smiled at him. "Yes, Danny," she said, "that's exactly what it is."

"What secret? Hey, what's he talking about? What does Danny know that we don't?" the other boys yelled, making the smaller child puff up with importance. His freckled face shone.

"Danny knows we're doing something special next week," Lindsay said. "It's going to be a treat for those of you who are spending the whole summer at the ranch."

"Oh, a *treat*," Clint muttered from the back of the room, his voice heavy with sarcasm. "Yippee."

"Shut up, Kraft," Lonnie said, brave for the moment because he was in a group with an adult present.

Lindsay knew that plump, easygoing Lonnie would never dare to rebuke the older boy if they were alone. In reality, all the Lost Springs residents, even Lindsay herself, were a little intimidated by this sullen, taciturn youth.

"Yes," she said calmly. "It's going to be a real treat. And I'm about to tell you what it is."

Danny edged closer, jumping from one foot to the other, his snake forgotten for the moment. Even his curly red hair seemed electric with anticipation.

"What is it?" he said. "What's the treat, Lindsay?"

"We're going on a trail ride into the mountains," she said. "We're going to take packhorses and camping gear and spend a whole week in the wilderness."

The boys, all except Clint, stared at her in wondering disbelief. For a moment the room was utterly silent, then broke into an uproar.

Lindsay help up a hand, smiling. "One at a time," she said in response to their shouted questions. "Yes, we'll cook all our own food, and you'll sleep out with no tents. We'll haul the horses in trailers over to the eastern side of the mountains and make a circuit there. Everybody gets to go."

Tim Bernstein was watching her with anxiety. Lindsay gave him a reassuring nod. "I'm making arrangements to take along an extra supply of your asthma medication, Tim," she told him. "And inhalers, too. You shouldn't have any problem."

The blond boy relaxed and began to talk excitedly to his brother.

Danny was still beside her, looking silent and downcast as the older boys chattered among themselves. Lindsay drew him close to her.

"Hey, what's the matter, cowboy?" she murmured. "Why such a long face?"

A tear slipped down his freckled cheek, followed by another. "You said…" He gulped and swallowed. "You said the surprise would be something I can do, too."

Lindsay stroked his hair. "Well, of course it is. You're coming along with us, Danny. I would never think of leaving you behind."

"I *am?*" His eyes widened. "I get to ride a horse and camp out with all these big guys?"

"Absolutely," Lindsay told him. "In fact you'll be one of the most important campers, because I want you to help me with the food. It takes a lot of supplies to feed six boys for a whole week."

"Five," Clint said from the back of the room.

The others twisted in their chairs to look at the boy, but Clint's eyes were fixed on Lindsay.

"You can count me out," he told her. "I got better things to do with my time than ride around in the trees with a bunch of snotty little kids."

Lindsay met his challenging gaze with deliberate calm, and was relieved when the tall youth was first to look away.

"I'm afraid you have no choice in the matter, Clint," she said. "Everybody's included on the trip. Since we'll all be gone, I'm using this opportunity to give the ranch staff a week's holiday before the fall term, so this whole place will be closed down. If anybody stayed behind I'd have to cancel the camping trip."

"So cancel it," he muttered, kicking at the floor again. "Because I'm not going on any stupid little trail ride."

The other boys turned back to Lindsay, their faces reflecting stunned disappointment.

"I'm not canceling the outing, Clint," she said quietly. "And I'm insisting that you go along because I need you.

Every boy will have a job to do, but yours will be the most important of all.''

''What kind of job?'' he asked suspiciously.

''We're putting you in charge of the horses,'' she said. ''You already spend more time working with them than anybody else, and you seem to be learning a lot. We'll need eight saddle horses and at least half a dozen spares to carry our packs, so that's fourteen animals to care for. I want you to pick the horses for us, and choose one of the other boys for a helper so you can make sure the horses are properly looked after.''

Clint looked up. Some indefinable emotion flickered in his dark eyes but was quickly masked.

Lindsay waited.

''Okay,'' the tall boy said at last. ''I'll pick Larkin to help me, then. Schneider's too lazy and the twins are just babies, not much better than *him*.''

He jerked a contemptuous thumb in Danny's direction. The little boy gulped nervously and edged closer to Lindsay, who gave his shoulder a comforting pat.

''Lindsay, will you be the only one coming with us?'' Allan asked.

''No, Rex is going to come along, too,'' she told the boys.

''Rex?'' one of them asked in disbelief. ''Can he even ride a horse?''

''Of course he can,'' Lindsay said with a good deal more confidence than she felt. ''He grew up here, you know, and took riding lessons from Sam just like all the other boys do.''

''But he's a big-shot lawyer,'' Tim protested, ''not a cowboy. It should be Sam going along with us.''

''Sam needs a holiday,'' Lindsay said. ''And Rex and I will be just fine as group leaders. We went on lots of trail rides when we were younger.''

"A lawyer and a woman," Clint scoffed derisively, lounging by the door. "Wow, this should be a great trip. Just great."

Lindsay was angered by his insolence, but decided not to make an issue of it in front of the others. Instead she ignored Clint, resolving to speak with him privately at the first opportunity.

"And the rest of you," she said as if he hadn't spoken, "will be assigned your jobs tomorrow. Think about what kind of duties you'd like, and any special research projects you might want to do while we're in the wilderness. Then we'll all meet back here in my office tomorrow afternoon at three o'clock to start planning our trip."

The boys whooped aloud and clattered from her office. All of them gathered outside on the grass to talk in a excited clump except for Clint, who strode off to the stables without a backward glance.

Even little Danny was part of the group, Lindsay noted with satisfaction as she watched them through the window. He stood in their midst, bouncing up and down as usual. Inside the glass jar his snake was also bobbing uncomfortably, and Lindsay made a mental note to coax him into releasing the poor thing that evening after their little talk.

Suddenly she remembered the purpose of the talk and grinned ruefully. She'd had discussions about sex with many of the boys over the years, and answered questions that would probably have thrown people with less experience into red-faced speechlessness.

But Danny was younger than the boys she was accustomed to working with, and she wasn't entirely sure what approach to take.

"Why so pensive, my fair lady?" a voice said near the door.

Lindsay glanced up, startled, then smiled when she saw Rex standing just inside the room.

"Danny and I are going to have a little talk tonight about the birds and the bees. And snakes."

"Snake sex?" He moved closer, his mouth lifting in the lopsided grin she'd always loved but seldom saw anymore.

"Well, I'm hoping I'll be able to make a smooth transition from snake courting to human sexuality before we finish. It's time Danny got a few of his questions answered properly, or God knows what the boys will start teaching him."

Rex hoisted himself lightly onto her desk, still watching her intently. "So, Lin, what are you going to tell Danny about sex?"

Something in his expression made her cheeks grow warm. She turned away, pretending to search through a filing cabinet.

"I'm going to tell him," she said over her shoulder, "that sex is a wonderful, loving thing adults do when they care about and respect each other, and with the right person it can be…"

She turned to find him staring at her with an unfathomable look in his eyes.

"What?" he asked when she paused. "What can sex be, Lin?"

"Lots of fun," she said with forced lightness, edging past Rex without touching him and sinking gratefully into the familiar safety of her desk chair. "But I do try to refrain from letting the boys know how much fun sex can be. At this age, anyhow."

"Do you find sex enjoyable?" he asked curiously, leaning back on the desk. "Are you a woman who laughs during lovemaking? I've always wondered about that, you know."

Lindsay felt a rising panic, along with a bracing touch of annoyance. "Well, you have no business wondering things like that where I'm concerned," she said crisply. "None at all."

"So you've never speculated about me?" he asked, balancing a stone paperweight in his hand. Lindsay had always liked Rex's hands, with their square palms and long, capable fingers. "Not even when we were kids, going out together?"

Lindsay shook her head. "Back then I was so innocent, I hardly knew what sex was. I had a big crush on you when we were teenagers, but surprisingly little idea what…what men and women did in bed."

He eyed her steadily. "It's a pity we never got the chance to find out."

A rush of desire sang through her body, warm and treacherous, making her feel full of yearning. She struggled to get her mind back on the stacks of paperwork.

"Rex, cut it out, okay?" she said, beginning to recover her equilibrium. "Just stop it." Lindsay glared at him directly, noting his clothes for the first time. Her mouth dropped open in shock.

He chuckled. "Hey, that's so cute. You look just like a guppy."

Lindsay closed her mouth and punched his arm. "Oh, shut up. Why are you dressed like that?"

Rex looked down at his jeans, boots and plaid shirt. "This?" he asked vaguely, as if he wandered around the ranch all the time in cowboy gear. "Do you like it? I bought a new Stetson, too."

"What gives? Are you having an early midlife crisis, or what?"

"Maybe I'm just getting in the spirit for our big trail ride," he said. "It occurred to me that I probably can't wear a suit and wing tips and carry my briefcase into the mountains, can I?"

Lindsay smiled at this image, relieved that the conversation had finally turned away from sex. "You could try," she said, "but it wouldn't be a really good idea. The boys are already pretty nervous about having you come along."

"They think I can't ride a horse anymore?"

"Something like that," Lindsay said dryly. "*Can* you?" she added, unable to resist.

"Lindsay," he said, looking into her eyes, "I can do a whole lot of things better than you ever imagined."

She held his gaze for a moment, almost mesmerized by the warm, lazy blue of his eyes and his unmistakable meaning.

"What a shame," he said, breaking the awkward silence, "that you didn't choose to have our bachelor auction weekend at that villa in Greece."

With sudden, dazzling clarity, she pictured a hot summer sun on Mediterranean vineyards, warm black nights under a shimmer of stars, romantic little dinners on a stone-flagged patio with cheese and bread, and bottles of wine wrapped in raffia.

And Rex alone with her, this new, disturbing Rex who kept looking at her so intently...

"I'm sure it'll be a whole lot more fun to camp out in the mountains and eat beans with the boys," she said.

What on earth had gotten into the man?

She'd known Rex Trowbridge practically all her life, and now he was acting so strangely. And her physical response to his teasing was also bizarre, almost beyond her control.

"Are you hitting on me, Rex?" she asked suddenly. "After more than twenty years of a pretty good friendship, have you decided to get ridiculous and mess our lives up completely?"

"What if I have?"

"Then I want to know why." Lindsay turned away from his probing gaze. "Have you decided you're a little bored this summer and I'm the last woman in Wyoming you haven't conquered?''

"Maybe I've decided..."

But Lindsay waved a hand to silence him when she saw her uncle striding across the ranch yard.

"So, Rex," she said with forced brightness as Sam climbed the steps and entered the office, "you're not worried about spending a whole week on horseback? Won't be too sore to move after the first day?"

"I've been doing a little practising today," Rex said casually. "Right, Sam?"

"What's that?" Sam looked thoughtfully at Rex's grin and Lindsay's flushed cheeks, then began riffling through a pile of mail on a side table.

"The mail is mostly catalogs," Lindsay told him. "Oh, and a personal note for you that I set over there. I don't know who it's from."

Sam picked up the note in its plain yellow envelope and studied it curiously. Lindsay was intrigued by the sudden flare of interest on his weathered face.

"Do you recognize the handwriting?" she asked.

"Hmm?" The older man looked up vaguely, then smiled at the envelope before putting it away in his shirt pocket. He even patted his chest a couple of times as if making sure the letter was safe.

Lindsay watched him, increasingly puzzled.

"I was telling Linnie how you've agreed to helping me learn to get on a horse again before this big trail ride of hers," Rex said.

Sam glanced at the younger man. A look passed between them, an expression of understanding and complicity that left Lindsay more puzzled than ever.

The old cowboy nodded and turned back to his niece. "That's true," he said. "I'm looking forward to spending

the odd half hour reminding this fancy city lawyer which
end of a horse you put the feed bag on.''

''Well, that's a good idea,'' Lindsay said. ''But do you
think he'll be ready in time? We're leaving before dawn
on Monday, you know.''

''Beats me,'' Sam drawled. Again she caught a glance
between the two men and a flash of humor in Sam's eyes.
''He may look the part right now, but these lawyers aren't
much good as cowboys. You might have to rig up a sling
and carry him.''

''Now, Sam,'' Rex said, grinning, ''don't be so hard on
me. You know I'll try hard to learn all the stuff I've forgotten.''

Sam chuckled, and Lindsay gave him a sharp glance.
''Hey, what's going on here, exactly?'' she asked, looking
from one man to the other. ''Do you two have some kind
of big secret?''

Rex's handsome face looked guileless. ''Why do you ask
that?''

''Because you're wandering around dressed up like a
cowboy for the first time in fifteen years,'' she said, ''and
Sam's acting like the cat that swallowed the canary. The
two of you keep grinning at each other, and I don't know
what the hell's going on here!''

''Poor cranky baby,'' Rex said indulgently. ''She really
needs a holiday, don't you think, Sam?''

He patted her head in the condescending fashion that had
always enraged her when they were teenagers. But now she
felt the warmth of his hand through her hair and it made
her tingle all over again.

''Look, get out of my office,'' she said in despair. ''This
minute, both of you, or I'll never get any work done. I have
tons of stuff to look after if I'm going to be away for a
whole week.''

"I've already booked off work till the end of August," Rex said. "I can come out tomorrow and help you, okay?"

"Oh, Rex, there's no need for that," Lindsay told him hastily.

The truth was, she would have welcomed some help, but she wasn't sure she wanted the man hanging around all day in the intimate confines of her office. Especially not the way he was behaving lately. His presence was too distracting and brought waves of the kind of feeling she hadn't dealt with for years.

Rex ignored her protests. "Of course I'll help. You need to finish up your regular paperwork as well as get all the supplies ordered for the trip and make sure the boys pack everything they need. I can take a lot of that burden off your shoulders."

He was right, those were all things she'd been concerned about, and it *would* be nice having somebody sharing the burden.

As long as he kept his hands to himself and didn't look at her with that disturbing intensity or talk about things like sex and lovemaking....

"Well, okay," Lindsay said at last when she realized he was waiting for her answer. "I guess I could use some help with the planning. You just...have to behave yourself," she concluded lamely.

"Behave myself?" Rex arched an inquiring eyebrow.

"You can't keep teasing me all the time. I thought we got over that stuff when we were kids."

"Maybe I'm not teasing," Rex said.

Lindsay tensed again and looked over at Sam, who was peering into his shirt pocket. She detected a ghost of a smile on his craggy features.

"Sam!" she said. Her uncle came to attention with a visible start. "If Rex comes out tomorrow, will you work with him planning the trail ride and ordering the supplies? Then I won't have to worry about it.''

"Sure thing," Sam said amiably. "Come on, Rex, let's go over and check out those horse trailers.''

The old man patted the letter in his shirt pocket again, then ambled out, followed by Rex, who paused in the doorway to give Lindsay a thoughtful glance.

"Go!" she said. "Leave me alone. I'm busy.''

"Wait'll I get you out there in the middle of the wilderness,'' he said. "You'll have to give me your undivided attention.''

"You and six boys," she scoffed, "and fourteen horses. Look," she added seriously, "stop all this nonsense, okay, Rex? I don't know why exactly you want to keep teasing me, but it makes me really uncomfortable. Just quit kidding around.''

"Sure, Lindsay," he said obediently. "Whatever you say.''

His face was sober, his eyes sparkling with laughter. Lindsay had to restrain herself from flinging something at the door as it closed behind him.

CHAPTER SIX

AN HOUR LATER, Sam and Rex strolled across the ranch yard to the lawyer's Cadillac. Rex opened the door and got in, then squinted up through the open window at the older man, who lounged against the fender.

"You're looking more like a real cowboy all the time," Sam said. "Even in this fancy buggy you drive."

"Maybe I'll have to trade it in and get a pickup truck," Rex said.

"Now, don't get carried away," Sam told him. "Just because you go out and rope a few steers, that doesn't mean you've knocked off fifteen years of rust."

"So you're another one who believes a lawyer can't be a cowboy?"

Sam studied the man's handsome face. "Well, you've traveled a whole lot of miles since you left this place, Rex."

"Too far to come back?" Rex asked.

"That depends. I'm not even sure why you want to come back. If you do."

Rex tapped his fingers on the steering wheel and looked across the paddock at a couple of grazing horses. "Maybe I'm lonely, Sam."

"Everybody's lonely." Sam felt a touch of sadness. "But trying to crawl back into your past...Rex, I don't believe that's the way to deal with it."

"You think that's what I'm doing?"

"I can't see what else you'd call it," Sam said. "Wearing jeans and riding horses, flirting with Lindsay...those were all things you did back when you were fifteen years old."

Rex glanced up at him. "You don't like me flirting with Lindsay?"

Sam scuffed a boot toe in the dirt and considered his answer carefully.

"Not when I can see how nervous it makes her. Look, son, you and Lindsay have had a good working relationship for years, and together you've done a whole lot for this ranch. I don't rightly know why you want to complicate things now. If it's just a joke, Lindsay doesn't seem to be getting it."

Rex shifted on the leather upholstery, picked up a pair of sunglasses and set them down again. "I'm not really sure what's happening myself," he said at last. "For the past year or two, especially since that bachelor auction, I've been doing a lot of thinking about my life. And it seems..." He paused, looking uncomfortable. "It seems my thoughts always come back to Lindsay."

Sam felt a growing concern. He cared deeply for both these young people, and had a feeling they were heading for big trouble.

Especially Lindsay, who seemed so fragile these days.

Rex watched him, obviously reading his thoughts. "I'm not going to hurt her, Sam," he said, "if that's what you're worried about. You should know I'd never hurt Lindsay."

"I'm not worried so much about that," Sam said slowly. "It seems to me somebody's already hurt her, and she needs her friends right now."

"So you're warning me not to try being anything but a friend?"

"Just don't keep teasing her," Sam said. "She's got enough on her mind, what with this trail ride happening just before the fall term. She doesn't need any more problems to fret about.''

Rex turned his key in the ignition. "Okay, Sam," he said, his face carefully expressionless. "I'll think about what you said.''

"So are you still coming out tomorrow?''

Rex nodded, his hands on the wheel. "I promised Lindsay I'd help her.''

"Well, good," Sam said, standing away for the car. "She could use the extra hand, I reckon.''

Rex waved and drove out of the ranch yard with sunlight flashing off the sides of his expensive car.

Sam watched him go and shook his head, wondering just what was going on in Rex Trowbridge's head, and how it was going to affect Lindsay.

But they were grown-ups, had been for long time. He couldn't meddle in their business any more than he'd done already.

With a sudden lift of spirits, Sam took the yellow envelope from his pocket, opened it and leaned against a fence in the sunlight, smiling as he read a handwritten note on flowered paper.

IN THE DOORWAY of the stable, Clint Kraft watched as the two men talked, then the lawyer drove off in his Cadillac. He turned aside with an angry scowl and kicked an empty pail, sending a hollow clatter echoing through the building.

He wouldn't be so upset about this stupid trail ride if that damned lawyer wasn't going along. Why couldn't it be Sam Duncan, instead?

Clint hated all lawyers for the power they had over people, and what they'd done to his own life. And Rex Trowbridge was a typical lawyer with his polished good looks, his fancy clothes and handsome face and easy, sophisticated manner.

Clint's anger rose, almost overwhelming him. He felt weak and sick with rage, and had to pause for a moment, leaning against a box stall until the emotion passed. Underneath the anger was pain so intense that he could hardly bear to think about his life during the past few years.

Nobody had ever noticed him much, not even when he was a little boy. Clint didn't know who his father was, and if he had grandparents or other relatives, he hadn't heard about them. But his mother had usually been around, providing a kind of shaky center to his life.

She'd been drunk or stoned most of the time, and had a string of boyfriends, most of whom treated young Clint with casual brutality. But at least she'd been there, until she was arrested and sent to jail on a drug charge when he was thirteen.

Clint had gone into a series of foster homes, but none of them had kept him for more than a few months. When he was fifteen he ran away and started living on the streets of Denver. He made his way with quick wits and hard fists, finally getting involved with a gang that gave him a harsh facsimile of the family he'd never known.

But during the past spring he was caught with two of his friends during an armed robbery. And *then* he fell into the hands of lawyers.

Clint kicked the pail again, his face darkening.

As a result of those lawyers and their finagling, he'd been sent far away from Denver to this dumb kiddie place.

He disliked everything about Lost Springs Ranch except the horses, and Sam and Lindsay Duncan. But especially he hated that suave polished lawyer who was director of the board. And the younger boys who acted so childish all the time.

Clint didn't hate Lindsay, though. He realized she was sincere and tried very hard to help all the kids at the ranch. But he was also frightened by the way she made him feel.

Sometimes when Lindsay spoke gently to him during meals, or came down to the stable to express an interest in his life and the work he was doing, Clint was worried by his own reaction.

He caught himself wanting to talk to her, to make her understand what his life had been like and how he felt about things, and how scared he'd been when he was involved in that robbery and the police caught him.

He abhorred this unaccustomed weakness in himself. It made him more resolved than ever to hold everybody at arm's length.

They couldn't keep him in this stupid place for more than another few months. If they tried, he'd run off and make his way back to Denver somehow. The streets were hard, and life inside the gang was brutal and scary all the time. But it was a different kind of fear from this soft, dangerous emotion that threatened to tear down all his defenses.

He wandered into the feed room and started filling pails with grain for the horses, still thinking about the upcoming trail ride.

Spending a whole week in isolation with a woman, a lawyer and five bratty little kids. What could possibly be worse? And they wanted him to be in charge of the horses. He was even supposed to select the ones they were going to use as saddle horses and pack animals.

Sam had told him how the horses at Lost Springs were trained for use by amateur trail riders.

"Our horses are taught all the trails around the ranch," Sam had explained, "so they're safe for anybody to ride. A group of boys can set out in any direction they like. When it's time to head back, they just have to give the lead horse his head and he'll find the way home to the ranch. That way, nobody ever gets lost."

Clint carried heavy pails of feed through the stable and

dumped chopped grain into all the mangers, still thinking about Sam's words. An idea began to form in his mind, an impulsive, mischievous thought that made his face break into a slow grin.

So they wanted him to pick the horses, did they? Well, that was just what he planned to do.

He strolled out into the corral next to the stable and looked at four horses who stood quietly against the white fence, flicking their tails at flies in the afternoon heat. Two were sorrels, one was a bay and one was a small buckskin. They were all gentle, well-trained horses, and the buckskin mare had been accustomed for years to having children ride her.

Lindsay and the lawyer could have the two sorrels, he decided. They were the biggest horses, and both had a bit of spirit. Clint himself would ride the bay, and he'd give the buckskin to little Danny.

He grinned again, tickled by the wickedness of his plan. He probably couldn't have gotten away with it a month ago but the old man seemed unusually preoccupied these days, more and more willing to leave the work at the stables to Clint. Sam shouldn't be too hard to fool.

Lindsay and the smart-aleck lawyer certainly weren't going to suspect anything. They didn't know the truth about these four horses.

Clint's smile broadened. He patted the little buckskin, scratching behind her ears while the mare closed her eyes in bliss.

"This is going to be fun, Daisy," he whispered to her. "Really fun."

For a moment his amusement was dampened by a tug of fear about the consequences of his action. Clint glanced into the ranch yard, almost hoping Sam would come talk to him about the selection of horses for the trail ride and forbid him to do what he was planning.

But Sam was leaving the ranch, heading off in his truck on some errand of his own. Clint stood there and watched the vehicle disappear from sight. Finally he let the four horses into the stable and opened the manger doors to give them all their daily feed of grain.

As SAM DROVE up the trail toward Rob and Twyla Carter's house, he tried hard to feel casual, as if this were a normal social call like any other. But his heart was pounding, and he felt as nervous as a boy.

When he neared the house, Sam saw somebody sitting on the porch. He caught a flash of white hair and the brightness of a pink cotton shirt, and it was all he could do not to stop, turn around and flee back to the safety of the ranch.

But she'd probably already seen him, in which case he'd look like a complete idiot if he ran off with his tail between his legs.

Sam gripped the wheel nervously, took a deep breath and parked near the house. When he got out of the truck, he realized with a sinking heart that Gwen wasn't alone. He could hear her voice and her warm bubble of laughter as she spoke to somebody.

She watched him approach and waved a greeting. Sam mounted the steps, carrying a plastic-wrapped package, and realized the other occupant of the porch was Gwen's small grandson, Brian.

He felt a surge of relief. Brian was a nice little boy, probably around the same age as young Danny at the ranch. And Sam Duncan had always been comfortable around boys.

"Why, hello, Sam," Gwen said. "How nice to see you again."

She sounded sincere, but maybe she was just being polite. Sam tipped his hat and smiled at the pleasant scene on the old front porch. Gwen McCabe and her grandson were shelling peas. They had a mountain of empty pods in a bushel basket between them, another basket containing full pods, and a couple of plastic pails brimming with freshly shelled green peas.

"Hello, Gwen." He settled into a rocking chair next to her. "Hi, Brian," he said to the little boy. "Are you having a good summer?"

Brian nodded gravely. "I'm on a baseball team. We've won six games."

"And he hit a home run last week, didn't you, dear?" Gwen ruffled the boy's hair fondly. He ducked away from her hand, making Sam grin.

"Once a feller gets to be a big baseball star," he said, "it's a lot harder for the womenfolk to fuss over him."

Gwen sighed. "I guess that's true. I have to keep reminding myself he's not a baby anymore."

Brian scrambled to his feet. "I have to go, Gram," he said. "I'm supposed to be over at Brody's house for batting practise."

Gwen looked at her watch. "All right," she said. "But dinner's at six o'clock. Don't be late, or your mother will worry."

The little boy took a baseball glove from a bin near the door and paused at the top of the steps, poised for flight. "I might eat at Brody's," he said. "They're having barbecue tonight."

"Only if you're invited," Gwen told him. "And if you are, be sure to call."

Brian clattered down the steps. At the bottom he paused, then ran back to hug his grandmother and kiss her cheek. He gave Sam a shy smile and headed off toward a group of houses down the road, arms swinging and bare legs pumping as he ran.

Sam smiled, watching the boy disappear. "They have so

much energy at that age,'' he said wistfully. ''Never walk when they can run.''

''And never work when they can play,'' Gwen commented dryly, reaching into the basket and taking out another handful of pods.

Sam tucked his wrapped package under the chair and took some peas as well, glad to have something to do with his hands. For a while they worked together in a silence that was oddly companionable. Pods opened with a gentle popping sound and peas rattled into the two plastic buckets.

He felt his nervousness begin to evaporate, replaced by a placid feeling of contentment. It was nice, sitting here with this woman at his side. Her company was pleasant and undemanding, and Sam didn't feel as awkward as he normally did around women.

''Are Rob and Twyla home?'' he asked after a while, glancing at the silent house.

''No, they're both at work. But Rob should be home in an hour or so,'' she added, ''if you'd care to wait that long.''

Sam looked at her in surprise, but she was bending over to gather more peas from the basket. Her movements were quick and graceful. He liked the way she looked in her jeans and pink shirt, and the quiet, competent way she handled this small household task.

In fact, he liked everything about her.

''I didn't come to see Rob,'' he said, lifting another handful of peas. Their fingers brushed and he felt a sudden thrill of excitement, as if he were as young and foolish as those boys back at the ranch.

She was looking at him curiously. ''You didn't?''

''I got your note today.'' Sam squinted at the climbing rosebush along the trellis, heavy with blooms. ''It was nice of you to send it, but you didn't need to apologize.''

Her face turned as pink as the roses in their tracery of

leaves. "I behaved like such an idiot," she muttered. "It was practically unforgivable. And you were so kind to me."

Sam hesitated, then reached under the chair and lifted his package, holding it out shyly. "I brought you something."

She looked at the package, then at him. "For me?"

"I picked it up in Casper yesterday when I had to take a horse to the vet."

She opened the plastic sack and peered inside. "It's a book," she announced.

"I know," Sam said gravely. "I bought it."

This small joke earned him another warm smile. His heart lifted with sudden happiness.

Gwen took the book from its wrapping, opened it and drew a quick breath. "It's about owls," she said, leafing through the pages. "Oh, my goodness. Look at these lovely pictures."

"I thought..." He moved awkwardly in the rocking chair and picked up another handful of peas, shelling them busily to hide his nervousness. "I thought if you could read about them and see how they make their nests and feed their babies, you might not be scared of them anymore."

Gwen touched his arm with a quick, shy gesture. "Thank you, Sam. That was a lovely thought. I'm really going to enjoy reading this."

Again she smiled at the book and began leafing through the glossy pages, looking as thrilled as if this were the finest volume ever published. Sam felt himself expand and glow, all his uneasiness banished by her warm reception of his gift.

He leaned over, brushing against her arm as he turned a few pages of the book on her lap. "The owl that scared you," he murmured, "I'm thinking it was probably a great gray owl. People call them the ghosts of the forest because they fly overhead so quietly. You see this big feller?"

He indicated a picture of a large bird with staring yellow eyes and a flat, circular face. She gazed at the page, and he could see how her hands tensed.

"They're rare out here," he continued, trying to set her at ease again. "You hardly ever see a great gray this far east of the Rockies. They have ears under that facial disk, you know," he went on, tapping the picture, "and they can turn their heads all the way around, as if they're on a swivel."

She smoothed the page, then flipped it over to study another picture of a gray owl on a nest, feeding its young.

"I was so horribly frightened." Gwen took a deep, shuddering breath. "You're right, it felt like a ghost. And it kept moving closer and closer to me."

Sam began to shell peas again. "I reckon," he said, "we're probably all a little scared of things that aren't familiar."

"Are you?" she asked curiously. "You seem like a man who wouldn't be afraid of anything."

Sam glanced up at her, startled. "I do?"

"You seem so calm and competent," Gwen said. "I'd guess there's nothing that could make you behave as foolishly as I did."

"Well, you'd be wrong," he said. "Some things scare me half to death."

"Like what?"

"Well, like coming here today," he said, not looking at her. "I was so scared, it was all I could do to drive my truck."

She laughed, a warm peal of amusement that made him smile, too, in spite of his embarrassment at having made such a confession.

"Well, I'm glad you managed to conquer your fear," she said at last, setting the book aside regretfully. "Because now I'm having some nice company and getting my peas shelled at the same time."

Sam grinned and went on working, amazed at how well this visit was going. He and Gwen were working together and having a conversation just like old friends. It was wonderful.

They kept shelling peas, chatting about the weather, Rob and Twyla and events around Lightning Creek. He was sorry when the bushel basket emptied and she got to her feet, lifting the two plastic buckets of peas. "Could I make you a cup of coffee?" she asked. "I've got some fresh carrot cake in the kitchen."

Sam got up as well and shook his head in regret. "I'd love to," he told her, "but I have to be back at the ranch by five o'clock. That horse I took to the vet is due for another dose of antibiotics."

"Well, maybe another time," she said.

Sam nodded and walked with her to the door of the house, then paused tensely at the top of the porch steps.

This was the moment he'd been dreading. But he had to speak now, because in a second she'd be gone inside the house and his opportunity would be lost. And she'd been so nice, so friendly and warm. He might just have a chance.

"Gwen," he said.

"Yes?" She paused, her hand on the doorknob.

"I was wondering..." He shifted his boots awkwardly on the floorboards and cleared his throat. "I wondered if you might like to go out with me sometime. We could drive to Casper and have dinner, maybe see a movie. It's been a long time since I..."

His voice trailed off when he saw the look on her face. Her expression had frozen, turned stiff and cold.

"I just thought..." Sam tried again, floundering miserably.

She gripped the plastic buckets and didn't answer.

"Look, it's okay if you don't want to," he said, drowning in embarrassment. "I understand."

What had possessed him to think this pretty woman might actually want to go out on a date with him? He was just a pure fool.

"Sam," she whispered, her face pale with concern. "I'm so sorry."

"It's all right." He turned away hastily and walked down the steps toward his truck.

"Really, Sam," she called in a strained voice. "I'd love to go with you, but I just…I can't."

"I understand." He climbed into his truck, anxious to be gone. "Don't give it a second thought."

He waved and put the truck into gear, backing up and heading away from the house. The last thing he saw of Gwen was her small figure standing unhappily in the doorway.

CHAPTER SEVEN

THAT EVENING, Lindsay and little Danny sat on the banks
of the creek in the dying sunlight, with the snake resting
between them in its jar.

She'd just finished telling him how snakes mated to pro-
duce babies, and confirmed the child's suspicion that these
events happened much the same way in the human popu-
lation.

Like most of the boys she had this discussion with, Lindsay realized that Danny already knew more than she'd expected him to, and that his ideas about human reproduction
were basically accurate, though they were also clouded by
a lot of misinformation and teasing from the older boys.

"Jason says…" His face turned red as he dug his toe
into the dusty bank of the creek.

"What does he say?" Lindsay patted the little boy's
mass of gingery curls, then smiled at a family of ducks
gliding along the surface of the water. A mother and almost
a dozen fluffy babies moved past them in stately procession
and vanished into the reeds.

Danny looked up at Lindsay, his freckled face pale with
alarm.

"Jason said when a baby gets born from a lady's stomach, it pops right out through her belly button and rips it
wide open."

"Well, that's just nonsense," Lindsay said firmly.
"There's a special place inside the mother for her baby to

live while it's growing, and another special place for it to come out.''

"Where are they?"

Lindsay told him, in a calm, matter-of-fact way.

The little boy stared at the water. "Does every lady have one of those baby places?"

"Yes," Lindsay said.

"Do you?"

"Of course."

"Then why don't you have a baby?" Danny asked.

"Because a lady needs a man to be the father of her baby, and I never..."

Lindsay had a sharp memory of sickening fear, of cruel hands and a harsh, jeering face. She closed her eyes briefly.

"I never found a man I liked quite enough to be the daddy, so that's why I don't have a baby."

Danny snuggled against her. "But would you like to have one?"

"Oh, yes, I certainly would." Lindsay hugged him with a fierce pang of yearning. "But in the meantime, I guess you'll have to be my baby, Danny. So do you think that's okay?"

"Sure," he said placidly, then paused. "But my snake..."

"Yes?"

"We don't know if it's a boy or a girl." He twisted to look up at Lindsay.

"That's right," she agreed. "I think you'd need to be an expert on snakes to figure that out."

"And if it's a girl," he said, his brow furrowed, "then she needs a boy snake to put the seeds inside her and make her babies grow."

"Yes, she does."

"So maybe..." He stared into the jar regretfully. Behind

the glass, his garter snake stared back at him with desperate yellow eyes.

"Yes, Danny?" Lindsay prompted gently. "What were you going to say?"

"Maybe I better let her go so she can find a boy snake to give her the seeds."

"I think that would be wonderful," Lindsay said gravely. "We could release her right here near the creek, because snakes love water. And someday when we're out for a walk, maybe we'll see her crawling by with a whole lot of babies."

"Just like that duck?" Danny was clearly trying to talk himself into letting his treasure go free.

"Just like the duck," Lindsay agreed.

Reluctantly, he unscrewed the lid on his jar, tipped it up and watched in sorrow as the snake tumbled out onto the ground in a mass of bright coils.

The animal stretched and writhed sluggishly, then gathered itself together and slithered off, vanishing into the tall grass along the creek.

Danny watched somberly, rubbing his nose to hide a sniffle. "That snake was my pet," he said. "I always wanted a pet."

Lindsay hugged him. "Well, soon you'll have a horse to look after," she said. "In fact, why don't you go down to the stable right now and ask Clint which horse is going to be yours for the trail ride? Then you can start looking after it and maybe even feeding your horse sometimes, so the two of you will be good friends before we leave next Monday."

As she'd expected, this suggestion was an immediate hit. Danny leaped to his feet, all his sorrow over the snake vanishing. He grabbed the empty jar and raced off in the direction of the stables.

Lindsay watched him go, smiling. Then she settled back

on the creek bank to watch the sunset colors reflected in the slow-moving water. The evening air had begun to cool and freshen. A breeze tugged at her hair and caressed her face.

She thought about her talk with Danny, and wondered how much of the sexual information she'd just given him would actually be retained.

Little boys were always such a mystery. Danny had absorbed her talk mostly in silence, then moved the conversation back to snakes. But Lindsay suspected he'd grasped what she was trying to tell him, and was relieved to know the truth.

In another few years it would be time to have the talk with him that she gave all the boys when they reached puberty. She told them the importance of respecting their own bodies and those of girls, as well; of being sexually responsible and not using their physical drives and urges to hurt other people in any way.

In any way...

She shivered and hugged her arms, tortured by harrowing memories and the knowledge of her own shameful, cowardly guilt.

But those things were far too painful to dwell on, and she'd had four years to practise shutting them out of her mind.

Instead her thoughts turned to Danny's question about why she didn't have babies, and her response that she'd never found the right man to father her children. Somehow the conversation had made Lindsay think of Rex's odd behavior in recent weeks, and the memory disturbed her.

She honestly didn't know what to make of the man these days.

Lindsay had always known there were two Rex Trowbridges in her life...the tough, streetwise teenager who'd been her friend and playmate so many years ago, and then the urbane lawyer whose life had moved off in a direction she could barely understand, let alone share.

But this new, troubling Rex was a bizarre combination of both, and she had no idea how to react to him.

Worse, she honestly didn't know what was motivating the man. Lindsay had been only half joking that afternoon when she'd asked if he was merely idling away the boring summer days by trying to seduce the last woman in Wyoming who seemed able to resist him.

If so, it was pretty shabby behavior on his part. Definitely a betrayal of their long friendship.

Lindsay's face hardened with resolve. She got to her feet, took the cardigan from over her shoulders and put it on, shivering as the sun dropped below the darkening line of trees.

Over at the stables, their figures etched with gold by the setting sun, she could see Clint Kraft talking to Danny, who had already shed his empty jar somewhere along the way.

Lindsay tensed, a little nervous about how the sullen older boy might react when he thought himself alone with the youngest child at the ranch.

But Clint appeared to be talking pleasantly with Danny. The two of them went out into the circular corral next to the stable, and Clint showed the little boy a buckskin mare standing near the fence.

Even at this distance, Lindsay could see the excitement in Danny's small body as he approached the horse. He glanced up at Clint, then reached out shyly to touch the mare's shoulder.

Clint lifted Danny with surprising gentleness and held him on the buckskin's back. Lindsay smiled at the proud lift of the little boy's chin as he sat astride the horse, supported by Clint's hands, and the look of wondering joy on his face.

This camping trip, she decided, heading back toward the

ranch house, was going to be a good experience for all of them.

Maybe it would even be good for Rex, she thought, remembering the surprising sight of the lawyer in blue jeans and boots, and his mysterious exchanges with Sam back in the office.

As long as Rex would just stop this ridiculous flirtation of his and go back to being an old school friend.

Maybe she'd talk seriously with him again tomorrow when he came out, and make him understand how upsetting his teasing was. Then they wouldn't have to deal with any such awkwardness on the trail ride while they had all those boys and horses to look after.

With sudden decision she quickened her steps and started back to the house, pausing on the way to tell Danny it was almost his bedtime.

REX LIVED in one of the few really upscale apartment buildings in the city of Casper, and had furnished his multilevel unit with the kinds of things he saw at the homes of his successful colleagues. The rooms were filled with black leather couches, side tables made of glass and chrome, twisted metal lamps and huge abstract paintings without frames.

Few people ever visited his home, but when Lindsay had seen it a couple of years ago, just after he moved in, she'd grimaced with characteristic frankness.

"You don't like it?" he'd asked.

"I know it's all very glamorous and expensive," she told him, glancing around the living room. "But it looks like…I don't know, Rex. A movie set or something. Certainly not the kind of cosy place where somebody could curl up on a rainy weekend and read all afternoon."

"On the rare occasion when I'm home for the weekend,

I spend cosy afternoons working in the den,'' he told her stiffly, a little stung by her criticism.

Tonight he remembered her words, and examined his costly furnishings with a touch of discontent.

Lindsay was right, there was little comfort in this place for a man who was feeling lonely and out of sorts. Still, it annoyed him that she could always judge him so unerringly, and wasn't at all reluctant to express her opinions.

But then, Lindsay had always been like that.

He settled on the leather couch and extended his legs, hands behind his head, thinking about their shared childhood.

For the first few years after his arrival at the ranch, Lindsay Duncan had been just like one of the boys. In fact, she could swim faster, shoot straighter and climb trees better than most of them, and even Rex had sometimes been hard-pressed to keep up with her.

But when she was about sixteen, things had begun to change between them. He'd been a year older, and suddenly both of them were conscious of their developing bodies and the powerful new urges they were feeling.

He remembered the first time he'd ever kissed her, under the big willow tree along the banks of the creek. She'd been away at boarding school and had just come home for summer holidays. It had been a shy embrace, awkward and tentative, and their noses had bumped together, making her laugh.

In the intervening years, Rex had held many women, a lot of them lovely, sexy and glamorous. But none of those conquests had ever thrilled him as much as that first kiss so many years ago.

He wondered if Lindsay remembered it, too.

For a long time she'd been treating him with offhand politeness, discussing the business of the ranch when necessary and avoiding any kind of personal conversation.

Busy with his own career, Rex had accepted her coolness without comment.

Besides, he'd been working for a long time on divorce and family litigation cases, and after all the things that went on within the privacy of his office, he was in no hurry to tie himself up in any kind of domestic situation. People within a marriage often treated each other with such breathtaking cruelty, it was hard to understand why anybody would risk getting themselves involved in a long-term relationship, let alone a family.

Not that he knew anything much about families, of course.

Frowning, Rex lifted a small leather cushion and turned it idly in his hands, thinking about his own years of abandonment and misery before he was sent to Lost Springs Ranch.

In many ways, young Clint Kraft reminded Rex of himself at that age, an angry and alienated boy without roots of any kind, only scars.

No wonder he'd never been anxious to get himself involved in a permanent relationship. As soon as things got serious with any woman, Rex found a way to extricate himself.

Nowadays he could hardly summon interest in the ritualized dance, the whole process of asking somebody out, searching for things to talk about, moving from lunches to drinks to dinner, all the while judging the right moment to make a sexual advance. Somehow it just didn't seem worth the trouble. Especially not when his mind seemed to be filled all the time with thoughts of Lindsay Duncan.

Hell, he was practically obsessed with the woman.

Rex leaned back moodily on the couch, still gripping the cushion, wondering how this had happened.

That ridiculous bachelor auction last year had set it off, he realized. It had made him look at her in a different light.

For years they'd been nothing but old friends who had little in common except their mutual concern for the ranch. But after the auction he'd started thinking about the reality of being bought and paid for by Lindsay, of going away for a weekend with her and devoting himself to her pleasure.

Now, even though she'd ridiculed the idea, he could hardly think of anything else.

Images filled his mind, pictures of the two of them walking along a silvered beach in the moonlight, pausing to kiss and caress, then moving on again, arms entwined as the tide crashed around their feet. Or Lindsay lying on a huge bed in some romantic hotel room, smiling with drowsy pleasure as he popped the cork on a champagne bottle.

Rex shifted awkwardly on the couch, hot and rigid with sexual need. Finally he lay full-length, staring at the black metal ceiling fan, then closed his eyes and allowed his fantasy image to grow.

She was wearing a negligee of some filmy white material. It fell open to show her small breasts, her slim boyish body and slender legs. Because they were in love, she trusted him completely and wasn't shy about revealing her nakedness to him.

Rex carried the two brimming champagne glasses to the bed and set them on the nightstand, then lay next to her. He was naked as well, and her eyes caressed his body, letting him know how much she wanted him.

"Champagne?" he whispered, drawing her into his arms and sliding the sliky fabric off her shoulders.

"Maybe later," she murmured. "Right now there's something else I'm thirsty for."

Her mouth roamed over his face and chest, moved lower on his body…

Rex groaned and sat up, then heaved himself to his feet and walked restlessly through the apartment. He switched on a few lights, glanced at the television listings and tossed them aside, brooded for a while over his collection of jazz and blues, but closed the CD cabinet without selecting anything.

He went into the stark white kitchen and got some orange juice, then settled at the counter to drink it, staring moodily at the walls.

He had no idea what Lindsay would be like in bed. Their childhood romance had never progressed beyond a few kisses. In those days he'd been too scared and awkward even to touch her firm young breasts, though he'd spent a whole lot of hours thinking about them.

But he suspected, in spite of her quiet composure, that Lindsay would be a warm, responsive lover. Something smouldered deep in her eyes, a kind of hidden fire that made him shiver whenever he thought of it. And there was her glowing, luminous smile, the sweet tug at the corners of her mouth that hinted at an impish, playful, inventive nature.

Rex thought about her talking with little Danny about human sexuality, and her comment that lovemaking was a lot of fun.

If she'd just loosen up and let herself go, they could have so much pleasure together.

He drained the glass of juice and set it in the dishwasher, then crossed the kitchen and paused by the phone.

Suddenly he was overwhelmed by the desire to call her at home.

No matter that she gave him no encouragement at all, and treated him as if he'd somehow turned out to be a disappointment to her. Forget, too, that Sam had warned him to stop bothering her, or that the two of them had nothing much in common anymore.

At this moment, he needed to talk to her so much that he'd die if he couldn't hear her voice.

His hands almost shook as he dialed the number from memory, then waited as the phone rang, thinking about the rest of their awkward exchange in her office that afternoon, and her demand that he stop teasing her.

But I'm not teasing, sweetheart, Rex thought grimly, waiting for her to answer. *I've never been more serious in my life.*

"Hello?" she said.

Rex's mouth went dry and he gripped the phone, his heart pounding as if he were sixteen again. Desperately he tried to think of an excuse for calling, something that wouldn't annoy her.

He pictured her at home, wearing whatever she put on to relax around the house in the evening.

Probably some kind of baggy shorts and T-shirt. She'd be sipping hot tea and listening to classical music, maybe reading, or working on one of the needlepoint designs she liked to do....

"Hello?" she said again. "Hello?"

Rex wanted her so much it was pure agony. He struggled to find his voice, but desire washed over him in a drowning wave. He needed to hold her and run his hands all over her body, reach under that shirt and cup her breasts, nuzzle the warm, silky place on her neck just below her ear....

"Is anybody there? Who is this?" she asked. He could hear the sharp note of fear in her voice, and it made him feel awkward and ashamed.

After waiting so long, there was no way he could speak now, he'd look like a complete fool. But he couldn't bring himself to hang up, either, and sever the tenuous connection between them.

Not while he hungered for her so fiercely.

"Look, whoever you are, stop calling me," she said, her voice shaking. "Leave me alone or I'll call the police!"

She hung up and he stood with the receiver in his hand, frowning.

At last he replaced the phone and wandered back into the living room. Rex settled on the couch, wondering what was happening to him.

How had he become so sexually obsessed that he'd begun making crank phone calls, terrifying this poor woman who was one of his oldest friends? Next thing he'd be driving out there in the darkness of the summer night, going right to her door and making an even bigger fool of himself.

He rolled over and buried his face in the pillow, lying painfully still and waiting for the storm of desire to subside. But he couldn't get her image out of his mind, or the fear in her voice when she'd terminated that phone call.

Was somebody else harassing Lindsay? If so, who was it?

Maybe that explained her cautious reluctance to get involved with anybody.

Or maybe, he told himself bleakly, it was just Rex Trowbridge she wanted to avoid.

CHAPTER EIGHT

"So, HOW MANY cases of beans?" Rex asked.

It was Saturday morning, two days before their camping trip, and he pored over a notebook as he lounged on the couch in Lindsay's office.

Behind the desk, Lindsay nibbled thoughtfully on the end of her pen.

"Well, let's see. We have eight people altogether, and lots of these boys can eat two cans in the blink of an eye, so let's say we need a dozen cans a day. That's about... eight dozen tins."

"Whew. That's a whole lot of beans," Rex said.

Lindsay grinned at his look of alarm. "We'll be out-doors," she assured him, "with all kinds of wide-open spaces. It'll be fine."

"That's a good point, but not exactly what I meant." Rex chuckled, then sobered. "I was thinking more about the weight of the tins. Don't you think we should be using something else? Maybe packs of freeze-dried food instead of all this tinned stuff?"

She considered and shook her head. "We'll take some freeze-dried food, but we have six pack animals, almost one for every rider. I don't think the weight of our supplies is going to be a major consideration. And tinned beans are such a nourishing high-protein food. Besides, the boys love them, even the picky eaters like Tim and Danny."

"Okay. We'll put beans on the grocery list and figure

out the rest of the food later, before I go back into town and pick up supplies.''

"When are you planning to do that?'' Lindsay asked, studying the ranch's list of available sleeping bags and groundsheets.

"Tomorrow afternoon.''

"But, Rex…that's Sunday.'' She glanced up at him. "Do you think it's safe to leave our shopping right until the last day? What if the local store doesn't have everything we need in stock?''

"I was thinking I'd take your list and buy all the supplies in Casper.''

"But we'll need them here on Sunday so the boys can help load the packs. I want them involved in every aspect of this.''

"Okay,'' Rex said. "I'll get the supplies first thing in the morning and bring them out here before noon. That should give you and the boys plenty of time for the packing.''

"That's good. Thanks.'' She looked through the papers in front of her, searching for an updated count on sleeping bags. "Too bad you don't have a truck,'' she said idly. "Maybe you could borrow one from the ranch tonight when you go home and leave your car here.''

"Do you think I'd look good driving around in a truck, Linnie?''

Something in his voice, an odd note of huskiness, made her glance up at him quickly.

Until now, Lindsay had been pretty successful at putting all his strange teasing and flirtation out of her mind. For the past couple of hours they'd worked on the details of the camping trip as if it were just another administrative problem at the ranch, like so many they'd handled together.

But now, with the sunlight filtering through the drapes

and gilding his blunt cheekbones, she felt a return of all the unsettling emotions.

Rex's face seemed thinner, and he was more tanned than he usually got in the summer when he spent his days stuck in that city office. Even his long body on the couch had a different look, lean and powerful and very masculine.

"It's got to be the clothes," she muttered, riffling hastily through stacks of paper.

"Beg your pardon?" He gave her a quick, alert glance. Despite the teasing, his eyes looked tired and darkly shadowed. Apparently Rex hadn't slept well last night, either.

But he wouldn't have been lying awake for the same reason she had....

Lindsay clenched her hands nervously into fists, then forced herself to relax and begin itemizing necessary nonedible supplies, like toilet paper and bandages.

"What did you just say about my clothes?" he asked, still watching her closely.

Lindsay felt her cheeks grow warm. "Nothing important. Just that you...you seem to look sort of different these days." She went on, floundering, "and I thought it must be the jeans and boots. I haven't seen you dressed like that in a long time, Rex."

"So you like it?"

"It's okay," she said, deliberately noncommittal, and returned to her list of first-aid supplies as if she had nothing else on her mind.

But in truth, this new Rex in his casual cowboy attire was so dangerously attractive, he seemed to fill the room. Lindsay couldn't find anywhere else to rest her eyes. Worst of all, he clearly sensed her discomfiture and found it amusing.

"Lindsay," he said at last, his voice soft.

"Yes?" she asked without looking up.

"What kind of sleeping arrangements have you made for this trip?"

She cast him a suspicious glance but he was studying the sheets of paper in his hands, making careful notations in the margins.

"It's a genuine campout," she said. "We'll take groundsheets and bedrolls and sleep under the stars. All the boys are crazy about the idea."

"No tents?" he asked idly. But Lindsay was well aware that Rex Trowbridge was not the kind of man who asked idle questions.

"I don't think tents are necessary in August," she said. "They'd add so much more bulk to our packs, and make it harder to set up camp every night. Besides, that would also keep the boys in little separate cliques, and I want them all to be together on this trip, sharing the same experience."

"But you'll need a tent for yourself," he said quietly.

"Me?" She stared at him. "Why?"

"Because you're a *girl,* Lindsay," he said with exaggerated patience. "Or have you been too busy these past few years to notice that little detail?"

"That's no big deal."

His steady gaze was so disconcerting. Again Lindsay felt her cheeks flare with sudden warmth.

"Look," she said, "on camping trips we always hang a blanket on sticks at one end of the camp and take turns getting dressed behind it. And, of course, we'll dig a latrine in the woods at every camping site. That's all the privacy I'll need."

Her companion looked briefly startled, as if he might be contemplating the reality of dressing in the chilly mountain air behind a blanket hung on posts, and using a dirt trench for a bathroom. His face expressed such deep gloom that Lindsay felt a bubble of amusement and a surprising urge to cross the room and give him an impulsive hug.

But her amusement vanished at his next words.

"You're going to need a tent," he said with an authoritative edge to his voice that probably worked really well around his office. "The boys can sleep out, and so can I. But I want you, at least, to have some privacy."

"Why?"

Rex leaned back and set the papers down at his side. He laced his fingers behind his head and stared through the window at the stable, where Clint Kraft's lanky figure could be seen among a group of horses.

"These kids aren't little boys, Lindsay," he said. "And you're a very pretty lady. Believe me," he added with a grin, "I can remember what it was like to be fifteen. So I think it will be more comfortable for everybody if you're sleeping and dressing inside a tent."

She thought it over, reluctant to give in. "In the past, I've always slept out on the ground with the boys and there's never been a problem."

"But those are younger boys who go on the little weekend campouts," Rex pointed out. "And this time we'll be gone for over a week. Just listen to me, Lindsay, and try not to argue for once in your life. I know what I'm talking about."

Though she hated to admit it, he was probably right. Lindsay said nothing, but she jotted a reminder to herself about checking into available dome tents in the supply room.

"Besides," Rex added casually, studying a scuffed area on the side of his leather boot, "what if you have company some night?"

"Company?" she asked, still thinking about the supply room. "What kind of company?"

"Overnight company." His eyes rested on her with unmistakable meaning. "It would certainly be best to keep a visit like that private, wouldn't it, Lin?"

"Look, I have…" Annoyingly, her voice caught and squeaked. She had to clear her throat and start again while he kept watching her intently. "I have no idea what you're talking about," she concluded with all the dignity she could muster.

"No idea at all, Linnie?"

She put the pen down and sat erect, folding her hands tightly on the desk in front of her. "I don't think you have this all straight yet, Rex," she said. "There will be no visitors in my tent on this camping trip. It's not going to happen. Do you understand?"

"But what if poor little Danny has a nightmare?" Rex's eyes sparkled with laughter.

"Then Danny would come into the tent and sleep with me, and bring his teddy bear," Lindsay said. "But he's eight years old. Anybody older than eight can spend the night outdoors."

"Even if one of the bigger guys has a nightmare?" Rex asked, his face deliberately sober, though his eyes continued to dance. "Like for instance, what if the biggest guy of all has a really bad dream, and needs some comforting in the middle of the night? Would you be coldhearted and turn him away, Lin?"

"In an instant," she said.

But her heart was pounding, her whole body moist with yearning as she pictured the deep shadowed woods, the starry blackness overhead, the scent of pine and the sleeping boys sprawled all around dying embers of a wood fire.

And Rex slipping silently into her tent in the moonlight, lying with her on the rumpled bedroll, holding her and kissing her, their naked bodies warm as fire in the chill of the night…

She got up abruptly and tossed her pen onto the desk. "I'm hungry," she said. "Let's go up to the house for some lunch, all right?"

Rex followed her from the office and ambled at her side toward the big log ranch house Lindsay had once shared with her father and mother, but now occupied by herself.

As they walked, she struggled to regain her composure, but she was still shaken and disturbed by all these wayward reactions of her body.

"Are you okay, honey?" he asked, taking her arm gently.

The touch of his hand on her bare skin was almost unbearable. Lindsay wanted to pull her arm away, but that would just start another uncomfortable discussion about her aloofness. So she submitted as if they were old friends who'd walked together like this a thousand times.

And that was true, of course.

But she didn't remember this tingling hunger, this wild song in her heart, the urgent desire to stop and burrow into his arms, press her face against his chest....

"God, I'm so tired," she said abruptly, climbing the steps to the veranda. "I'll bet I didn't sleep more than two hours last night."

"Why not?"

Lindsay held the door open and went into the house behind him, heading for the kitchen. "I had a breather on the phone just before bedtime," she said over her shoulder. "It really spooked me."

"A breather?" Rex asked behind her.

"Oh, it's not the first time." Lindsay washed her hands at the sink, then rummaged through the fridge, taking out cold cuts, bread and lettuce. "This guy calls me from time to time and then just...sits there. Never says a word. It's so unnerving."

With the ease of long familiarity, Rex moved through the kitchen taking plates from the cupboards, getting out a knife and cutting board.

"Do you know who it is?" he asked.

"No," Lindsay said curtly. She arranged slices of bread on the countertop and reached for the butter. "My call display always just says it's a private call, the same way it does from your unlisted number. I haven't the foggiest idea who it might be."

But that was a lie, she thought miserably. It was true she didn't know the man's name, but she certainly knew his face.

And the feel of his hands, and the sound of his voice…

She shivered and paused in the middle of the kitchen, hugging herself to ward off a sudden chill.

"Linnie?" he asked, looking up quickly. "What's the matter?"

She gave herself a little shake and began buttering the bread with quick nervous strokes. "I'm just worn-out, and it's pretty stressful to plan this whole camping trip on top of everything else. Rex, would you rather have mayo or mustard on your ham?"

He reached out and grasped her hand, the one holding the knife. "Honey, you're shaking like a leaf. Come on, tell me what's going on."

"There's nothing going on! I'm stressed out, that's all."

She paused, conscious of him watching her in concern, and forced herself to meet his eyes.

"Rex, I really want to thank you for helping me with all this, and being such a good sport. You're taking a huge load off my hands, and I appreciate it."

He grinned in reply. But the smile didn't touch his eyes, which remained thoughtful and worried. "Hey, what choice do I have?" he said lightly. "Like you told me, I'm bought and paid for, right?"

Lindsay felt a touch of sympathy. "Are you really going to hate it? Going on this trail ride for a whole week with a bunch of boys?"

"And you," he said casually, breaking chunks from a

head of lettuce. "Don't forget the most important part. *You're* going to be there, too."

"But that doesn't mean anything," she said, trying to match his casual tone. "It's been such a long time since my presence or absence made any difference to you."

"How do you know that?"

Lindsay glanced up at him in surprise, conscious again of his maleness, the hard planes of his face, the sculpted line of his lower lip. She had a sudden urge to touch him, to caress his cheek and run a finger over his mouth.

The image was both distressing and embarrassing. She turned hurriedly back to her work, hoping Rex hadn't noticed.

But even when she wasn't looking at him she could sense his nearness as he lounged by the counter, his physical strength, even the pleasant scent of his aftershave. The room had an intensely intimate feel, as if they were the only two people in the world.

Lindsay had been alone with the man hundreds of times, but she'd never been so aware of him.

"I'm still worried about this guy who calls you and breathes on the phone," he said at last, breaking the awkward silence. "Are you sure it isn't just a wrong number or something?"

"I'm sure," she said briefly. "Let's not talk about it anymore, okay?"

Rex turned away to slice mushrooms and green peppers on top of the lettuce, making a salad. "Sometimes," he said over his shoulder, "people can dial a number and then get interrupted or forget what they were going to say, so they just hang up without saying anything. Hell, I've even done it myself."

"So have I," Lindsay said. Despite her agitation, she was touched that he kept trying so hard to reassure her. "But it isn't like that, Rex. This guy calls me..." She paused, gripping the knife tightly, and felt her heart begin to pound. "Never mind," she said. "Please, let's talk about something else, okay?"

He went to the fridge and got out the salad dressing, giving her another worried glance. "Have you told the police?" he asked.

Lindsay stared at him.

Tell the police, a voice echoed inside her head. *Tell the police, tell the police....*

She took a deep breath and stacked the sandwiches on the cutting board, slicing them raggedly with her knife. "What am I going to tell them? This guy phones from time to time and says nothing, and it scares me? I'm sure they'd be really impressed with that."

As she spoke, Lindsay pictured herself talking to the police, telling them the whole truth, easing the terrible burden on her heart.

That interview with the police was a fantasy she'd had for almost four years.

But Lindsay knew she was never going to do it. She was such a pitiful, contemptible coward....

"I know a female detective in Casper who has great advice for this kind of thing," Rex was saying. "You know what she always tells women if they're being upset by crank calls?"

Lindsay arranged her sandwiches on a plate and set a couple of places at the table in the sunny eating nook. "What does she tell them?"

Rex brought over the salad and a pair of small wooden bowls. "She says to keep a police whistle right beside the phone. When you know your caller's on the line, blow it as hard as you can right into the mouthpiece. The sound hurts like hell. It'll be a while before this guy wants to call you again."

Lindsay looked over at him, startled. "Hey, that's not a

bad idea," she said slowly. "In fact, it's great. I wonder if one of the boys has a really loud whistle."

"Don't worry, I'll buy you a good one tomorrow when I pick up the supplies."

Lindsay watched as he took an electronic organizer from his breast pocket, flicked it open and punched in a notation.

There'd been a time, and not too long ago, when she would have looked on such an action as affected and pompous, a deliberate display of Rex's sophistication. No doubt she would even have been vaguely annoyed.

But Lindsay realized she'd been unfair to this man in recent years.

Now he was sitting across from her in jeans and boots, planning a campout in the mountains, expressing concern about her welfare. And she found his pleasure with his electronic organizer had a boyish quality that was actually endearing.

"You men," she said, smiling at him. "You sure do love your toys, don't you?"

Rex frowned, concentrating on setting the alarm to ping as a reminder. "Toys?" he asked.

"Like it's so hard to carry a notebook and pen," Lindsay scoffed. "You need your stuff on a memory chip or it doesn't count."

But she didn't feel sharp or scornful. And she knew there was a note of indulgence, almost affection in her voice that unnerved her.

Rex looked up and met her eyes in obvious surprise. Then he smiled, a warm grin that made his whole face light up. Suddenly he was the same boy she'd known so long ago, with his mercurial shifts from brooding anger to a cheerful, sexy ebullience that used to take her breath away.

Their sandwiches were briefly forgotten, along with the conversation. For a long moment they smiled at each other as the warm bars of sunlight slanted through the window blinds.

CHAPTER NINE

LINDSAY WAS the first to turn away, her heart pounding. "Come on," she said with forced casualness, "have a sandwich. If they're left over, I'll just have to eat them for supper."

"Do you ever get lonely here?" Rex asked, looking around at the pleasant ranch-style house. "How do you spend your evenings?"

"Lots of nights I bring things home from the office. When I don't have any work to do, mostly I read, or listen to music and do my cross-stitching."

"Don't you watch television?"

"Not much, just a few shows that I really like. The rest of the time I turn it off."

"That's what I should do," he said. "I watch far too much junk. But if the television's not on, my place seems so lonely."

Lindsay glanced at him, surprised by this unexpected glimpse into his private life. "Somehow I never pictured you sitting around watching television," she said. "I thought you were always out on the town with some glamorous woman."

He laughed with genuine amusement, then shook his head. "Oh, Linnie," he said, his voice suddenly husky. "If you only knew."

She was about to ask him what he meant when a knock sounded at the front door.

"Come in," Lindsay called, knowing it would probably be one of the boys. "Who's there?"

"It's me," Danny responded from the entry foyer.

"Take your shoes off and come in, Danny," Lindsay told him. "We're having lunch."

He arrived in the kitchen, padding softly in his stockinged feet, and came over to lean against Lindsay's chair as he always did.

She put her arm around the little boy and hugged him. "Those socks are full of holes," she told him. "Where are the new ones I bought you?"

"In the wash. Rosemary took them," he said, referring to the pleasant, motherly woman who looked after the boys' dormitory.

"All six pairs?" Lindsay asked while Rex looked on, smiling.

Danny snuggled against her and examined the sandwiches. "Maybe not all of them," he said evasively. "But these were the only ones I could find this morning."

Lindsay sighed and made a mental note to do another check of his wardrobe. If she didn't stay on top of it all the time, he soon looked like a ragamuffin.

"Danny, I don't know what to do with you. I really don't."

But Danny wasn't listening. Gravely he selected a sandwich from the plate that Rex offered, then sank into a chair between them.

"This is nice," the little boy said after chewing and swallowing a huge bite. "It's like eating with a real family."

"A real family?" Lindsay asked.

"A mom and a dad."

"Oh, sweetheart." Lindsay reached out to give the little boy a hug, then became aware of Rex's thoughtful glance.

Her cheeks flamed with embarrassment, and she sipped hastily at her glass of water.

Danny continued to eat, placidly unaware of the discomfiture he'd caused. "Clint says…"

Lindsay touched his shoulder gently. "Don't talk with your mouth full, sweetheart."

Rex smiled at her, his eyes crinkling warmly. He seemed relaxed and at ease in this setting, which surprised her a little.

Even in his late teens when he was the acknowledged leader of the other boys at the ranch, Rex Trowbridge had always been big, prowling and predatory. And in later years when he became a "corporate animal," as Lindsay often teased, he'd seemed even more formidable, though in a glossy, sophisticated kind of way.

Despite the closeness of their long friendship, she had to admit he was even a little scary in his city lawyer mode. But now, relaxing in the sunny kitchen with Danny between them, the man didn't seem imposing at all, just pleasant and approachable.

Lindsay found herself liking this new, casual Rex. In fact, she liked him a lot.

Except when he started looking at her with such disturbing intensity, or teased her about their long-ago, childhood relationship….

"What does Clint say?" she asked Danny to break the silence.

"He says you and Rex should come over to the barn and look at the horses." Danny sat erect in the chair, beaming with importance at being the one to deliver this message. "Clint says he needs the final list checked off or something."

Lindsay and Rex exchanged another puzzled glance.

"Are you sure he wants us to do it?" Rex asked the

little boy. "Wouldn't Sam be the one to approve the riding horses?"

"Clint asked, but Sam said for you to do it," Danny reported. "Clint said Sam didn't feel like bothering about the horses."

Lindsay met Rex's eyes again, frowning. "That sounds so odd. Rex, do you have any idea what might be wrong with…"

Rex raised an eyebrow and nodded imperceptibly toward Danny. "Not a clue," he said. "But there's definitely something going on there. I'll see what I can find out, okay?"

"Something going on where?" Danny asked, then took a thirsty swig from the tumbler of milk Lindsay brought to him.

"Now you've got a milk moustache," Rex said. "Here, let me fix it."

He took his napkin and swabbed gently at the little boy's mouth. Lindsay sat down again, watching the tender competence of his hands. Suddenly her heart melted with emotion. She got up hastily to clear the counter and load the dishwasher.

"What's your rush?" Rex asked, leaning back in his chair to watch her. "Don't we have time for coffee and a chat?"

Lindsay avoided his gaze. "We really should go right away to look at those horses. Then we have to finish the supply list and print another one for each of the boys so they can get their packs ready for inspection. The truck is leaving with all their equipment at five o'clock tomorrow evening to rendezvous with us Monday morning at the trail head, so we only have…"

"Lindsay," he said.

She stopped and turned to him.

"Quit fretting and rushing around," Rex told her calmly. "There'll still be lots of time to get everything done."

He extended a long arm and drew Danny close to him, scooping the little boy from his chair. "Come sit on my other knee, Lindsay," he said over his shoulder. "I'll tell both of you a story."

Danny bounced happily on the big man's lap, but Lindsay turned away, annoyed once more by the teasing sparkle in Rex's eyes and his slow meaningful grin.

"No stories today," she said curtly. "There's far too much to do."

Danny tipped his head back. "Tell me the story," he said to Rex. "What's it about?"

Rex hugged the little boy and rested his chin on Danny's mass of gingery curls. Lindsay smiled privately, watching from the corner of her eye as the lawyer searched his mind for a story that might be suitable for an eight-year-old boy.

"This story's about me when I was your age," he said at last, "and I had dog called Scout."

"Oh, *boy,*" Danny breathed. "I love stories about kids and dogs."

Lindsay kept stacking dishes, listening intently. Despite their long friendship, she'd never learned much about Rex's boyhood days. She was always curious to learn what his life had been like before he came to Lost Springs Ranch as a wild, sullen twelve-year-old.

But he set Danny gently on the floor and ruffled the boy's hair. "Later I'll tell you the story," he promised. "When we're on the trail and have all kinds of time to fill in."

"Not now?" Danny asked, clearly disappointed.

"Right now Lindsay says we all have to keep busy, and she's the boss."

"Are you the boss?" Danny asked her gravely, watching as she spooned detergent into a little compartment in the door of the dishwasher.

"I certainly am." She hugged him briefly. "And don't you forget it, young man. Either of you."

Rex chuckled and got up to begin putting his salad makings away in the fridge. He lifted Danny and sat him on the counter, where the little boy sat swinging his stockinged feet.

"I like it here," Danny said wistfully. "You guys are so nice. When my mom and dad were... Before they..."

Suddenly his face reddened and contorted. Tears began to stream down his cheeks as he gulped and sobbed. Lindsay moved toward him, but Rex was too quick.

He gathered Danny in his arms and carried him out through the house toward the veranda. "We'll just rock and talk for a while," he called over his shoulder. "Come out when you're ready, Lin. Okay?"

"All right." As Lindsay worked, she listened to the low murmur beyond the screened front door. She could hear Rex's deeper rumble, punctuated by Danny's tear-choked words. Gradually their voices stilled and a feeling of midday contentment stole over the log house.

She wrung out the dishcloth and hung it next to the towel, then steeled herself to go outside.

It was getting harder all the time to deal with this new Rex, both his teasing and his surprising tenderness. The sight of him holding and comforting Danny had practically wiped out the last of her defenses.

Ruefully, she examined her flushed, bright-eyed reflection in the hall mirror.

If Rex Trowbridge kept behaving this way, he wouldn't even have to invade her tent under cover of darkness. She'd be more likely to leave the flap wide open as an invitation.

The thought was alarming to her on several levels. First of all, she couldn't behave so wantonly with a man who was one of her oldest friends. Besides, the life Rex had built for himself was not at all the kind that appealed to her.

Mostly, though, Lindsay couldn't bear the thought of being touched intimately or held by *any* man.

Not after…

She turned abruptly, grabbed her sweater from the bench in the hall and went out onto the veranda where Rex sat in the rocking chair that had once belonged to her father, Danny cuddled in his lap. So many boys had been rocked and comforted in that same chair in years past.

The child's storm of tears had subsided, and the summer afternoon was still and peaceful.

"All set?" Rex asked, looking up at her.

Lindsay nodded and cast a questioning glance toward Danny's red curls.

"This cowboy's just fine," Rex said. "Aren't you, son?"

"I'm fine," Danny replied. He wriggled to look up at Lindsay. The blue eyes were still red-rimmed, but his tears had been carefully wiped away, and he looked almost like his old cheerful self.

"Well then, let's go see the horses," Lindsay suggested. "You lead the way, Danny."

Rex set the boy on his feet, and they both watched as he scampered down the steps and across the yard toward the barn. Lindsay and Rex followed more slowly, strolling along in the sunshine.

"Thank you for taking care of him," she said. "I had no idea you could be like that."

"Like what?"

"So…tender," Lindsay said awkwardly.

He took her arm and drew her closer. "I keep telling you, Linnie, there are such a lot of things you need to learn about me."

This time she pulled away hastily, alarmed by the storm

of feeling he aroused in her. "I don't want to learn any-thing, thanks," she said a little stiffly. "I think after all these years, I know as much about you as I'm ever going to need."

She was spared his reply when Sam wandered toward them with the bereft look he'd been wearing since yester-day. Her uncle carried a bit of wood and was whittling on it aimlessly as he headed toward his own little house near the creek.

Lindsay reached out to stop him. "Why don't you come to the barn with us, Sam?" she said. "Clint wants us to check out the horses for our trail ride, but it's been years since I had very much to do with that part of the business. I really don't have a clue which horses would be best for us to take."

Sam kicked the toe of his boot idly in the dirt. "I reckon young Clint's on top of things," he said. "The boy spends all his time down there, and he takes real good care of the horses."

"But…" Lindsay exchanged a glance with Rex, feeling helpless and worried. "But does he really know the horses well enough to pick safe mounts for all these boys?"

Sam shrugged, a wholly uncharacteristic gesture. "One horse is pretty much like another, I guess. None of them are going to buck, and they all know how to find their way back home, so I don't suppose it matters which ones you take."

Rex tightened his grip on Lindsay's arm, giving it a squeeze of warning. "Okay, Sam," he said. "Lindsay and I will go down and work things out with Clint. You have a nice lunch."

"Is it lunchtime?" Sam looked vaguely at his watch, then tried to smile. "When a feller gets this old, he starts to lose track of time."

He shambled off toward his cottage again while Lindsay

watched in concern. For the first time, her uncle really did look old, and his aimless, lonely air tore at her heart.

"I wish I knew what the problem was," she said in an undertone to Rex.

"It must be something that just happened recently. He's been this way since yesterday."

"But, Rex…you probably won't get a chance to talk to him before we leave."

He patted her shoulder. "We'll only be gone a week. We're not going to the ends of the earth, Lin, just west into the mountains."

"I guess you're right." She smiled wanly. "But with all the supplies on this list, it sure feels like we're going to the ends of the earth."

They both paused at the entrance to the barn. Danny had vanished inside to find Clint, and the two of them followed.

CLINT GLANCED UP, suddenly tense when he saw the man and woman silhouetted in the square of sunlight at the door of the barn. He was sitting on a bale of hay as he repaired a torn saddle blanket, mending the leather edging with a heavy curved needle and the neat stitching that Sam had taught him.

Danny arrived and stood at his side, watching with interest. Clint grunted at the boy, then pretended not to notice as Rex and Lindsay drew nearer.

"Hi, Clint," the lawyer said. "Sam wanted us to check in with you on your list of horses for the trail ride."

Clint kept stitching, deliberately finishing the edging of the blanket. "Okay," he said, after a lengthy pause that stopped just short of outright rudeness. "I'll be right with you."

He glanced up covertly, watching as the three of them wandered outside into the corral. Then he knotted and snipped the coarse thread.

It gave him a lot of satisfaction to keep the big-shot lawyer waiting.

Clint had cooled his heels in a lot of lawyers' waiting rooms over the past year. And whenever he finally got into their offices, they'd pushed him around and pretended a concern they obviously didn't feel. He enjoyed the chance to give one of them the same treatment for a change.

But Lindsay looked tired and frazzled, and Clint couldn't help feeling a bit of sympathy for her. She was working really hard on this dumb trip, wearing herself out. Clint wanted to tell her not to bother, that the little kids and the lawyer weren't worth so much effort.

Part of him also wanted to warn her that if they went ahead with the trip, something bad was almost certain to happen.

He set his jaw and got up, tossing the sewing supplies into a big wooden box near the tack room.

The welfare of this group wasn't his responsibility. If they insisted on hauling him off on some kiddie expedition, they deserved whatever they got. Their problems were going to be funny to watch, Clint told himself firmly. In fact, he was going to get a real kick out of the whole thing.

He ambled out into the corral, carrying a prepared list of horses. On Clint's roster, an individual horse's name was matched to each of the eight people going on the trail ride, while six others were designated as pack animals.

Lindsay glanced over the list, then looked up at him. "Can you show us which horses these are, Clint?"

"Sure." He moved over to the corral fence and gestured across the pasture. "The Bernstein kids are riding those two pinto mares over there." He pretend to consult his list, although he knew all the horse assignments by heart. "Larkin gets Prince," he said, "and Lonnie will ride Duchess."

"Is Duchess still around?" Rex asked. "I remember riding her when I lived here."

"She's such a sweetheart." Lindsay smiled at the old roan mare. "Most of the boys still learn to ride on Duchess."

Clint checked the list again, feeling a cruel lift of amusement. It appeared this was going to be even easier than he'd expected.

"I'm giving you two those sorrel geldings," he said, pointing, "and I'll take the bay. Danny here..." He patted the little boy's head. "He's going to ride that little buckskin mare."

"Her name is Daisy." Danny jumped from one foot to another in excitement. "Clint lets me ride her around the corral every day, and Rosemary gives me carrots to feed her. Daisy loves me. Doesn't she, Clint?"

Clint felt Lindsay's eyes resting on him with startled approval. Again he felt guilt and a touch of unease, and firmly suppressed the emotions.

"Are these new horses?" Rex was studying the two sorrels Clint had selected for him and Lindsay. "I don't recognize either of them."

Clint tensed. "Pretty new," he said casually. "Sam bought them at a horse sale a while ago. He says he likes both of them a lot. They've been trained to be really gentle."

The lawyer nodded, and Clint felt a cold touch of scorn.

The guy might look tough, but he was as easy to fool as any other adult. None of them paid any attention to what kids were doing. They deserved whatever they got, all of them.

But he kept his face expressionless, going on to point out the horses he'd selected for the pack string. All of them were gentle saddle horses, as well, so they'd have spares in case any of the designated mounts came up lame during the trip.

Finally Lindsay initialed Clint's list and gave him a

warm smile that made him feel clumsy and nervous. He watched as they took a last look at the horses in the corral, then left and headed back to the office. Clint saw the lawyer reach out to put a hand on her arm as they walked. Lindsay pulled away, but there wasn't much conviction in her resistance. In fact, these days she seemed flustered and emotional whenever Trowbridge was around.

And it was easy to see how much the man wanted her.

Clint's eyes narrowed as he turned back to the barn.

The lawyer was probably going to get her, too. Rex Trowbridge was the kind of man who always got everything he wanted, including all the pretty women.

Well, just let him wait a few days, Clint thought grimly. Let him get out on that trail and have a few little problems, and see what a big shot he was…

"Can I ride Daisy now?" Danny said, materializing at his side.

"Not now," Clint told him. "I have to run an errand for Sam. Maybe you can ride her after supper, okay?"

"Then can I come with you while you do the errand?"

Clint looked down with touch of exasperation at the boy's eager freckled face.

"Oh, all right," he said. "I'm just going over to Rob Carter's to pick up some first-aid supplies for the trail ride. Hop in the truck."

CHAPTER TEN

GWEN MCCABE WAS in her accustomed chair on the veranda. Brian sprawled on a rug at her feet, reading a book with his baseball glove nearby, while a couple of dogs drowsed next to them in the shade.

She was working on a knitted afghan, inserting cable needles and twisting the yarn into a complex pattern as she frowned through her reading glasses at the intricate mass of instructions.

"Knit two back," Gwen muttered, "and purl two forward. But that's what I just did. Now, what do you suppose they mean by…"

Surreptitiously she glanced up at the dusty road for a moment, then returned to her work, feeling nervous and embarrassed.

But even though she'd been keeping watch most of the afternoon, Brian was the first to notice the approaching vehicle.

"Somebody's coming," her grandson announced a few minutes later. "It's a truck."

Gwen peered anxiously down the road again. Both dogs had lifted their heads, as well, and were looking on with drowsy interest. Her heart began to pound when she recognized the blue vehicle from Lost Springs Ranch that Sam Duncan always drove.

He was coming back after all, she thought, feeling a joyous rush of happiness.

Sam had decided she wasn't a total idiot. He was giving

her a second chance. And this time she wasn't going to squander the opportunity.

No matter how embarrassing it was, Gwen intended to explain to Sam just what was wrong with her, and beg him for his understanding. She liked the man far too much to give him the wrong impression or hurt his feelings another time.

"Brian..." she began, anxious to get the little boy out of the way so she and Sam could talk privately. "My goodness, sweetheart, I think it's just about time for you to go over to Brody's. I know you have batting practise today."

"Not for a while, Gram," Brian said. "Brody had to go to the dentist today. Hey, look," he added, brightening. "Danny's here."

Gwen's anticipation turned to cold disappointment when she saw a boy and small red-haired child get out of the truck and approach the veranda.

Earlier that morning Rob had prepared several kits of first-aid equipment for Lindsay Duncan's trail ride and left them with Gwen when he went off to work at his clinic. She'd been watching the road ever since, hoping Sam would be the one to come over from the ranch and pick up the medical supplies.

But obviously Sam never wanted to see her again. He thought she was rude and unkind, not worth a moment of his time.

Gwen shivered when she recalled that last dreadful, uncomfortable meeting, after he'd been kind enough to bring her the beautiful illustrated book about owls. Sam had been so sweet, asking her out for dinner like a shy teenager. And when she refused without an explanation, he'd looked as wounded and embarrassed as Brian did when somebody hurt his feelings.

Oh, Sam, she thought in agony. *I wish I could tell you how sorry I am....*

Gwen realized the newcomers were standing at the foot of the veranda steps, looking up at her expectantly.

"I guess you've come for the first-aid supplies?" she asked.

"Sam told me Rob was getting them ready, and I should come and pick them up this afternoon."

The older boy's voice was surprisingly deep. He looked to be about sixteen and had a dark, withdrawn air.

"I have them in the kitchen." Gwen put aside the knitting and got to her feet. "Just sit yourselves down for a minute and I'll go fetch them."

"Gram," Brian said, "can I take Danny to see my rabbits?"

"Of course, dear," Gwen said with automatic courtesy. "And maybe these two fellows would like some lemonade and cookies?"

"We have to get back to the ranch," the other boy said. "There's a lot of work to do, getting ready for the trail ride."

But the two smaller children had already vanished around the back of the house.

Gwen smiled. "Well, it looks like you might as well sit down for a minute," she told her visitor. "When little boys start looking at rabbits, it usually takes a while to distract them. What's your name?"

"Clint Kraft." He mounted the steps and sat awkwardly in one of the chairs, reaching to pat the spaniel who lay at his feet.

"I'll bring out those first-aid kits and a bit of a snack. By the way," she added, "my name's Gwen McCabe. I'm Rob's mother-in-law."

"Hello." The boy gave her a quick, expressionless glance.

Gwen smiled, but he'd already turned away and was patting the dog again. She couldn't decide if he was sullen or just shy.

She went into the house and piled some oatmeal cookies on a plate, set out a jug of lemonade and four glasses and carried them onto the veranda, placing the tray on a little wooden side table.

"Help yourself," she said to her silent visitor. "I'll get the first-aid kits."

He still said nothing, but when she peeked back from inside the house, Gwen saw him munch one of the cookies with obvious appreciation, and immediately reach for another.

She returned with the plastic kits and stacked them at the top of the stairs. "Rob says to tell Lindsay he packed everything she might possibly need, including antidote for snakebite. If she has any questions, she's supposed to call him."

"Okay," the boy said curtly, reaching for another cookie.

Gwen sat in her chair again and poured herself a glass of lemonade. "Are you going along on this trail ride, Clint?"

"I have to. They say nobody can stay behind at the ranch."

Gwen cast a glance at his withdrawn expression. "But you're not excited about it? I'd think this would be a terrific adventure."

He scowled and stared at his feet. "It's a stupid thing," he muttered bitterly. "The other kids are just babies. Even *Danny* gets to go."

She could sense his anger, along with depths of underlying pain that tore at her heart. "So you'd rather just stay at home than camp out for a week in the wilderness?" she asked, wondering what had happened to alienate this boy.

"I'd rather be a thousand miles away from this place," he said. "I hate everything about it, except for the horses."

Gwen hesitated, a little reluctant to probe further. All the boys at Lost Springs Ranch had sad stories of pain, loss and abandonment, and she knew it might not be wise to ask questions.

But her concern won out over caution.

"Where were you living before you came here?" she asked.

"I was in Denver. I ran away a couple of years ago, after my mother went to jail."

"Where did you go?" Gwen asked, listening to distant peals of laughter as the two little boys played behind the house.

He shrugged. "Nowhere. On the streets."

Gwen tried to picture her beloved grandson just a few years from now, surviving by himself on the streets of a big city, but her imagination couldn't even encompass the idea.

"Oh, Clint," she said. "That must have been so hard for you."

"Yeah, it was hard." His voice was still brusque, but Gwen could sense that he was getting more involved in the conversation, responding to her sympathy.

The poor boy probably never talked much to anybody around him. Maybe it was easier to open up to a stranger, especially when that person was a harmless gray-haired grandmother who sat on a shady veranda and served him cookies.

"So how did you survive?" she asked.

"I got into a gang. We stole things so we could buy food. When I got busted, they sent me here to this dumb place."

Impulsively Gwen put a hand on his arm. He flinched a

little at her touch, but didn't get up and stalk away as she'd half expected.

"Have another cookie," she said. "There are more in the kitchen."

He obeyed, chewing and swallowing in silence as both of them stared at the vivid flower garden beyond the picket fence.

"Weren't you scared?" Gwen asked at last. "It seems to me that would be such a terrifying way to live, especially for a young person."

His dark glance flicked over her. "Sure I was scared. All the time. You don't even know what it means to be scared, living in a nice place like this."

"Oh, but you're wrong," Gwen said. "I know what it's like to be scared, Clint. I'm not frightened of the same things you were, maybe, but I live with terror every day of my life."

For the first time he looked at her directly, and the sullen, brooding expression lifted for a moment. "You do?" he asked. "What are you afraid of?"

"Everything." Gwen wondered why she was telling him this. "I have panic attacks whenever I try to leave the house."

"What's a panic attack?"

"I get so scared, I feel as if I'm going to faint. My throat closes up so I can't breathe, and my head starts to spin."

By now Clint was apparently so fascinated that he'd forgotten about being rude and withdrawn. "What makes you scared?"

"I have a medical condition called agoraphobia," Gwen said. "That means I'm afraid of open spaces."

"So you get scared like that whenever you go anywhere?" he asked.

"I don't go anywhere," Gwen told him simply. "I can't leave the house."

She realized it was the first time she'd told this truth to anybody outside the family.

By now she understood she was giving Clint Kraft the explanation she'd wanted so much to tell Sam Duncan. She was telling Clint about herself because Sam hadn't come to see her, and he never would again.

"You can't leave your house?" the boy asked in disbelief. "But that's crazy."

"I guess it is," Gwen said with a humorless smile. "But that doesn't make it any less real if you happen to be the one who's suffering from it."

"How do you… What kind of life do you have?"

"Quite a lonely one," she said. "And it makes me feel even worse when I realize I'm a burden to my family because of these ridiculous fears. But I still can't seem to get over them."

Clint munched thoughtfully on another cookie. "What causes something like that?" he asked at last.

"Usually some kind of panic or trauma in a person's past life," Gwen said, thinking of her husband's tragic death. "I've had…some pretty awful experiences. I think they hurt me so much that something just snapped inside me, and it seems to be taking a long time to repair, no matter how hard I try."

He glanced at her again. For a moment the boy's scornful mask dropped away, and she could see the deep hurt in his eyes.

"I guess everybody reacts to things in a different way," he said at last, staring at the garden again.

"What do you mean?"

"Well, you've been hurt," Clint said, "but now you keep beating up on yourself, right?"

Gwen considered, then nodded. "I suppose that's what I'm doing."

"Well, some people are different. They…"

"Yes?" she prompted when he fell silent.

The boy cleared his throat. "Some people, when they've been hurt, they'd rather take it out on other people. They want to see somebody else get hurt the same way."

All at once Gwen felt a chilly touch of danger, almost a warning in his voice. "Do you feel that way sometimes, Clint?" she asked softly.

But his dark face looked shuttered and cold again, and she knew their strange moment of closeness had passed.

"When people push you around," he said, getting to his feet, "they shouldn't be surprised if you push back." He looked directly at her. "Because they deserve whatever they get."

Again Gwen thought she detected a note of warning in the boy's voice. She stared up at him, wondering what to say.

"Come on, Danny," he shouted toward the back of the house. "We have to go."

The little boys rushed around the corner of the shed, and Danny set up an immediate protest when he realized they were leaving before he had a chance to be served cookies and lemonade.

"Just put some of those cookies in your pocket," Clint told the child, striding toward their truck with the first-aid kits tucked under his arm. "I can't waste any more time."

Gwen smiled apologetically at Danny as she filled his pockets with cookies. Then she stood by the railing to watch as he climbed into the truck and the two boys drove off, heading back to Lost Springs.

Brian waved, then wandered back around to the rear of the house where his rabbit cages were kept.

After the ranch truck disappeared behind a grove of trees, Gwen sat down and twisted her hands nervously in her lap, wondering what to do.

Gwen McCabe was no stranger to pain. She realized

Clint Kraft had suffered terrible things that twisted his soul, although she also suspected he had a core of decency and might be worth salvaging if somebody was willing to spend enough time with him.

But she was also troubled when she remembered the look on his face.

Clint Kraft had enough pent-up anger to be dangerous, and he was soon going to be isolated in the mountains for a week with five younger boys and a couple of adults. At some level, Gwen had the feeling he'd been trying to remind her of that fact.

Particularly because he'd said these things to a virtual stranger, she thought perhaps he'd been warning her, almost begging for somebody to intercede and stop him before he could do something destructive.

Gwen wondered if she had the responsibility to tell somebody her fears.

If she didn't, and as a result some kind of harm came to any of the people on that trail ride, she'd feel terrible.

Finally she settled back in her chair and picked up her knitting, wondering if anybody would even pay attention to her. Most likely they'd think she was just a silly old woman whose imagination was working overtime because she never left the safety of her own house.

And probably they'd be right.

Frowning, she tried to concentrate on the complicated pattern. But all she could see was Clint Kraft's angry young face, and the cynical twist of his mouth as he talked about hurting people.

THE FOLLOWING AFTERNOON Rex and Lindsay were outside the rear entry to the Lost Springs Ranch office, making their final arrangements before embarking on the trail ride the next morning.

Loads of supplies had already been leaving throughout

the afternoon. Clint and one of the ranch hands were hauling the horses over to the Bighorn Ranch, where they would be kept overnight so the animals would be fed and rested, eager for an early start on the trail the following day.

Along with the horses, Clint was also taking all the equipment, the bedrolls and cooking equipment and supplies of food. On the square of lawn behind Lindsay's office, each boy was required to display his own pack and have it approved before Clint loaded it on the truck.

Rex had finished itemizing their itinerary and now sat on the office steps, watching as Lindsay checked through duffel bags and backpacks.

The day was hot and windy. She wore a brief cotton sundress printed with big yellow flowers and a pair of leather sandals. This attire was something of a novelty to Rex, who was accustomed to seeing her in jeans or khaki shorts and businesslike plaid shirts.

"Lonnie," she said, her voice drifting up from the lawn, "you can't take all these granola bars! Look, there must be three or four dozen of them in here."

Lonnie Schneider looked anxiously at the bulging zippered pack in her hand. "But I need proper nourishment," he said. "What if we get stranded out there and run out of food?"

"C'mon, Schneider," Jason Bernstein said. The Bernstein brothers' neat packs were both already approved, but the boys still hung around watching. "You could live off your fat."

"Until Christmas, at least," Jason's twin brother chimed in, grinning.

All the boys laughed, but Lonnie still looked deeply alarmed when Lindsay set the pack of rich treats aside on the grass.

"Lindsay," he pleaded, "come on, I can't get along

without granola bars for a whole week. The doctor says I need the fiber.''

"Fiber! Hey, Lonnie needs *fiber*.'' The other boys hooted in delight.

Rex smiled privately, enjoying the warmth of sunshine on his face and the lively group arguing down on the lawn. He watched with interest to see how Lindsay would handle their conflict.

She was so damned good with all these boys.

"Fiber is good for you, but do you need six bars a day?'' she asked Lonnie.

Lonnie shifted uncomfortably and looked down at his dirty sneakers. "I'm just worried about running out. That always scares me a lot.''

When Lindsay turned to exchange a quick glance with Rex, he could tell what she was thinking by the soft, troubled look in her eyes.

Lonnie Schneider had been sent to the ranch when he was ten years old. He'd been found living in an alley behind one of the trendy restaurants in Jackson Hole and scavenging food from a nearby garbage bin. Lonnie's mother was dead and his father, they learned, was a migrant farm worker who'd abandoned him, claiming the boy wasn't his biological child.

In the days soon after the social worker brought Lonnie to Lost Springs Ranch, he wouldn't talk to anybody but he ate all the time, greedily and voraciously, as if every meal set in front of him was the last he would ever see.

Now, four years later, Lonnie Schneider was plump and amiable, easygoing and lazy, bearing few apparent scars from his childhood ordeal. But they knew he was still terrified by the prospect of running out of food.

Rex watched with interest as Lindsay wavered, holding the pack of granola bars. "Okay, I'll tell you what,'' she said to Lonnie. "You can take your granola bars if you promise to share. There are enough bars in this pack for every single boy, including you, to eat at least one of them a day."

Lonnie's round face drained of color. "But if everybody eats one, they'll be gone in no time!"

Lindsay hugged the boy and patted him soothingly as Rex watched.

"Lonnie," she said, "listen to me. We have tons of food. Most of the pack horses are carrying nothing but food supplies. There's not a chance in the world of us running out."

He drew away and looked up at her, obviously struggling with his own fears.

"So what'll it be, Lonnie?" she asked. "Are you going to share your snacks, or will you leave them behind altogether?"

The boy kicked sullenly at a clump of grass. "I guess I'll share."

Lindsay patted his arm and smiled her approval. "Then your pack is fine. Stack it inside the office with the others and Clint will load it up later when they make their next trip."

"Okay." Looking relieved now that he'd made the painful decision to sacrifice his treats, Lonnie marched past Rex and into the office, depositing his pack next to the others by her desk.

Rex watched, still smiling, as the plump boy disappeared around the side of the office with the Bernstein twins.

Lindsay came up to sit on the steps beside him, stretched her legs wearily and rested her head against the door frame.

They were alone in the warm summer afternoon, with nobody else in sight. Rex felt himself tingling with sudden excitement at her nearness. She looked so pretty in that little scrap of a dress, with her shapely tanned legs and graceful shoulders, her windblown curls...

"I guess Lonnie was the last one," he said. "Or is there another boy waiting?"

"No, that's it. All six examined and accounted for. Now the poor things just have to fill in the time somehow until we leave tomorrow. I'm letting them go into town after supper and see a movie."

Rex felt a brief touch of worry. "Is Danny going with them?"

"You really like Danny, don't you?" Lindsay turned to him, smiling.

For some reason her question made Rex vaguely uncomfortable. "I just wondered," he said, "because he seems awfully small to be hanging around with that gang of teenage boys."

Lindsay frowned. "I know he does, but I can hardly exclude him from everything they're doing. If I don't let him go to the movie, he'll have to sit around in the dorm and watch television with Rosemary like he does every other night."

"Maybe you and I could take him somewhere," Rex said, remembering their comfortable lunch in Lindsay's house, and Danny's heart-rending comment that it felt just like a real family.

And then that storm of tears, and the warm feeling of holding the little boy while he cried, comforting him and stroking his hair…

Lindsay rolled her head against the door frame and watched him with a quizzical expression.

"What?" Rex asked. "Why are you looking at me like that?"

"I'm just…wondering, that's all."

"Wondering what?"

Lindsay frowned and plucked a blade of grass from the lawn. She leaned back, chewing on it thoughtfully.

"What's going on with you, anyhow?" she asked. "For

years and years you've been coming out here in a suit and
tie to check the books and preside at meetings. Then you'd
always go barreling back to the city so fast I couldn't see
you for dust. But now…''

He waited while she stared at the creek winding slowly
past them, its surface shimmering with broken bits of light.

''Now all of a sudden you're hanging around in cowboy
clothes, offering to take little kids on outings, teasing me
as if I were—''

''As if you were what?'' he asked when she stopped
abruptly.

She looked down at her hands, obviously unwilling to
continue. Rex waited, holding his breath, aware that something of monumental importance was on the verge of happening between them.

Something that could change their lives forever.

CHAPTER ELEVEN

LINDSAY'S CHEEKS were pink with exertion, and she looked as pretty as a wild rose. The heat of the day coupled with the hard work of lifting the boys' packs had made her warm. Rex could see a delicate shimmer of perspiration on her upper lip.

Another drop of moisture glistened like a satiny jewel on her golden skin, rolling down toward the smocked bodice of the yellow sundress and into the shallow cleft between her breasts.

Rex reached out to touch it, letting his hand rest on her bare skin for a moment. He raised his finger and licked the salty moisture, looking directly into her face. She stared back at him, wide-eyed, like a little bird hypnotized by a snake.

"You taste so good, Linnie," he whispered. "Flowers and sunshine."

"Rex…"

He put an arm around her and drew her close, holding her gently, loving the feel of her warm silky body in his arms, the fragrance of her hair.

While she nestled against him, Rex reached out to run a hand down the length of her bare leg. He caressed the smooth curve of her calf, then eased his hand back up onto her thigh just beneath the brief hem of the dress.

"So pretty," he whispered in her ear. "You've always had the sweetest little body."

He could feel her tension, but she didn't move or try to pull away.

"Kiss me, Linnie," he murmured. "Not like an old friend, either. Kiss me for once as if you really meant it."

She shook her head against his chest, keeping her face hidden.

"Kiss me," he urged her, his voice husky. "You know you want to, Lin, and I'm dying for you. Come on, just one kiss."

She raised her face and his mouth found hers in an explosion of feeling. Rex was astonished by the intensity of his own need. Her lips were so soft, so sweet and yielding. He could feel her straining toward him, and sense the rising passion in her.

His only coherent thought was that he wanted this woman more than he'd ever wanted anything in his life. He wanted her now, immediately, right here on the sun-warmed grass.

Barely aware of what he was doing, Rex began to whisper urgently and tug at her dress. He reached under the smocked bodice to caress her shapely breasts, ran his hand under her skirt to find the edge of her panties, slipped a finger beneath the elastic edging at the leg to touch her moist warmth.

He heard her gasp, felt the way she shuddered in his arms. For a few moments she responded, opening her mouth wide and driving her tongue against his. The deep kiss sent him even wilder with passion.

But then, as abruptly as the storm had come upon them, it was over.

Lindsay whispered something and pulled away from him. Scrambling to her feet, she rushed inside the office. A few minutes later when she came out again, her clothes were in order, her face tight and composed.

"Well, I have a lot to do," she said over her shoulder

as she walked past him down the steps, ''and I'm sure you're busy too, so I guess we'll see each other bright and early tomorrow morning.''

He remained on the step, watching thoughtfully as Lindsay hurried up the path in the direction of the ranch house.

A casual onlooker would think their searing moment of mutual passion had never happened, that his kiss had meant nothing at all to Lindsay. But Rex could see the unnatural stiffness of her shoulders as she walked away from him, the slight trembling of her hands, and he knew better.

He leaned back against the door frame, still watching with narrowed eyes as her dainty yellow-clad body disappeared from view.

During that embrace he'd felt her brief uninhibited response, and he knew she wanted their sexual union as much as he did. Whatever was holding her back, it seemed to be getting weaker.

Rex was winning.

And now they'd have a whole long week on the trail, with private walks in the woods and long starry nights, and all kinds of other opportunities for intimate talks and caresses.

Rex smiled dreamily, resting his head against the office door and lifting his face to the warmth of the afternoon sun.

His body was still on fire, aching with need, but both his heart and mind were full of the woman he'd just held. He wanted to drown in her sweetness, to spend a lifetime holding her and learning everything he could ever know about the mysteries of this one person. He knew well enough how lust felt, but his yearning for Lindsay Duncan went far beyond that.

He loved her.

The sudden realization was stunning, but also strangely liberating. It explained his solitude all these years, his restlessness and inability to commit to much of anything in his life.

But now that he knew the truth, Rex intended to act on it without wasting any more time. Before they returned from the mountains, he and Lindsay Duncan were going to have things sorted out between them, and all the obstacles removed.

The thought made him so happy he couldn't lounge in the sun any longer. He got up from the steps and jogged along the path toward the barn, moving easily, as carefree and full of anticipation as when he'd run along these same trails as a young boy.

THE DAY OF THE camping trip arrived in a whirl of activity.

Lindsay was up just after four in the morning. She rushed into jeans and sweatshirt, made herself a hasty breakfast in the predawn light and did a last-minute check of her own duffel bag, making sure she'd packed everything she was likely to require for a whole week in the wilderness. It was a relief to be so busy that she had no time to think about what she and Rex had done the day before.

She hauled her equipment down to the office building where the boys already milled around, shouting and laughing. Little Danny was so tense with excitement that his face looked pale and all his freckles stood out in sharp relief.

Lindsay smiled and hugged him, checking to be sure he was warmly dressed.

Finally she tossed her duffel bag into the van with the rest of the equipment and settled in the front seat next to Sam, who was going to drop them off at the foot of the trail where their horses waited.

"So, are you wishing you could come along?" she teased, looking fondly at her uncle's profile under the old Stetson.

He tossed her a rueful glance and jerked his thumb toward the back, where a good deal of scuffling and yelling could still be heard.

"You're joking, right?" he said. "A whole week on the trail with these young hellions? I'd rather be skinned and hung out to dry."

She laughed, pleased by the touch of humor in his voice. Sam hadn't found much to joke about lately, for some reason.

Lindsay turned and glanced into the back seat where Jason Bernstein and Allan Larkin were arguing loudly over how to read a compass. Lonnie Schneider sat next to his friend Allan, munching furtively on something. When he caught Lindsay's eye, he hid the food hastily in his pocket and looked out the window.

Tim Bernstein sat with his twin brother, his finely drawn features tense with anticipation. He coughed a couple of times and Lindsay rummaged hastily in her pack, making sure she'd remembered to bring enough of the boy's asthma medication.

In the rear seat of the van, Clint Kraft sprawled with legs extended and eyes closed, looking bored and detached. Beside him Danny bounced up and down, red cowlick waving like a flag as he strained against his seat belt to see out the window.

If Danny got any more excited, he was in danger of flying into little pieces.

Lindsay settled back, still smiling.

This trip might have been a tremendous amount of work, but it was worth all the effort just to see the look of wonder on that small freckled face and feel the surges of excitement from the older boys.

All except Clint, of course, who still gave the impression of being bored to tears.

"I wonder if Clint really hates this whole idea as much

as he lets on,'' she murmured to Sam under cover of the noisy uproar from the middle seats.

''He's a hard one to read,'' Sam said. ''A closed book. Most boys I can get figured out before too long, but not that one.''

Lindsay gave him a thoughtful glance but her uncle didn't seem disposed to talk further. She nodded after a moment and rested her head against the back of the seat, letting her eyes drift shut as she thought about Rex and their passionate kiss the day before.

She still didn't know what had come over her. After all her firm resolve to keep him at arm's length and not allow herself to get involved in his silly, upsetting game of seduction, she'd practically thrown herself at the man. In another few minutes they would both have been naked on the grass.

Lindsay grimaced and hugged her arms, trying not to remember the feel of his hands on her bare skin, his probing tongue and hard mouth.

They'd kissed a few times when they were teenagers, but it had never been anything like that.

Lindsay knew it was important to keep reminding herself Rex Trowbridge was no longer her childhood playmate. He was a grown man now, powerful and sexy and dangerous.

Far too dangerous. But so desperately attractive…

''What was that?'' Sam asked.

Lindsay opened her eyes and looked over at him. ''Beg your pardon?''

''I thought you said something just now.''

Lindsay shook her head, feeling prickly and embarrassed. ''I was just…thinking out loud, I guess.'' She glanced restlessly out the window. ''I hope Rex is going to be there to meet us. Are you sure he knows the right time?''

''Don't worry,'' Sam told her. ''His secretary is driving him out from Casper to meet you all at the ranch. He said he'd be there by 6:00 a.m. to help load the packhorses, and I expect he's going to keep his word. Rex was always reliable.''

Lindsay wondered how she was going to react when she saw him for the first time after their embarrassing kiss. She could almost feel the heat of his lazy blue eyes and see that meaningful grin.

A whole week on the trail, she thought, turning to look bleakly out the window at the countryside flowing past. A week of days to avoid talking with him about anything significant, and nights of lying alone in the tent with him so close by.

"Jason!" she said sharply, turning to look over her shoulder again. "And Allan! Stop that yelling, both of you."

The boys glanced at her, clearly startled, then lowered their voices and continued to argue passionately over the compass.

Lindsay turned back, avoiding Sam's curious glance, and watched as he pulled off the highway and started up a graveled road that led to the ranch at the foot of the mountains.

REX WAS THERE when they arrived, just as he'd promised. His secretary had already left, heading back to the city. He sat on a fence rail in the pale morning light wearing jeans and a denim windbreaker, his duffel bag at his feet, talking with Karl Fuller, the rancher who'd boarded their horses overnight.

When Sam and Lindsay drove up with their lively crew of passengers, Rex climbed down from the fence and ambled over to the van. He stood with an arm on Lindsay's window ledge and smiled at her while the boys tumbled out and began to run across the ranch yard in a wild excess of high spirits.

"Hi, Sam," Rex said. "Good morning, Linnie. Are you ready for this?"

She was painfully conscious of his nearness. "Ready for what?" she asked, pretending to rummage under the seat for her belt pack.

"Well now…ready for whatever happens on the trail." His eyes sparkled with teasing laughter. "I'm thinking something might…come up."

Her cheeks warmed painfully. Lindsay opened the door in his face, scrambled out past him and headed toward the small knot of boys who crowded by the fence with their equipment.

Rex followed her and they both stood watching as Sam pulled the ranch van around, then drove back onto the graveled road with a final wave of his arm.

Lindsay frowned at the van as it vanished beyond a grove of trees. "Why isn't he staying to see us off?" she asked Rex. "I thought he'd at least want to do a check of all the horses and packs before we left."

He rested an arm casually around her shoulder. "I guess Sam thinks we're grown-ups who can look after things by ourselves."

"Of course we can." She drew away, not looking at him. "But it still seems odd that he has so little interest in anything these days."

Rex walked beside her toward the barn where their horses were being prepared for the trip. The pack animals were loaded first, the weight of their burdens carefully distributed to avoid galling or laming the horses. Then, under the supervision of Clint and the neighboring rancher, each boy settled his own bedroll and pack in position and attached them by tying the cantle strings.

Finally, after more than an hour of careful preparations and several last-minute checks, the group was ready to start their first day's journey into the rugged mountain range.

By now the sun was higher in the sky, and the air had begun to warm, although a fresh breeze still tugged at Lindsay's hair. She took off her jacket and tied it with the bedroll at the rear of her saddle, then swung herself up onto the big sorrel gelding, who danced and sidestepped a few paces, adjusting himself to the unaccustomed burden of rider and pack.

She reined him in patiently, allowing her mount to get used to the feeling of the long flapping bedroll at his sides. Then she turned around to watch Rex helping Danny onto his little buckskin.

A telltale froth of orange welled around the small mare's bit, and Lindsay smiled privately, realizing Danny had slipped his horse a smuggled carrot. Sam didn't normally allow any of the horses to be fed treats while they were working.

But Sam wasn't here.

Her smile faded as she remembered the way he'd driven off without a backward glance, and hadn't even stayed to watch as they set out on the trail.

It was so unlike her uncle. Lindsay resolved to have a talk with him as soon as she got back, and try to find out what was going on in his life.

As she watched, Rex checked Danny's stirrups and cinches, then moved toward his own horse. By now all the boys were mounted and waiting.

Only Rex remained on the ground. Lindsay watched him, holding her breath.

This was the moment of truth. Rex Trowbridge might look like a cowboy in his jeans and windbreaker, and he had a commanding air that made all the boys look up to him. But would he be as impressive when he was on a horse for the first time in almost fifteen years?

As the group watched, Rex gathered the reins, placed his boot in the stirrup and swung himself easily into the saddle.

Once mounted, he wheeled his horse around and walked forward a few paces while he settled himself more comfortably.

Lindsay's eyes widened in amazement.

The man looked as if he'd been born on horseback and never left. His tall body was easy and relaxed, his hands low and gentle on the reins. He urged his horse into a trot and jogged across the field and back, pulling up next to the little group.

"Feels great," he said with a casual grin. "If everybody's ready, I guess we can start."

His laughing eyes caught Lindsay's, and she realized she must be staring at him in utter shock.

Rex looked so confident and at home on that big horse. In fact, he looked wonderfully, incredibly desirable.

"Lindsay," he said, "you take the lead, since you're the one who knows the trail, with Danny right behind you where we can all see him. The rest of you boys fall into place behind Lindsay and Danny. Clint and I will ride at the back and lead the pack horses."

The boys moved to obey, stringing out behind Lindsay on the trail in single file. Rex and Clint took up the rear, each of them in charge of three pack horses.

They waved goodbye to Karl Fuller and the Bighorn Ranch and set out west toward the range of mountains, passing from open spaces onto a trail thick with pine needles and dappled by sunlight filtering through branches. Magpies scolded from the trees overhead, and squirrels chattered at them noisily as they passed.

Otherwise the silence was profound and rich, almost palpable. Lindsay felt herself lulled and soothed by the gentle rhythm of hooves, the occasional bursts of happy conversation from the boys behind her, the soft creaking of saddle leather and the rustle of the wind in the trees.

For a while she forgot about Rex and their troubling kiss the day before.

She even put aside the painful memories that tormented her every day of her life, and gave herself over to the utter peace and stillness.

CHAPTER TWELVE

REX LOUNGED ALONG at the rear of the group, leading his three horses. Just ahead of him he could see the bulky outlines of the other loaded pack animals, and beyond them Clint's slumped young body in a red plaid shirt and black Stetson. The younger boys were all strung out in the middle of the group with Danny riding far ahead, just behind Lindsay.

She'd attached a string to Danny's cowboy hat that tied under his chin. The little boy had protested bitterly, arguing that none of the bigger guys had their hats tied on like babies. But the wisdom of Lindsay's action was immediately apparent, because Danny's hat almost always hung down on his back, and without the string would have been lost far behind on the trail.

Rex smiled as he watched the flare of Danny's red curls against the dark-green of the pine branches.

Far in the lead was Lindsay, so distant that she was usually hidden from Rex's eyes by curves in the trail. But even when he couldn't see her, Rex could remember every detail of her appearance that morning.

The sunny golden hair, her striped collar above a green sweatshirt, her faded jeans and the leather riding boots she'd been wearing for so many years that they clung to every line and angle of her small feet.

God, how he loved her.

He was hardly able to cope with this enormous flood of tenderness and yearning. In the past he'd felt lustful desire for a lot of women, but that was more like an itch, a purely physical urge that eased as soon as it was dealt with.

With Lindsay he felt utterly different. He wanted passionately to sleep with her, of course. But he also longed to hold her and talk about everything in the world from politics to movies to favorite foods. He wanted to share thoughts and dreams and memories.

What he really wanted, Rex realized, was to have her with him every day, waiting for him when he came home at night, sharing treats and holidays and lazy Sunday breakfasts.

He wanted Lindsay Duncan to be living with him in his house.

Or hers, he reminded himself, thinking about the pleasant log ranch house she'd once shared with her parents. But if Lindsay didn't want to leave Lost Springs, would he be prepared to give up his city home and lucrative legal practise and move back to the ranch to be with her?

In a New York minute, he would.

Rex shook his head. He could hardly believe these stunning changes in himself. It was so bizarre, like looking inside his head and finding a stranger had taken up residence there, somebody he needed to acquaint himself with all over again.

Or could it be...

He shook his head slowly.

Could this home-loving, monogamous outdoorsman be the *real* Rex Trowbridge? Had he actually been living as an imposter all these years?

Rex shifted in the saddle, then stood up briefly and rested his weight in the stirrups to stretch his legs. He sat back and looked around at the peaceful beauty of the mountains.

The trail was growing steeper and the horses picked their way with increasing care. On their right, a narrow gorge plunged downward so far that they rode level with the treetops filling the valley below. To the left of the trail, little springs trickled from the mountainside and made their way down over twisted roots and mossy outcroppings, gathering strength as they plunged into the depths below.

Rex leaned ahead to make sure all the boys were navigating this treacherous stretch carefully and letting their horses pick the trail as they'd been taught.

"Take it easy, boys," he called. "Everybody stay in line, and don't stop."

Clint cast a brief contemptuous glance over his shoulder but the other five heads nodded earnestly in unison, concentrating on the trail.

Rex settled back in the saddle and returned to his thoughts.

This was something he often wondered, just what kind of person he really was, and what he might have become if his life hadn't taken such a bitter turn early in his childhood.

He'd never really known his father, although the man had stuck around long enough to sire a brother three years younger than Rex. But then, not too long after Dane's birth, the old man had taken off and they'd never seen him again.

Deanna Trowbridge, Rex's pretty young mother, had cried without ceasing for about two months after her husband left. But then she'd picked herself up and tried to go on.

His face tightened as he recalled those early years. They'd lived in trailer homes and motels, working the onion fields in southeastern Washington State, and once they spent a whole winter in a shed at the back of the place where Deanna was doing housework.

The only bright spot in Rex's life during those years had been his brother. He loved Dane, who was a fat, good-natured baby and followed his big brother everywhere with unquestioning adoration.

For his part, Rex had taken tender care of the youngster. He'd protected Dane and fought hard to keep him safe.

But not hard enough…

Rex's face tightened with pain. He strained wistfully forward in his stirrups, trying to catch a glimpse of Lindsay, but she was out of sight around a bend in the trail.

Like somebody unable to resist probing a sore tooth, he let his mind go back to that last nightmare day when Deanna's boyfriend came to their trailer. She always had a lot of boyfriends but most of them were good to the two little boys, bringing candy and gifts for the kids to please their mother.

This man was different, an oil rigger with a sneering, handsome face. Deanna was crazy about him, but even ten-year-old Rex could tell the man was bad trouble. He tried to warn his mother, but she never listened. Her face would get all hot and misty whenever the man was around. She even walked different.

But the last time Deanna's boyfriend came to their trailer, he brought a gun. He was drunk and enraged about something, furious with her for a flirtation he kept accusing her of having with the manager of the trailer park.

When Rex realized the danger he began to fight with the man, struggling with all his boyish strength to wrest the gun away and run off with it. For a while Deanna's boyfriend had just laughed at him, standing arrogantly in the kitchen and letting young Rex fling himself in vain against that big hard body.

But at last, tiring of the game, he set to work to beat the boy within an inch of his life. All Rex could remember of that terrible hour was an eternity of crushing, sickening pain.

He woke up under a bed, hurting in every bit of himself. When he crawled out to assess the damage, his mother was dead, and so was Dane.

Rex closed his eyes and groaned softly at the memory he seldom allowed himself to recall, even all these years later.

But there was something about this place, the placid gait of the horses and the ageless, eternal mountains all around, that seemed to bring a man's life into sharper focus.

Out here you couldn't hide from the things in your heart, because there were none of the distractions that city life offered.

But, mysteriously, along with the hurtful memories somehow came the balm to make them endurable. No wonder people said wild places were healing.

He heard a shout from the boys farther up the trail and saw them pointing downward. Rex followed their signals to see a flock of wild turkeys descending the slope in stately procession, their dark plumage and red wattles glittering like jewels in the morning sunlight.

He smiled and waved back at the boys, then turned to check the packhorses at the rear of the line.

After Deanna's death, welfare officials had tried to find a foster home for him, but Rex hated all of them. He was still sick with loneliness for his mother and little brother, and he couldn't talk to anybody about what had happened.

When they caught him after his fourth time running away, he was put into juvenile detention. As soon as Rex was able to escape from that place, he headed for the streets. He'd been eleven years old, living by his wits in downtown Spokane, at a time when homeless people were still a relatively uncommon sight.

Rex looked at Clint's slouched body jogging ahead of him in the red shirt and wondered how many life experiences he and this sullen boy had shared, and how surprised Clint would be to hear about them.

By the time Rex Trowbridge was brought to Lost Springs Ranch, he'd been just twelve years old but as tough and hard as whipcord. He'd understood the laws of the jungle as well as any animal, and trusted nobody.

Lindsay's parents, Robert and Karen Duncan, had worked hard, along with Sam, to earn the boy's trust. Then, slowly, they'd begun to civilize him. And Lindsay had helped a lot, too, with her tomboyish sweetness and innocent trust.

By all outward appearances, they'd succeeded beyond their wildest dreams.

But nowadays Rex often wondered how much of that tough, hungry, desperate little boy he'd actually left behind. Maybe it was the miserable child he'd once been who now drove him to succeed in his profession, to buy big impressive cars and expensive clothes and take lavish holidays he knew his friends would envy.

But that same child, the terrified boy who'd lain shivering under the bed while his mother and little brother were being murdered, had kept him from ever loving anybody else.

How could you give yourself to a person who might be cruelly torn away from you while you looked on in helpless pain? Better to remain free and invest your emotion in cars, works of art and other costly possessions that you were able to buy or sell at will.

Things that could be covered by insurance, because life held no guarantees.

Rex wasn't sure how much of the truth Lindsay knew about his boyhood. She'd been just a little girl when they brought him to the ranch.

He grinned, remembering her angular body and her immense capacity for imagination and daring. Nothing had scared Lindsay back in those days. She could come up with better, wilder, more exciting games than anybody. If she'd been conscious of being a girl, and different from her playmates, it never showed until she was fourteen or fifteen and began to develop shapely little breasts and a pair of curving hips.

Oh, Linnie, Rex thought, his heart aching. What a darling you were....

He wondered if she'd ever had a chance to peek at his case file. Robert Duncan always kept the boys' records under lock and key in his office. But when Rex became the director of the board at Lost Springs Ranch, he'd looked up his own file and removed it so nobody would ever learn that sad story of pain and terror, or be able to read about the humiliating times he'd broken down and sobbed when talking to the ranch psychologist.

Ancient history, he told himself grimly, sitting erect in the saddle. All of it was ancient history. No point in thinking about it...

"Hey!" He glanced at his watch and called forward, up the line of riders. "Somebody pass the word to Lindsay that it's time to start looking around for a place where we can stop and have our lunch."

"All *right!*" Lonnie Schneider called back, so eagerly that the other boys began to torment him with good-natured teasing.

AT THE END of the first day, they stopped to camp in a high meadow when the wind began to freshen and the shadows fell long and silent across the trail.

The group dismounted and each rider unsaddled his own horse and gave it a rubdown. The boys hobbled around for a while, avoiding each other's eyes, everybody trying not to show just how stiff and sore they felt after a long day in the saddle.

Lindsay watched them in amusement, noting that even surly Clint was limping just a little, though he did his best to hide it.

Rex, though, seemed amazingly fresh. He carried the

sacks of cooking supplies and food over to her and set them on the grass with a flourish.

She watched him with approval. "Nobody would ever suspect you were a lawyer in real life. You look just like a cowboy."

He grinned and leaned toward her. "That's good, Linnie," he murmured, lowering his voice so none of the boys could hear. "Because I hear you've got the hots for cowboys."

"Not after ten hours on the trail." She turned away to hide her smile. "By that time, the only thing I'm lusting after is a soft bedroll and a good sleep."

"How about a soft bedroll and some good company?" he suggested.

"Rex..." she began warningly.

But he was already gone, striding off across the campsite and directing the saddle-weary boys to their various tasks.

Despite howls of protest, everybody fell to work with surprising efficiency. Clint, Rex and Allan concentrated on the horses, getting them fed, brushed and settled. Under Rex's supervision the two boys made an impromptu corral by stretching a couple of rows of lariat rope around a circle of tree trunks. As an extra precaution, they staked out a couple of the livelier horses on ground hobbles.

Lindsay worked with Lonnie and Danny to make the cooking pit and start preparing their meal. Meanwhile the Bernstein twins dug a latrine in a thick grove of trees just down the slope, made an ingenious sling to keep food supplies suspended out of reach of bears, and set up Lindsay's tent at the edge of the camp, discreetly removed from the rows of sleeping bags.

"We'll do Lindsay's air mattress," Jason called out, getting the little pump from his brother's pack. "And maybe Danny's. But the rest of you guys have to look after your own."

"Thank you, Jason," Lindsay said from across the campsite, where she was emptying cans of beans into a big cooking pot.

Danny crushed each can when she finished with it, stomping it flat with his little boots and putting it away carefully in the waste sack.

"Good campers don't leave one single thing behind," Lindsay told the boy. "We'll carry out everything we use, so nobody can even tell we were here. That way the wilderness stays pure and clean for other people to use."

Danny watched, round-eyed and solemn, as Tim Bernstein inflated an air mattress, then arranged Danny's small bedroll on top of it, complete with teddy bear.

"I can't believe I'm really going to sleep out here all night," he breathed. "Right in the mountains."

Lindsay emptied the final can of beans and set it down on the grass for him to squash. "Are you afraid, sweetheart?"

"'Course not," he said scornfully.

But she sensed some hesitation in the little boy's manner, and wondered if he would be quite as brave when night fell across the mountains.

THEY FINISHED their meal of bread, cheese, beans and fruit, then made pots of black tea that the boys drank with lashings of powdered cream and brown sugar.

By the time the camp was tidied and the waste materials stored away, the woods had filled up with inky darkness that seemed even denser beyond the glow of the big campfire.

Noises drifted in from the woods. They heard squirrels chattering overhead, the hooting of owls and the high-pitched singing yelps of distant coyotes. The boys gathered around the fire, their young faces ruddy in the glow of leaping flames as they told the kind of stories dear to the hearts of boys everywhere, scary tales of corpses and monsters and massacres.

Lindsay sat in front of her tent on a blanket, sipping a mug of the hot sweet tea. Rex lay next to her with his hands folded behind his head, booted feet casually extended, gazing upward at the sky.

"Too bad it's so cloudy," he commented. "There'll be a full moon in a few nights, you know. But it looks as if we won't get to see it for a while."

Lindsay cast him a sideways glance, conscious of his nearness with every fiber of her being. "That's just as well," she said, taking another sip of tea. "The full moon makes the horses restless. This way we'll sleep more peacefully."

"But it's not nearly as romantic."

"Romantic!" she said, trying to scoff. "Who thinks about romance on a trail ride with six rowdy boys?"

"I do." Lazily he reached up to rub her back, stroking and kneading the aching muscles.

Lindsay sighed with pleasure. For once she didn't move away. In fact, she edged a little nearer to him.

"That feels so good," she murmured. "I thought I was in pretty good shape, but it still takes stamina to spend ten hours on horseback."

"Do you have lots of stamina, Linnie?" His voice was teasing, but with a husky edge. Out of sight of the boys he slipped his hand under her sweater, then her shirt, and began to caress her naked back.

His touch seemed to chill and burn at the same time. This time she forced herself to pull away, trying to look casual as she tucked her shirt in again.

"Don't you think it's bad for Danny to listen to all those scary stories?" she asked. "What if he has nightmares?"

"I don't think he's even listening," Rex said. "Look, he's practically asleep."

Lindsay smiled fondly, watching the little boy drowsing against an upturned saddle.

Danny was trying so hard to be one of the big boys. But he was clearly exhausted by the day's ride, the fresh air and food and the warmth of the fire. His ruddy head wobbled from side to side, and his eyes kept dropping shut.

"I'll look after him," Rex said when Lindsay started climbing to her feet. "You just relax."

She sank back gratefully, still sipping her tea, and watched as Rex skirted the fire, plucked the smallest, sleepiest camper from the group of boys and carried him over to the row of sleeping bags.

Working skillfully, he stripped off Danny's jeans and boots, tucked the child into the sleeping bag and settled the teddy bear in the crook of his arm. Rex patted and kissed the flushed cheek, murmured a few last words and returned to Lindsay.

"Sound asleep before I zipped up the bag," he reported.

"You're so sweet with him," Lindsay said, still moved by his tenderness. "Where did you ever learn to look after a little boy like that, Rex?"

He sprawled beside her and reached for his own tea. "I had a brother once, a long time ago."

Lindsay turned to look at him in surprise. "Really? You never once told me that, and I've known you more than twenty years."

"I keep telling you…" he said, his eyes glittering in the shadows.

"…there are all kinds of things I don't know about you," Lindsay finished for him. "I know that, Rex. And most of those things will have to remain a mystery."

She turned away deliberately, her heart pounding, but his hand was toying with the hem of her shirt again.

"Aren't you going to be lonely in that tent all night?" he whispered. "What if a bear gets in there?"

"If I find any bears in my tent, I'll scream really loud," she said without looking at him.

"But what if it's just a big friendly bear who likes to kiss and cuddle?" His fingers were roaming over her bare skin again, stroking and caressing.

"If you're going to insist on doing that," Lindsay said in a low voice, "then rub the small of my back, please. It feels so tight and sore."

Obediently he began to work his strong fingers just above her belt, while she sighed with pleasure and lifted her face to the warmth of the distant fire.

"Rex," she said at last.

"Hmm? Linnie, you have such beautiful skin. Just like warm silk."

"Does this trail seem a little bit strange to you?"

"I thought you were the one who knew these trails. Does this feel good?" he added, probing a muscle along her spine.

"It feels heavenly. In another minute I'll curl up and purr and start shaking my leg."

He chuckled. "So why are you worrying about the trail?"

"I don't know." She frowned. "It just seems to me that we're getting awfully high, almost as if we've already crossed the first range of mountains."

His hands continued their gentle ministrations. "But that would never happen, Lin. Sam says the ranch horses are all trained to pick their way around these trails on the eastern slope, and start working their way back toward Karl Fuller's place."

"I know." Lindsay backed closer to him, loving the soothing feel of his hands. "Sam told me I didn't need to worry about the trails at all, just give the lead horses enough rein and let them pick their way. And that's what

I've been doing all day, but it still feels like we've climbed too high."

"Tomorrow when the sun comes up, we can get a fix on our position," Rex said casually. "It's hard with all this cloud. I can't see any stars tonight, either."

"You're right," she said in relief. "As soon as the sun comes up, we can make sure we've started working our way north instead of heading further west into the mountains."

"It sure wouldn't be much fun to get caught off a trail in the mountains with all these kids. Would it, Linnie?"

"It would be awful," Lindsay agreed. "But Sam has always said not to worry about it, because our horses know how to take us home. Oh, God," she added, "that feels so wonderful."

"Wait until later," he whispered, "after all the boys are asleep."

"What happens then?" she asked, grateful for the sheltering darkness that hid her flushed cheeks.

"Leave your tent flap open around midnight and you'll get the deluxe treatment," he murmured. "The full-body massage."

Lindsay was suddenly breathless with sexual yearning and hot with desire.

"Come on, sit up," she told him. "I'll do your shoulders."

He sat up and moved ahead of her on the blanket so she could rub his back. Lindsay flexed and worked her fingers in the flat bands of muscle across his shoulders, stunned by the wildness of her emotions.

This was Rex, her old childhood friend, but he seemed new and exciting, like a man she'd just met.

A man she was going to sleep with tonight, Lindsay realized, and give her body to. Already she could almost feel the warm silky nakedness of his skin against her own, and the hard thrusting strength as he entered her...

"I can feel it in your hands," he whispered.

"What?" she asked

"How much you want me."

"Oh, Rex..."

One by one the boys grew weary of gore and horror. They rolled onto their bedrolls, leaving the fire to die down. Rex and Lindsay waited, hardly speaking, lost in a world of dreamy anticipation as the logs burned and smoldered and the fire died to a ruddy glow.

By now the shadows were deep enough that he moved back and took her into his arms. Their kiss held all the yearning passion both of them were feeling, and went on and on until they were startled by a sudden noise.

They were wrapped together so passionately that it took a while for them to separate, to control their ragged breathing and tuck their clothes back in place.

Eventually Lindsay realized the sound came from Danny's bedroll. She went over to find him sitting upright, crying and trembling in the aftermath of a nightmare.

"I couldn't leave him out here," she told Rex, making her way back across the campsite with the little boy sobbing in her arms. "I have to take him into my tent with me."

Rex stood up painfully, his jeans still bulging at the groin.

"Oh, hell," he muttered. "Lindsay, couldn't we just..."

"Tomorrow," she promised shamelessly, holding Danny close to her. "By tomorrow he should be able to sleep out with the other boys and not be afraid."

Rex had to be satisfied with that, but his tall figure looked tense and miserable as he strode off into the woods to check on the horses.

Lindsay watched him go. Then she carried the little boy

inside her tent, went to get his bedroll and air mattress and sat next to him, smoothing his rusty curls until he settled and feel deeply asleep again.

Part of her ached with sexual frustration, but another, deeper part was grateful for the interruption. If Danny hadn't wakened and cried, she would certainly have gone to bed with Rex tonight.

And as much as she wanted him physically, Lindsay wasn't at all sure her emotions were ready for that experience.

Not yet. And maybe not ever...

She tucked Danny's teddy bear close to his cheek, then peeled off her jeans and sweater and settled in her own bedroll, where she lay for a long time staring at the ghostly moving shapes against the taut canvas.

CHAPTER THIRTEEN

LIFE WAS ALWAYS peaceful around Lost Springs Ranch in the summertime, but Sam could never remember a silence as profound as this. Lindsay and the boys had only been gone a little more than a day, but it seemed like months.

The rest of the staff were all off on vacation while he stayed alone in his little cottage, listening to the grass grow. Sam had been looking forward to a whole week of rest and solitude, but now the quiet seemed to weigh on him, making him feel lonely and old.

The second day of the trail ride he sat on his porch, whittling at a block of wood as he watched the sun setting behind a bank of clouds that wreathed the distant mountain ranges.

No doubt they were having a cloudy ride up there. But that always made a trail ride more pleasant, in Sam's opinion. The clouds and mist enclosed you, and they muffled other sounds, making you feel like the only person in the world.

As long as it didn't start raining, he thought. A little rain could be fun on a trail ride but when it went on too long, life started to get pretty miserable.

He squinted at the clouds with a practised eye, then went back to work with his jackknife, frowning as he shaped a miniature grizzly bear with one paw raised.

In addition to his worry over the eight horseback riders up there in the mountains, he still couldn't shake his depression over the abrupt way Gwen McCabe had rejected him.

Sam knew his behavior was childish, but it didn't help to scold himself. The pain was so intense, especially after the amount of courage it had taken him to get up enough nerve to ask her out in the first place.

Worst of all, he still couldn't understand her refusal. He was pretty sure she hadn't found him repulsive, because she'd smiled and chatted in such a warm, friendly manner. And a deep instinct told him Gwen McCabe was as lonely as he was.

But it appeared the woman wasn't lonely enough to spend an evening in his company....

The phone shrilled inside the cottage. For a moment Sam considered letting it ring; he had no desire to talk to anybody. But it might be ranch business, and he was the only person around. Finally he hauled himself from the rocking chair and wandered inside to pick up the receiver.

"Lost Springs Ranch," he said.

There was a long silence. "Sam?" a voice said tentatively. "Is that you?"

He gripped the phone, his heart pounding. "Yes, this is Sam Duncan."

"It's...this is Gwen McCabe calling. I didn't know if I'd be able to catch you at home, but I..." Her voice trailed off.

Sam felt almost light-headed with relief and excitement. She'd changed her mind!

Maybe Gwen was just really shy after all, and when she had time to think it over, she'd decided there were worse things than having dinner with Sam Duncan.

And she was such a pretty woman, so pleasant and delightful to be with.

His mind whirled with plans. Sam hadn't been to a nice restaurant in quite a long time, and Lindsay wasn't around to confer with. He'd have to look through the phone book and see if there were...

But her next words chilled him like a dash of cold water.

"I hope I'm not being a bother," she said with odd formality. "I won't keep you long. There's something that's been worrying me and I just wanted to mention it, if you don't mind."

"Worrying you?" Sam asked cautiously.

His mind still clung to warm images of himself and Gwen McCabe, dressed up and dining out, chatting and smiling at each other over a good steak, maybe even taking a whirl around the dance floor.

But it appeared he'd jumped to conclusions. The disappointment was hard to endure.

"Yes," she said. "The other day two of your boys came here to pick up the first-aid kits for their trail ride in the mountains. One of them was a little red-haired boy about Brian's age, and the other was a tall young fellow with dark hair."

"That would be Danny and Clint," he told her, wondering what this was all about. "Did they cause you some kind of problem, Mrs. McCabe?"

She hesitated a moment at this formal mode of address, but didn't protest. "No," she said. "They were both very polite. But I just..." Again her voice trailed off nervously.

"What?" Sam asked.

"That bigger boy...Clint," she said at last.

"What about him?"

"He seemed so angry. There were real undercurrents of tension in him, and a sort of...attitude."

"The boy's had a tough life," Sam said.

"I just wondered if he might...do something."

"Like what?" Sam asked, increasingly puzzled.

"I don't know." She sounded distraught and embarrassed. "I just wondered if the others were safe out there in the mountains with him."

"You think Clint might *hurt* somebody?" Sam said in astonishment.

"I don't know. Look, this is probably just silly. I'm so sorry to have bothered you, Sam."

"But I…"

"Good night," she said hastily, as if anxious to wind up the conversation. Before he could say anything more, the phone clicked in his ear. Sam stood for a while looking at the receiver, then replaced it and wandered back out onto the porch.

Hearing her voice had upset him all over again—especially when it was clear she had no desire to talk to him. She was just worried about young Clint, for some reason.

Moving heavily, Sam settled himself back in the rocker and stared thoughtfully at the ring of clouds above the mountains.

RAIN BEGAN TO FALL during their third afternoon on the trail, a cold silver drizzle that seemed to hang in the air like mist.

"Liquid sunshine," Rex told the boys at noon. "Let's all get into our sweaters and slickers and try to stay warm."

Lindsay was grateful for his good cheer, though the group's spirits didn't seem to be dampened by the bad weather. They all put protective covers on their hats and shrugged into long plastic raincoats slit to the waist to fit comfortably over their saddles. Then they mounted up and headed out on the trail again.

She could hear their cheerful voices behind her, calling and shouting to one another as she led the way deeper into the mountains.

By now the boys were completely absorbed in this adventure, bonded with each other and lost in their imaginations. All of them except Clint had smeared their faces with mud, then woven twigs and leaves into their hatbands to create a camouflage effect. They were explorers, brave outdoorsmen, the first people ever to venture into a forbidden land.

Lindsay grinned privately as she glanced back at them. But her smile faded again when she looked around at the trail.

It was years since she'd ridden in these mountains, and she was a little surprised how hard it seemed to get her bearings, especially when they hadn't seen the sun since the first day. The path they followed was still fairly well marked, but it no longer seemed familiar.

Still, her sorrel horse had chosen each fork without hesitation, and she knew they had to be making a wide circle on the lower slopes of the range. For the past two days they would have headed almost due north. Tomorrow they would reach the farthest outpost of the trail, where they would spend two days fishing in Lost Lake and exploring an old abandoned miners' camp before picking their way back toward the Bighorn Ranch.

But the trail was getting so rough. In some portions it seemed as if they were in the mountains rather than the foothills, with steep gorges falling away at their feet, and fewer trees among the rocks.

Lindsay would have liked to talk with Rex but he was at the rear of the group, a quarter of a mile behind her, still supervising the packhorses and keeping an eye on the noisy group of boys.

The rain continued as they set up camp for the night in a dense stand of pine that gave some shelter. Under Rex's supervision, the boys hurried to build rough structures from pine boughs and dragged their bedrolls inside, shouting with excitement.

As Lindsay and her helpers prepared the meal, she found herself fascinated by this changed man.

One of the boys had smeared Rex's face as well. He looked like a painted warrior with his blunt cheekbones and flashing eyes. By now there was nothing left of the city lawyer with his briefcase. He was a big, grown-up version of the boy she'd played with and loved so many years ago.

He caught her glance across the campfire, his eyes very blue and full of intensity above the smeared markings on his cheeks. Lindsay stared back at him, drowning in emotion, and knew that tonight he was going to come into her bed.

Danny had spent the second night, as well, in the tent with her. Poor Rex, clearly frustrated, had been forced to remain in his bedroll.

But their smallest camper had adjusted to the adventure and by now was as wild and carefree as the other boys, excited at the prospect of sleeping with Clint in one of the makeshift pine shelters.

Lindsay would be alone in her tent while the rain pattered in the trees overhead....

"I'm getting worried about the trail," she said aloud as they sat around the fire with their meal of stew and dried fruit.

"Why?" Rex asked, sipping his tea.

"It just doesn't look right," Lindsay said. "My horse is still choosing the way, and I know it's been years since I've ridden these trails, but I'm worried. It feels like we're getting too high."

Rex frowned while the boys ate in silence. "But to be getting higher," he said, "we'd have to be heading straight west. I thought we were bearing north, going laterally along the middle slopes. Sam told me that's how the trail runs."

She nodded, giving Lonnie another helping of stew. "I

know. That's what I thought, too, and it's probably right. I just can't shake this uneasy feeling.''

"But we *are* heading west," Jason Bernstein said. "We've been going straight west ever since we left the ranch.''

The others stared at him. Jason looked nervously at his plate.

"At least I think we have," he said. "According to my compass…''

Allan Larkin hooted with laughter. "You don't know how to read a compass, Bernstein," he said. "You couldn't find your way out a paper bag. Where'd you get that thing, a popcorn box?''

Lindsay relaxed and drank some tea.

"We've never bothered to use a compass up here in all the years we've been taking boys on campouts," she said. "Our horses know these trails so well, they could circle them blindfolded.''

But Rex stood up and moved around to where Jason sat. "Let me look at your compass," he said.

Jason handed it over with a bitter scowl at Allan, and Rex flipped open the lid. He held the compass up, moved a few paces into the trees and came back, squatting next to Lindsay.

"According to this thing, Jason's right," he said. "We've been heading due west for three days.''

"But that's impossible." She stared at him, her anxiety returning. "Rex, none of our horses would head straight up into the mountains like that. Sam told me to…''

She was interrupted by a harsh peal of laughter from the other side of the fire. All the campers turned to look in astonishment at Clint, normally so silent, rocking with merriment.

"You should see your faces," he choked. "God, this is rich.''

Rex moved around the fire and stood above the tall boy. "What's so funny, Clint?" he asked quietly.

Clint leaned forward, howling with laughter, then sat back and wiped his eyes. "It worked like a charm," he said, still gasping. "I couldn't believe nobody caught on, after three whole days."

Without even being sure of what he meant, Lindsay began to sense a cold, sick feeling in the pit of her stomach.

Clint's fit of laughter passed. He glared up at Rex, the firelight glinting on his dark features.

"Some leader you are," the boy sneered. "Big lawyer with mud on your face, trying to look after a woman and a bunch of little kids. Somebody should be looking after *you.*"

Lindsay and the younger boys watched, wide-eyed, as Rex reached down and drew Clint roughly to his feet. Rex didn't seem to exert any particular force, and he said nothing at all. But his big, lean body was taut with controlled fury.

Clint stood uneasily in front of the man, no longer able to meet his eyes.

"What's going on?" Rex asked softly, gripping the boy's shoulder so tightly that Lindsay could see Clint wince. "Because if you've done something to hurt these people…"

Rex's voice dropped even lower.

"If you have, Clint, I hate to think what I'm going to do to you."

All Clint's swagger and bravado vanished along with his laughter. He now looked much younger, like a frightened boy.

"Hell, it was just a *joke,*" he muttered.

"What kind of joke?"

"Those lead horses that Lindsay and Danny are riding, and yours and mine, too—they're not Lost Springs horses."

Clint glanced defiantly at Rex, then looked down again while the significance of his statement slowly dawned on Lindsay.

"Where are they from?" she asked with another cold clutch of fear.

Clint turned sullenly in her direction. "Sam bought them a couple of months ago at a horse sale over in Wolf River. All four of them were working on a dude ranch there."

"But Wolf River…that's right over on the other side of the mountains," she said, increasingly horrified as understanding dawned. "Rex, these horses have been going *home!* They've been taking us straight west every day, all the way into the mountains."

The other boys were pale under the smears of mud on their faces. Danny clearly had no idea what was going on, but seemed on the verge of tears.

"I can't believe Sam let you outfit us with unfamiliar horses," Rex said.

Clint gave another sharp bark of laughter. "Sam didn't even look at the horses. He doesn't care what's going on anymore."

"But we trusted you," Rex said. "Lindsay gave you the responsibility of choosing safe horses and you let her down. That's contemptible behavior."

Clint stared at the big man for a long time, trying to look casual and offhand. He was the first to turn away, his cheeks flushing darkly.

Allan Larkin finally broke the edgy silence. "So what's the deal? Are we lost?"

"Of course not," Rex said, taking charge of the situation again. "We came this far on a well-marked trail, and we can just follow the same trail back out. Tomorrow we'll turn around and start heading back down. It'll be a whole lot easier," he added in a comforting tone, sitting down and gathering Danny onto his lap, "because it'll be all downhill."

"But we won't have the nice trip we'd planned," Lindsay said bitterly. "We won't be able to stop at the miner's cabin or spend a day resting and fishing at the lake. In fact we'll just barely have time to get back, now that we've come so deep into the mountains."

"It was just a *joke,*" Clint muttered.

The other boys glared at him coldly.

"Some joke," Lonnie Schneider muttered. "We could have got lost and run out of food."

The other boys echoed Lonnie's sentiments for once. Tim Bernstein looked especially frightened and began to cough, his body shaking. He relaxed a little when Lindsay assured him she had plenty of asthma medication and they would still get home from their trip on schedule.

But the rest of the group shunned Clint pointedly as they got ready for bed and settled down inside their pine shelters. The tall boy actually seemed grateful to have Danny crawl in under the branches with him.

From her tent Lindsay saw Clint murmur softly to the little boy, then tuck Danny's teddy bear close to his face and draw the blankets up around him.

She let the tent flap drop and got ready to crawl into her bedroll, torn by conflicting emotions.

IT WAS AFTER MIDNIGHT and the boys were all sound asleep when she heard Rex's voice outside the closed tent flap.

"Lin," he whispered. "Are you awake?"

Her throat went tight with alarm. She clenched her hands into fists, listening tensely.

"Lin?" he whispered again.

She wanted to ignore him, to pretend sleep so he'd go away. But she was still anxious, a lot more worried about

Clint's startling disclosure than she wanted the boys to know.

This was a good chance to talk with Rex about the situation in private.

Finally Lindsay sat up and opened the tent flap, annoyed by the shaking of her hands.

He crawled in rapidly, his big body filling the small enclosed space. He smelled of wood smoke and pine, and his shoulders glistened with raindrops in the faint light of the fire.

"At least you've washed all that mud off your face," she whispered as he stripped off his coat and stored it at the foot of the bedroll.

"Don't you like me in jungle camouflage?" His teeth flashed white in the darkness.

"Actually, it's kind of flattering." Lindsay settled back on her pillow and gazed up at him. "You looked very primitive. Intriguingly savage."

He laughed and pulled off his jeans, then stripped away his shirt.

"Hey, isn't this just a bit presumptuous?" Lindsay asked. "I don't remember inviting you to get naked."

"I'm so cold," he said. "I've been out for more than an hour checking the horses and having a look at the trail. With this rain, I'll bet the temperature's barely above freezing. I'm hoping you'll be generous enough to warm me up."

She touched him in quick sympathy and realized he wasn't exaggerating. His teeth chattered, and his arms and shoulders were like sculpted ice.

"Come here," she murmured, unzipping her big sleeping bag and holding it open. "Hurry. Oh, poor Rex."

He crawled in next to her and pulled another blanket up over their bodies. She stifled a little scream as his chilly length enfolded her.

"God, I'm sorry," he whispered. "This must be awful for you."

He still shivered violently and his teeth continued to chatter. Lindsay realized he was rubbing his hands together behind her back, trying to warm them before touching her skin.

"Oh, for goodness sake." She tugged at his arms. "Give me your hands."

"Honey, they're like ice. I don't want to…"

"Give them to me!"

Reluctantly he offered his hands and she held them in both her own, rubbing and chafing them, distressed by their coldness. At last, slowly and deliberately, she placed them between her thighs and drew his body close.

"That's the warmest place I can offer," she whispered against his shoulder.

"Oh, sweetheart…"

"Rex, tell me the truth. How far into the mountains do you think we are? Did Clint…"

"I don't want to talk about that little bastard right now," he muttered through gritted teeth. "I just want to get warm."

He lay in her arms, their bodies touching and pressing together from head to toe. Gradually her warmth began transferring to him, and his shivering stopped.

As they cuddled, Lindsay's concern evaporated. In its place came a singing excitement and a wondering sense of joy. She'd never been so close to him, never held his naked body in her arms, and yet it felt so right.

His hands were warm now. One of them crept out and around to her back under her T-shirt, drawing her closer. The other remained between her thighs, but it began to move and quest upward.

"You're right," he whispered hoarsely in her ear as he

tugged her panties away and continued to explore with gentle fingers. "This is the warmest place in the whole world."

"Well, you're certainly feeling much better." Lindsay smiled against his shoulder. "I guess you can probably go to your own bedroll now."

"I don't think so," he muttered. "It's best if I stay here for a while, at least."

"Why?"

"Because it seems I've got the tent pole."

He took one of her hands and placed it on himself. She gasped at his size and hardness. "My goodness, Rex," she whispered. "What on earth is *that?*"

"You've never run across one of these, Linnie?" he teased.

"Not quite like this one." Mesmerized, she stroked him, feeling her body begin to open with excitement.

"Oh, you little flatterer." He chuckled, then moaned with pleasure at her touch.

He was fondling her now, one hand caressing her body with long gentle strokes while the other continued to play and tease between her thighs.

She was amazed at herself and her body's response to the rich sweetness of their love play. The warmth of the tent enclosed them, and the rain pattered on the waterproof cover overhead, beating a steady rhythm to their rising passion. From outside, firelight flickered and danced against the curved nylon sides.

Lindsay pressed against him, her mouth seeking and questing, all the tortured memories wiped from her mind for the moment. It was such a blessed relief to be simply a woman, alone with a man she desired, and not have to think about anything else.

Their bodies moved together with slow purpose, arousing each other to an unbearable frenzy. When he entered her, Lindsay felt a brief alarm, even a flash of pain.

"Are you all right, darling?" he asked, instantly concerned.

"I'm fine," she whispered. "It's just…it's been a while for me, Rex."

Well, that was certainly an understatement, she thought grimly.

"But don't stop!" she whispered, pounding at his shoulder. "For heaven's sake, you can't stop now!"

He laughed and continued his gentle thrusting rhythm. By now all the pain had vanished, swallowed up in a warm, rich tide of happiness.

Though Lindsay had known this man for most of her life, Rex felt strange in her arms, different from what she'd expected. He was bigger and his body was so hard. Even his chest was hairier than she remembered from long-ago summer days at the swimming hole.

And he made her feel so delicious…

Lindsay closed her eyes and thought about how he'd looked earlier that day. Dreamily she pictured those blue eyes glittering above the smears of mud on his blunt cheekbones.

"My warrior," she whispered as he moved within her. "My big sweet savage…"

He was lost in passion now, his face taut, and she sensed the iron control he was using to keep from reaching his climax. Lindsay had a fleeting moment to think about his unselfishness, another thing that surprised her.

Then her own release flooded over her, pulsing and ebbing in rich bursts of pleasure that carried her off into a world of dreams where sunlight glowed on her face, redgold and shimmering.

CHAPTER FOURTEEN

WHEN SHE RECOVERED, Rex lay spent in her arms.

She patted his back gently, then wrapped her arms around him, feeling weak with tenderness. "That was so nice," she whispered.

"Nice?" He nuzzled her shoulder drowsily. "Is that the best you can do?"

"Well, how would you describe it?"

He drew her closer, kissing her hair with a gentleness that astonished her. "Earth-shaking," he suggested huskily. "Monumental. Life-altering."

"Oh, go on," she scoffed, though she was deeply moved by his words. "I'll bet you say things like that to all the girls."

"I've never said anything like that to a woman in my whole life." His arms tightened around her, and his voice was suddenly sober and intense.

"Rex..."

But he was still holding her, running his hands slowly up and down the curve of her back. "I feel like such an idiot," he muttered. "After all these years I finally get to sleep with my princess, and then I forget everything I should be thinking of."

"Like what?" she asked.

"Like birth control, and some kind of responsible protection. I just jumped on you like a horny teenager. I'm so sorry, Lin."

She drew away, looking at him. "Do I need some kind of protection besides birth control?"

"Oh, no. Not from me." He drew a forefinger down the line of her nose and lips. "I'm a really clean guy, sweetheart."

She relaxed and smiled, moving back into his arms again.

"In fact," he said, holding her close, "you'd probably be surprised how boring my sex life is. I haven't been with anybody for a long, long time."

"No kidding? That *is* a surprise to me."

He continued to stroke her hair. "You know, there's always one major flaw with any woman I date."

"What's that?"

"She isn't you." He bent to kiss her again.

Lindsay pulled away to stare up at him in the flickering darkness. "I had no idea you felt that way about me, Rex."

"I guess I didn't, either," he said. "At least not until last year at that bachelor auction, when you let me know spending a weekend with me was just about the most ridiculous idea in the world. Because when I started thinking how much fun that weekend might be, I was a goner."

She smiled against his chest. "Really?"

"I've been nuts about you over this past year, Lin. Out of my head. Every minute of the day, I find myself thinking about you. I even started taking team roping lessons from Sam so I could impress you with what a great cowboy I was."

She sat up and looked at him in astonishment. "You didn't!"

"Yeah, I did." Rex reached up with a lazy hand to caress her breasts. "Every evening I lie around my house and think about you. I daydream like a kid about having you there with me."

She was genuinely amazed. "Rex, I can't believe all this."

"Wait, there's more," he said, looking abashed. "I even phoned you just to hear your voice, and then hung up because I couldn't think of anything to say and I was too embarrassed to let you know what I'd done."

Her eyes widened in shock. "When?" she said, clutching his arm. "How many times did you do that?"

"Just once, a couple of weeks ago. Hey, I may be a lovesick puppy, but I'm not a pervert."

Chilly fingers of dread touched Lindsay's spine and curled into her stomach. She nestled back under the covers again and pressed close to him, but the fear wouldn't go away.

"Lin?" He kissed her ear and the nape of her neck. "Are you all right?"

"I'm fine."

"We should have used some kid of birth control," he muttered. "Darling, what if you get pregnant?"

"It's the wrong time of month." She hesitated, searching for words. "But if it happened, what would you think about that?"

"If you got pregnant with my baby? I'd think I was the luckiest guy in the world. I'd be over the moon with happiness."

"Oh, Rex," she whispered.

"Let's get married, Lin," he said. "We don't need to know each other any better, we've been friends all our lives. And we're not getting any younger, you know. Let's get married and start making a baby."

She felt tears stinging behind her eyes, and a weight of misery too cold and heavy to bear.

"Hey," he said, "what's wrong? Don't you want to have babies? Because if you don't, that's all right. We'll just adopt Danny instead."

Lindsay thought about a bassinet lined with silk, and a fat baby with Rex's blue eyes and crooked grin. She pictured the log house on the ranch with herself and Rex living there together, and Danny as their son, and other children running and playing.

She was sobbing now, holding him so tightly she could feel him wince.

"Lindsay?" He sounded terrified. "Darling, what's the matter? What did I say to hurt you?"

She knew this was the time to tell him. Here was her opportunity to let him know the truth about her own terrible cowardice, and ask for his help in dealing with the terrors that plagued her.

But Lindsay had been afraid so long, she didn't know how to change.

"You aren't hurting me," she said when she was able to speak. "I'm just…a little overwhelmed by all this, I guess."

"You're so lovely, darling," he murmured, touching her face. "The most beautiful woman in the world. God, how I love you."

He began to caress her with more purpose, and Lindsay's body responded though her mind was still in turmoil. Soon they were making love again, and it was even sweeter than the first time.

There was poignancy, too, a shattering feeling of precious, fleeting happiness.

Because Lindsay knew beyond a shadow of a doubt that when they left the mountains, this sweetness was going to end. She would tell Rex goodbye, and she would never hold him again.

For more than four years she'd kept her painful secret. The knowledge of her cowardice was lodged at the very center of her being, destroying her life and blocking the possibility of an intimate relationship with anybody. Until Lindsay could bring herself to deal with the terrible thing that had happened to her, she could never move on to a normal life.

She didn't deserve a man like Rex Trowbridge. And he certainly didn't deserve the kind of pain and danger that she would undoubtedly bring into his life.

THEY FELL ASLEEP and drowsed together for a few hours in a warm, sweet tangle of arms and legs.

Rex woke and looked around in confusion for a couple of seconds, wondering where he was. Then he remembered and his heart soared with happiness.

The dying campfire flickered beyond the tent, barely giving enough light to make out her golden mass of hair and the delicate lines of her face.

"I love you," he whispered under his breath because he didn't want to wake her. "My sweet darling, I love you so much."

He kissed the pillow by her cheek, wishing he could wake her up and make love. The memory of their night together had aroused him all over again. His groin was stiff and hard, aching with desire.

He rolled away from her and sat up to reach for his shirt, shivering in the morning chill.

Rex knew he was never going to get enough of this woman, even if they lived together for the next fifty years. Always she would fascinate him, tantalize him, thrill him with her loving and that elusive, teasing essence she'd had since girlhood.

Quietly, trying not to wake her, he pulled on his socks and jeans, wondering about Lindsay's odd moment of withdrawal and tears the night before.

He'd always thought of her as a home-and-hearth kind of woman, the kind of woman who'd want a family. She had the boys at the ranch, and she genuinely loved little

Danny, but Rex suspected she also longed for a husband and babies of her own.

So why had she sounded so distraught when he broached the topic? Was it possible she didn't love him after all, that after their rich night of sex she would reject him?

He felt a chill of alarm and looked at her small body cuddled under the plaid blanket.

He couldn't believe she didn't want him. Lindsay was such an honest person, and she hadn't been faking her responses the night before. He'd felt the intensity of her orgasm all the way to the core of himself.

Remembering, he started to feel aroused again.

If he didn't get out of there right away, he was going to be all over her.

Hastily he grabbed his jacket and boots, opened the tent flap and crawled outside, then did the flap up carefully behind him.

Sitting on the ground sheet in front of Lindsay's tent, he laced his boots, zipped his jacket and stood up to look around.

The rain had stopped sometime during the night, although the sky brooded with heavy clouds. It was still very early, with the first pale light of dawn beginning to wash over the mountain peaks.

All the boys were deeply asleep in their rough pine shelters as Rex walked among them. The Bernstein twins lay huddled close together for warmth. Lonnie and Allan were back-to-back in their bedrolls, and little Danny snuggled in the shelter next to Clint, still clutching his teddy bear. Danny seemed comfortable and must be having happy dreams, because he smiled in his sleep.

For a moment Rex gazed tenderly at the little boy, whom he was rapidly growing to love as much as Lindsay did. He bent to toss a few more logs on the fire, then looked around.

The camp all seemed to be in order, and he wasn't sure why he had such an uneasy feeling. Maybe he was just bothered by Lindsay's inexplicable moment of sadness the night before.

Or it could have something to do with Clint's confession about that bonehead trick with the leading horses.

Rex's face hardened with anger. He'd tried not to show Lindsay how upset the boy had made him, or his worry about their situation.

It was true that they had a well-marked trail to follow back down to the base of the mountains. But if they somehow lost the trail or it was washed away in heavy rain, they could be in real trouble. This was rough country and they were a long way from anything familiar, thanks to Clint's cruel prank.

He went across the campsite and into the trees to check on the string of horses. They had been carefully roped and tethered in a small meadow about a hundred yards from the camp.

But as Rex drew nearer there were no welcoming nickers, no sound of stamping hooves. His heart lurched with fear. Before he stepped into the clearing, he knew what he was going to see.

All their horses were gone.

LINDSAY STOOD at the edge of the clearing with the little group of boys, gazing blankly at the shredded ropes, the empty hobble stakes and trampled, muddy ground.

"But…what happened?" she asked Rex.

He squatted near the trees, studying the ground intently. Tim Bernstein was beside him, a camping handbook open in his hand.

"Black bear," Tim said briefly, coming back to Lindsay and pointing at one of the tracks on the page. "A great big one, maybe even two of them. Their pawprints are all over the place.''

"Did the bears eat our horses?" Danny asked. He stood at Lindsay's side, clutching her hand. His eyes were wide with terror. "Did the bears eat Daisy?"

He began to cry, and Lindsay knelt to hug him. "No, no, sweetheart," she said. "Daisy is fine. None of our horses were hurt.''

"How do you know?" Danny asked, gulping.

"Because there's no blood around," Tim told the younger boy. "The bears just scared our horses so they broke the corral and ran off. Horses are really terrified of bears. They can't even stand the scent.''

Rex came back across the clearing, his face drawn with worry in the pale light of dawn. "It happened sometime during the night," he told her. "I blame myself, Lin. I should have been out here keeping watch.''

She knew what he was thinking. The horses had been frightened away while they were inside the tent, lost in their lovemaking.

Lindsay met his eyes steadily. "Don't feel that way, Rex. You can't stay awake twenty-four hours a day. Everybody has to rest sometime.''

Clint stood silently at the edge of the group, looking chastened, even fearful. None of the other boys spoke to him.

"I checked farther up the trail," Clint said at last, clearing his throat. "And Larkin went back the way we came. There are lots of tracks in both directions, but no horses.''

Rex nodded. "So the Wolf River horses are still heading home through the mountains, and ours are going back toward the Bighorn.''

Fear made Lindsay's anger flare, almost choking her. "I honestly don't know how you could do such a terrible thing, Clint!" she burst out. "Of all the cruel, childish—''

Rex put a hand on her shoulder and squeezed it gently. "Getting mad at Clint isn't going to help anything now," he said. "We have to keep a clear head and decide what we're going to do. Any suggestions, men?"

"Can we catch up with the horses?" Jason asked. "Only four of them are still heading west. The other ten are going back to the foot of the mountains, right? So maybe we can track them down, and then we'd still have a riding horse for each of us, plus a couple of pack animals."

"That's good thinking," Rex said, "except I doubt if we can catch up with them on foot. Remember, they're traveling downhill without saddles or packs, and they'll be anxious to get home. Besides, they're at least four or five hours ahead of us."

Lonnie's plump face registered sudden alarm. "If we've got no pack horses," he said, "how are we going to carry the food?"

"Or the bedrolls?" Tim asked.

Rex shook his head and led the way back to their camp. He settled by the fire and gestured for the others to sit. "Let's have a big breakfast," he said, "and while we're eating we'll have a powwow."

The boys obeyed, their faces pale with the seriousness of their plight.

"Now, we're not sure how high we've come," Rex began as they ate, "but we're safe on a well-marked trail. It's going to take us at least three long days to walk back out, and that's assuming we can all keep up a good steady pace. We might have to take turns carrying Danny for part of the time."

"I'll carry him the whole way if I have to," Clint said gruffly.

This was Clint's first sign of apology or contrition. Rex and Lindsay exchanged a quick glance, then Rex went on talking.

"We'll have to leave most of our supplies up here and come in later to get them. Each boy will put together his own pack with just the bare essentials, something light enough that he can carry it on his back."

"But we'll still need our bedrolls, right?" Jason said.

"Yes, and some extra clothes and socks because it's getting colder every night. That should leave you enough room to pack a canteen of water and some freeze-dried food, but not much. I'm afraid we'll all be pretty hungry by the time we get back."

"Maybe somebody will come and rescue us," Lonnie said, looking glum at the prospect of these severely diminished rations.

"I doubt it." Rex glanced at Clint again, then looked away. "Even if some of our horses begin to straggle into the base ranch in the next day or two, they're not going to come looking for us way up here. Sam will expect us to be farther north, on the lower slopes of the mountain."

Clint looked down and kicked his toe unhappily in the ashes of the fire.

"Well," Lindsay said at last with forced brightness, "I guess we all know the plan. Danny and Lonnie, help me clean up the breakfast stuff and then we'll decide what we can take. Rex and Clint are the biggest, so they'll carry extra supplies of food. The rest of you start getting your own packs ready."

She moved around the camp, trying to energize the frightened boys with cheerful conversation. Once when she passed Rex, he caught her arm and looked into her eyes with a questioning expression.

"Are you all right, darling?" he murmured.

"Of course I am. This is a real adventure, Rex. In years to come it'll be a great story for these boys to tell."

"I love you so much, Lin." He watched her closely for a moment, then dropped her arm.

Lindsay turned away, feeling sad. Both of them knew there would be no more nights of secret lovemaking. A tent was a luxury too heavy to carry when they had six young boys who needed food and other supplies.

And after they reached the safety of the base camp, Lindsay intended to resume their easy, casual friendship. It would be as if that night of sweet passion had never happened.

Tears burned in her eyes, blurring the trees and the campfire in a haze of color. She bit her lip and set grimly to work, trying to concentrate on sorting and packing their food supplies.

CHAPTER FIFTEEN

AN HOUR LATER the camp was fully dismantled, and painful decisions had been made about what to take and what to leave behind. The boys hoisted the extra supplies into more of the bear-proof slings overhead, hoping Sam would be coming up soon with fresh horses to recover their gear.

Lindsay helped to outfit each boy with a pack and bedroll. Then Rex loaded a massive bundle on his own back and another on Clint's that contained extra food supplies and one of the first-aid kits.

Over Rex's objections, Lindsay also carried a larger pack than the boys, but much of its bulk consisted of additional dry clothes for the rest of the group.

Even Danny had a small pack containing a change of clothes and some dried food. He set out bravely on the trail, his small legs pumping as he marched along behind Lindsay.

To add to their misery, a chilly rain began to fall a few hours after they began their homeward trek. They were able to stay reasonably dry in their slickers and plastic-covered hats, but the rocky trail grew increasingly slick and treacherous.

Lindsay remained in front, picking her way carefully, trying not to think about the miles and the cold wet days and nights ahead of them before they reached any kind of safety.

As she walked, her mind kept filling with images of Rex,

who was now far behind on the trail, bringing up the rear of their long file of hikers.

The night in his arms had been so wondrous, so sweet and utterly fulfilling. Lindsay knew by now that she'd been in love with him all these years and never allowed herself to realize it, because she'd disapproved of his life-style and the choices he was making.

But who was she to disapprove of anybody, or make any kind of moral judgments?

At a point where an old rockfall nearly covered the path, she pushed her miserable thoughts aside and stopped walking.

"Let's take a break, guys," she called to the straggling file of boys behind her, trying to keep her voice cheerful. "Everybody find a rock and sit down for ten minutes."

Gratefully they slumped onto the boulders, stretching their legs and leaning back against the rock face beside the path.

Lindsay looked in concern at the row of pinched young faces, then at Rex, who sat down next to Clint.

"How are you managing with those heavy packs?" she asked. "It must be so hard for both of you."

Clint grunted something, avoiding her eyes. Rex gave her a jaunty smile. "It's a piece of cake," he told her. "These packs are nothing for a couple of tough mountain men like us. Right, Clint?"

The boy glanced up, clearly startled at Rex's friendly tone, and seemed on the verge of speech. But he nodded and looked down again, shifting his feet awkwardly.

Lindsay smiled back at Rex, feeling weak with love and sorrow. "I had no idea you lawyers were such marvelous physical specimens."

"You didn't?" He gave her a glance of warm significance over the heads of the tired boys. "Then it was about time you found out, right?"

She met his eyes for a long moment, feeling her cheeks turn hot.

"Danny," she said automatically, turning away, "be careful, darling. Don't go too close to that bank, it's really steep."

Danny was near the edge of the trail, peering down into the misty gorge below. "I saw something moving around down there," he said. "It was big and brown. Maybe it's one of our horses."

"Or one of the bears that scared them off," Jason suggested dryly, blowing on his chilled fingers.

"I think it's…" Danny moved closer to the edge of the precipice. "Now it's gone," he reported, pointing. "But it was right down there, in the trees by that…"

Lindsay leaped to her feet and grabbed for him, but she was too late.

In one horrifying instant Danny's boots slipped on the rocky ledge, he uttered a startled cry and vanished over the edge of the trail, his small body sliding and tumbling into the void below.

All the boys shouted and began to crowd toward the place on the trail where Lindsay stood, trembling with shock as she stared down into the mist that had swallowed Danny.

"Oh, Rex!" She clutched at his arm. "What are we going to do? I can't even see where he is!"

Rex was already shrugging out of his pack. He gave her a brief, reassuring hug, then moved to the edge. "I'll go down and get him," he said. "You wait here. Danny and I will be right back."

"But…" Lindsay stared at him, her heart pounding with terror. "Rex, we can't even see where he landed! It's so steep. How will you…"

In front of all the frightened boys, Rex gave her a kiss and another smile. "Don't worry, sweetheart," he murmured. "Just stay here with the boys. I'll take care of Danny."

Before she could protest further, he allowed himself to slide feetfirst down the rocky slope, vanishing almost instantly into the mist below. Lindsay stood waiting, her teeth clenched with fear, her throat tight. The Bernstein twins waited silently on either side of her. Tim clutched her hand, while Jason held her other arm.

After what felt like an eternity, she heard a distant shout that seemed to echo up from miles beneath them.

"What was that?" she asked the boys frantically. "Did anybody hear? I can't make out what he's saying!"

Clint made a curt gesture and knelt to listen, his dark face taut with concentration as he stared into the misty void.

The muffled shouts came again.

"I think Danny's hurt or something," Clint told Lindsay at last. "Rex says he can't bring him up the cliff face, so we have to go down there."

She stared at the boy. "But...Clint, it's so steep. We'll never be able to climb back up that slope."

"Probably not," he agreed. "I'll have to take Rex's pack down with me, just in case."

"You can't carry that huge pack," Lindsay protested. "You're already overloaded."

"But what if we can't get back up here? We're going to need our supplies," Clint argued. "And most of the food is in Rex's pack. I don't want to leave any more of our stuff behind."

After a brief, tense discussion, they decided to double up Allan Larkin's load, giving him Lonnie's burden, as well. Lonnie, who was the next biggest among the boys, shouldered Rex's heavy pack, his plump frame quivering with effort.

He gave Lindsay a brave smile that tore at her heart. "I don't mind," he told her. "I like carrying all the food."

"Okay, everybody line up." Clint stood at the edge of the trail and looked them over.

In Rex's absence he'd automatically assumed command. Lindsay was so distressed and worried over Danny that she was grateful to the taciturn boy for making decisions.

"If you guys are ready," Clint said, "we'll go one at a time. Tim, you start off, then Jason. Lindsay and I will come last."

Tim peered down reluctantly. "It's so steep," he muttered. "And I can't even see the bottom. What if I just keep falling forever?"

"Rex didn't keep falling," Clint told the boy, giving his shoulder a casual, comforting punch. "And neither did Danny. There must be some kind of ledge down there. Just start out feetfirst like Rex did, go completely limp and let yourself slide."

Tim turned to the rest of the group with a gloomy expression, then lowered himself carefully over the edge and vanished into the swirling mist, his shouts growing fainter and finally vanishing altogether.

One by one the other boys followed, until only Lindsay and Clint stood on the trail's edge.

"Go on. I'll be right behind you," he told her with a shy, encouraging smile that briefly lighted his hard young face.

She glanced at him, startled, wondering if she'd ever seen Clint smile before. Then she shifted her pack into a more comfortable position, took a deep breath and let herself begin to hurtle downward through the shale and wet tufts of grass.

The journey seemed endless, a blind plunge into billowing mist. She slid for long time, her body jarred and buffeted by uneven terrain and jutting rocks. At last she landed with a thump just a few feet away from a looming boulder.

Lindsay sat up, rubbed her legs and felt for her pack,

which seemed miraculously intact. She looked around, realizing she'd slid through the mist into an alpine meadow bordered by stunted trees and rich with wildflowers. She almost sobbed with relief when she saw the little knot of boys nearby, and Rex running toward her.

He knelt beside Lindsay, touching her anxiously. "Are you all right?"

She struggled to her feet. "I think so. Did everybody make it down?"

"The boys are all here now. Everybody's okay except Danny."

Lindsay hurried to the group of boys and knelt by Danny who lay on the grass, his freckled face white with pain and one leg twisted at an unnatural angle.

"His leg's broken," Rex muttered at her side. "But it looks like a simple fracture. We'll have to splint it, then rig up some kind of stretcher to carry him on. I don't think he has any internal injuries."

"Oh, God," Lindsay whispered. She touched Danny's face and smoothed his hair. "You'll be all right, sweetheart," she told him, trying to smile. "Don't worry, we're going to look after you."

Clint had arrived and was already rummaging through his pack in search of the only first-aid kit they'd been able to bring with them. While Lindsay continued to comfort Danny and the other boys huddled together, looking hushed and panicky, Clint and Rex arranged their medical supplies in a businesslike manner.

Rex gave Danny a sedative and waited for it to take effect, then splinted the small leg with pine boughs and bound it with rope supplied by Allan. Under Clint's direction the boys used blankets and additional branches to rig up a makeshift hammock for Danny that they would take turns carrying between them.

The little boy was asleep by now, still deeply under the

influence of the sedative, and some color was returning to his cheeks.

"But he'll be in terrible pain when he wakes up," Rex told Lindsay, "and we only brought one of the first-aid kits with us. I'm afraid we won't have enough painkiller to last the trip, unless we get going right away. I want us to cover as many miles as we can before nightfall."

While Clint organized the rest of the boys, checked their packs and arranged for transport of Danny's litter, Lindsay saw Rex approach Jason and have an urgent whispered conversation.

Jason handed something over and Rex looked at it, frowning, then slipped it into his pocket.

Lindsay went over to him, feeling a growing alarm. "What's going on?" she murmured. "What did Jason give you just now?"

"He gave me the compass." Rex looked down at her, his face grim and tense. "We can never climb back up to the trail, Lin. Somehow we're going to have to find a way out of here on our own."

FOR LONG, exhausting hours they trudged and struggled through increasingly difficult terrain, with Rex using the compass to lead them in an easterly direction back down the mountain.

But the valley where they now found themselves was nothing like the lofty, rock-strewn trails they'd been riding on previous days. Down here the woods were deep and still. Tree branches often hid the sky so they seemed to move through a series of hushed green tunnels dappled with shifting light, and shadows that deepened as the day wore on.

The ground was littered with fallen trees and ancient uprooted stumps. Occasionally they traversed areas where springwater bubbled from the rocks and made the ground slick and treacherous.

They all took turns carrying Danny's hammock, trying hard not to jar his pain-racked body.

"Hey, this is a *lot* better," Lonnie said late in the afternoon, obviously determined to cheer Lindsay, who trudged along just ahead of him. "Down here in the trees we're getting lots of shelter from the rain. I'm hardly wet at all."

She turned to hug the plump boy impulsively. "You're such a ray of sunshine, Lonnie," she murmured. "A born optimist."

"As long as the food supplies hold out," he told her with a weary grin.

Rex kept them pressing onward late into the summer evening. By nightfall they were all so exhausted, the task of making camp seemed almost impossible. But Rex and Clint rallied the boys, encouraging them with promises of food and hot tea.

With a final burst of energy they all worked together, constructing three pine-bough shelters to protect them from the constant drizzle of rain that trickled from the tree branches overhead.

Lindsay boiled pots of water to make tea and soup from freeze-dried packages. They had little else except nuts, trail mix and Lonnie's dwindling stash of granola bars, since most of the heavier supplies had been left behind at the upper camp when the horses disappeared.

She worried as she served out the rations, knowing every one of the boys could have eaten three times as much, though nobody complained. After the meal they were too tired to sit around the fire and talk. Wordlessly, the boys dispersed to their rough shelters under the trees. Lonnie shared with Clint, and Allan climbed in with Tim and Jason. Lindsay and Rex took Danny into the largest shelter, placing him carefully between Lindsay and the wall nearest the fire. They rolled up a blanket as a barrier to prevent her from inadvertently jarring his splinted leg.

Rex got up to do a final check of the camp and their supplies. Lindsay watched as he threw more wood on the fire to keep it aglow, discouraging predators. Then he came back and ducked under the pine boughs, stretching his long body out next to her.

She leaned up on one elbow, watching the glitter of his eyes in the darkness. "Rex, I'm so scared," she whispered.

He gave her a warning glance and gestured at Danny's still form, then gathered her into his arms and whispered in her ear.

"I'm scared too, darling. But we're going to get ourselves out of this mess, and all the boys are going to be fine. We've already covered a lot of ground today, you know."

"But it's such rough going, and it all looks the same," Lindsay murmured against his throat. "How can we be sure we're not just going around in circles?"

"Because I'm following the compass. Remember when we started out the first day, and we crossed that road near the Bighorn Ranch?"

She nodded against his chest.

"Well, it runs pretty much north and south. If my calculations are right, we'll stumble across it again tomorrow or the next day, and then we can just follow it south to the ranch."

Lindsay thought about the rough deadfalls, crevices and bogs in the woods they were traversing. "That would be so wonderful, Rex."

He held her gently, stroking her hair.

Lindsay smiled bitterly. "All those things I thought I wanted in my life, the goals we chase after and things we worry about…they don't mean anything at all, do they? Right now, I'd give up everything I ever dreamed about, just to be able to walk on a road."

He drew her closer. "What have you dreamed about,

Lin? And what kind of things make you worry? I want to know everything.''

Even under these harsh and exhausting conditions, foot-sore and dirty and aching from hunger, Lindsay felt her body begin to respond to him. She sighed, imagining what it would be like to be back in civilization with a bathtub, a comfy warm bed, a kitchen stocked with food.

And Rex there with her…

"If we were alone together somewhere more comfort-able,'' she whispered against his cheek, ''we'd never get a single thing done. We'd just be all over each other from morning to night.''

He chuckled, a warm sound in the stillness of the night. "You know what? That's called a honeymoon, darling. And I think we'd better go on one right away, don't you?''

"Rex…''

"Marry me, Lin,'' he said, his voice husky.

He began to kiss her, his lips moving over her eyelids and cheeks, her mouth and throat and into the opening of her shirt.

Lindsay lay tensely, holding him, feeling the softness of his hair as it brushed against her breasts.

"Say yes,'' he urged in a muffled voice, his breath warm against her skin. ''Tell me you'll marry me as soon as we get out of here. If you'd say it, Lin, I'd be so strong, I could carry Danny and all the supplies and the rest of the boys on my back, too, if I had to. Just tell me you love me.''

She was silent. Tears burned in her eyes and began to trickle down her cheeks, but Rex didn't notice. He was still intent on kissing her breasts.

At a sudden sound from Danny, she sat up and leaned to touch the little boy's forehead, then turned back to Rex in alarm. "He seems to be getting warmer,'' she whispered. "I'm afraid he may be getting a fever, Rex.''

Rex reached across her body to touch the little boy's face and neck. Lindsay could see him frowning in the dim flickering glow of the campfire.

"You could be right," he muttered, "but it doesn't seem bad to me. At least he hasn't gone into shock, and that's what I was most afraid of. We'll take his temperature in the morning and give him some aspirin along with the painkiller if we need to."

"Do we have aspirin?"

"A bit," he said grimly. "Not very damned much. I hope none of the other boys get sick on us, or we'll be in big trouble."

They settled back into their embrace, huddling close together for warmth.

"Do you think any of the horses could be back to the ranch by now?" she asked. "It's been almost twenty-four hours since they ran away."

"I think a few of them could probably start to straggle in tomorrow, if they've kept up a steady pace. They'll be cold and hungry, anxious to get home. But like we told Clint, that's not going to help us much even when they start sending out search parties."

"Because Sam will think we're farther north on the lower slopes?" she asked.

"Well, he sure wouldn't expect that we'd be riding straight west into the mountains. And even if they do fly over us, how could we signal? Most of the time this tree cover's so heavy, they'd never see us down here."

Lindsay frowned, thinking. "But once we get lower and come out onto some of the open slopes, we'll be a lot easier to see, even if we are on the wrong trail."

"That's what I'm counting on." He stretched his long body, still holding her in the crook of his arm. "I only hope Danny can hold on till then."

As if in response to his name, the little boy stirred and

muttered something. Lindsay watched him in concern but he settled almost at once, his face twisting and grimacing occasionally with pain.

"Poor little sweetheart." She kissed him and felt the tears begin to gather in her eyes again. "He's being so brave."

Rex continued to hold her with one arm, staring up at the interlaced boughs above their heads. "Lindsay," he whispered.

"Yes?"

"Why do you keep dodging the issue whenever I talk about our future?"

She felt a rising panic. "Rex, this is pretty sudden, you know. Up until a few weeks ago, we'd never even considered such a thing. Now you want an answer from me right away?"

"It's hardly as if we just met on a blind date," he said quietly. "We've been friends for more than twenty years. I love you, and there's nothing about your life or background I don't know."

The words echoed hollowly in her mind.

There's nothing about your life or background I don't know....

Lindsay shivered and gripped her arms tightly. She could feel him watching her.

"Do you love me?" he asked.

She didn't answer.

"Look, that's not so much to ask," Rex said in a reasonable tone, though she could hear the tightly suppressed emotion behind his words. "Last night, I got the impression you had a lot of feeling for me. I'm pretty sure you weren't faking it. I just want to know for sure how you feel."

"I..." Her voice caught, and she swallowed hard.

"Say it," he urged.

"I love you, Rex," she whispered. "I really do love you."

The words released a floodgate of emotion. She ached to hold him, to nestle close and feel the comfort of his naked body against hers, to make love so he could fill and soothe and protect her. She wanted to tell him what she feared the most.

But she wrestled her feelings under control and lay stiff in his arms, gazing miserably at the fire beyond their shelter.

"Then will you marry me?" he asked again. She could hear the caution in his voice, and knew that he already sensed something was wrong.

Rex had always understood her so well.

"No," she said, choking on her tears. "No, Rex, I won't marry you."

"Why not?"

She shook her head in despair. "I can't talk about it while Danny's here with us," she said at last.

"He's sound asleep."

"I still can't. Tomorrow," she promised. "Somewhere on the trail, come and walk with me for a while and I'll tell you everything. It's a horrible story, Rex. You'll hate me after I've told you."

Even as she said the words, Lindsay felt a sickening wave of reluctance. She could hardly imagine herself telling him all the things that would need to be said, letting him know just what a wretched coward she'd been.

But Rex was entitled to the truth. Even if he wanted nothing to do with her afterward, it was no more than she deserved. At least he would know, and then there'd be an end to all this sweet teasing and talk of love and marriage.

"Let's get to sleep," she said, turning her back on him. "We've got another horrible day ahead of us tomorrow. We need some rest if we're going to get through it."

"Sleep," he muttered bitterly. "You think I'm going to be able to sleep after what you just said?"

"You have to."

"Tell me now, Lin," he whispered, gripping her shoulder. "You'll feel better, and we'll both be able to sleep."

"I've had to live with this for four long years," she said, staring at the glimmer of firelight on Danny's bright curls. "So what's one more night?"

"Lindsay, sweetheart…"

But she ignored him, pulling the blanket up tight around her shoulders and pretending to sleep. Silence fell in their little shelter, broken only by distant sounds of rustling trees and animal cries.

In spite of her bone weariness, it was a long time before Lindsay could get to sleep. And even as she drifted off, she was conscious of Rex still moving and turning restlessly beside her.

CHAPTER SIXTEEN

MIDAFTERNOON ON the following day, Sam pulled his blue pickup through the Bighorn Ranch gates at the base of the mountains, his hands tight on the wheel, feeling sick with tension.

He parked near the corrals where a group of men stood on one of the lower rails, looking at a milling group of wet, muddy horses. Then he hurried across the damp grass and climbed onto the rail next to the other cowboys.

"You've got some more of them here now?" he asked in alarm.

Karl Fuller nodded. "That's six altogether. The first one got here about an hour after lunch, and I phoned you right away. Another three wandered up half an hour later, and two more just came in out of the trees a few minutes ago."

Sam looked at the knot of horses drinking thirstily at an open trough. "They're ours, all right," he said grimly. "Which one got here first?"

"That big roan mare over there," the rancher said, pointing.

"That's old Duchess." Sam looked at the mare with narrowed eyes. "She must have brought all the others home. Duchess has been circling these same trails for twenty years."

He studied the horses, feeling puzzlement and a growing worry.

"One of them was still dragging broken hobbles," a cowboy said. "We took them off."

"A horse in hobbles?" Sam turned to stare at the man. "Then they must have run off during the night. I wonder how far they've come."

"It shouldn't be hard to find your boys," the rancher said. "We know which trails they were using, and we have a pretty good idea where they planned to be camping every night."

Sam continued to stare at the little herd of horses. "I don't like this," he muttered. "I don't like it one bit. Why aren't the…"

Before he could finish his thought, there was a shout from one of the men.

Four more horses straggled in from the line of trees bordering the meadow. When they saw the corral and the other horses, they nickered joyously and began to canter though the damp swaying grass.

One of the cowboys climbed down from the fence and opened a rail gate to let the newcomers into the corral, where they crowded their way to the trough and began to drink thirstily.

"More of ours," Sam said, watching the new arrivals. "And there's another one in broken hobbles."

"That's ten altogether," the rancher said. "How many horses did they take?"

"Fourteen." Sam was still examining the herd, trying to remember something. "They had eight riding horses and six under pack."

"So now they've got four horses for eight people?" one of the cowboys muttered.

"Four horses." Sam looked at the milling animals. "But which ones?"

The rancher stared at him. "Sam, I never thought there was an animal that left Lost Springs Ranch without your approval."

Sam shifted uneasily on the corral rail. "I've been…sort

of busy lately," he muttered. "Didn't pay much attention to their plans for this trail ride."

"Something's real strange here," one of the cowboys said. "I'm wondering about those hobbles."

"What's funny about hobbles?" the rancher asked. "They were staked out overnight when something scared them. Likely it was a bear, and then the horses all ran off together."

"Except for four," the cowboy said.

"Maybe the kids caught those four, or else they didn't run away in the first place. Or it could be they'll wander in later."

"But we don't know how long these horses have been traveling," the cowboy pointed out. "If they just ran off last night, they wouldn't have been able to make it back here already. And if they got away one of the other nights…"

He didn't finish his statement, but the other men stared at each other anxiously.

"If they got away on one of the earlier nights," Sam said at last, breaking the uneasy silence, "then those poor kids have already been on foot in the rain for a long time."

"Here comes Jerry," the rancher said, turning to point at a light plane that circled above the ranch and swooped in for a landing on the private airstrip beyond the corrals. A stocky man climbed out of the cockpit and came hurrying toward them, heedless of the rain that pattered on his sheepskin coat.

"Hi, Sam," he said, then nodded to the other rancher and the silent cowboys.

"Did you see any of the kids?" Sam asked tensely. "Are they up on the western trail?"

The pilot, who was a neighboring rancher, shook his head, looking baffled. "I can't figure it out, Sam. I flew over the whole trail two or three times, all the way out to the lake and the miner's cabin. There's not a trace of them anywhere.''

BY THE TIME darkness fell, the base ranch swarmed with people and the meadow near the corral was filled with vehicles. Most of the residents of Lightning Creek had driven down to help with the search. Many brought horses in trailers, and several more light planes had spent the evening scouring the network of trails at the base of the mountain range.

Sam worked with local police and forest service personnel who had organized an impromptu command post in the ranch's living room. Maps were taped to the walls and above the rock fireplace, marked with felt pen to indicate trails that had been searched.

The big kitchen had been taken over by a bustling group of women who made sandwiches and brewed gallons of coffee. In spite of the darkness, dozens of people were still out on horseback, riding the trails and reporting back to the ranch at intervals for a rest, some food and coffee and a change into dry clothes.

As soon as a team returned to the corrals, now lit with floodlights and filled with milling groups of people, another group would set off.

One by one the weary groups of riders checked in at the search headquarters to report their lack of success, along with the fact that rain was falling harder with every passing hour, and the temperature was falling to dangerous levels.

Sam prowled restlessly around the room. It was four o'clock in the morning and his eyes felt gritty with fatigue, but he would have given anything to be out on a horse himself, riding the trails, doing something besides twiddling his thumbs. He studied the maps and charts with baffled frustration.

''We've already covered most of the area close to the

ranch," he muttered to the room in general. "And a bunch of planes have flown over the turnaround point where they should have been by now. Even if the horses ran off two nights ago, those kids should be back in sight by now. So where in *hell* did they get to?"

Rob Carter put a hand on his arm. "Take it easy, Sam," he murmured. "We'll know a whole lot more when the sun comes up and we can send the planes out again."

Sam stared at the map without speaking.

"And there's some more good news," Rob said. "Jerry just told me Jamie Tailfeathers is driving up from Cheyenne. He'll be here before daybreak."

At this bit of information, Sam felt a brief surge of relief.

Jamie Tailfeathers was a Wyoming artist who was famed throughout the western states for his realistic depiction of cowboy life. But he was also one of the most expert trackers in the country, trained by his old Lakota grandfather to detect the smallest signs of human and animal passage.

As quickly as Sam's spirits lifted, they began to plummet again.

"Even Jamie couldn't find any tracks in this rain," he muttered, waving a hand toward the rivulets that lashed the darkened windowpane. "It's getting worse all the time. God, those poor kids. What if some of them are hurt out there? And Lindsay..."

His voice broke. Rob put an arm around him to steer him toward a couch. "Sit down for a while, Sam," he said. "I don't want to deal with you having a collapse on top of everything else."

"I'm glad you came, Rob," he muttered, allowing himself to be lowered gently onto one of the leather couches. "When did you get here?"

"Just a half hour ago." Rob sat next to Sam and stretched his legs wearily. "I was out past midnight delivering a baby, and then it took Twyla a while to find someone to look after Brian so she could come down with me. We finally had to wake up Brody's parents and leave him there.''

The words registered gradually on Sam's tired brain. "Why didn't you just leave Brian with his grandmother?" he asked.

Rob gave his friend a brief smile. "Well, that would have been a lot easier, but there was no way Gwen would stay behind. When she heard about those boys lost and on foot out there in the woods, she insisted on coming along with us.''

Most of Sam's weariness vanished in a flood of nervous excitement. "You mean she's here?" he asked. "Gwen is here right now?"

Rob nodded, looking puzzled. "She's out in the kitchen, making sandwiches. Why?"

Sam leaned back on the couch, feeling a whole array of conflicting emotions. He had a hunger to be close to her, to look into her face and see her smile. Desperately, he wanted to feel Gwen's gentle hand on his arm and hear her voice saying this wasn't his fault and everything was going to turn out just fine.

But he was afraid to go and look for her. The disappearance of the campers and their horses coming back without riders had shaken him to the core. Sam knew he couldn't bear any more pain tonight.

And that last blunt rejection from Gwen McCabe was definitely not the kind of hurt he wanted to endure another time.

Rob was on his feet, moving away to talk with one of the forest rangers. Though they kept their voices low, Sam could hear them discussing the danger of possible hypothermia among ill-equipped young campers stranded in the rain.

He thought of Lindsay, whom he loved more than all the world.

And little Danny with his cowboy hat dangling from a string and his face sparkling with excitement as he chattered about the upcoming trail ride.

Sam groaned aloud and passed a hand over his face, then felt a gentle touch on his arm.

He looked down to find Gwen McCabe sitting next to him in the seat Rob had just vacated. She was offering him a tray containing two hearty sandwiches and a mug of coffee.

"I think I got it right," she told him, trying to smile.

Her face looked tired and strained, actually frightened, but he could also see the deep concern in her eyes.

"It's pretty strong, but I thought you could use it," she said.

Despite Sam's wary caution, her very presence was a comfort to him. "This is all my fault," he told her without thinking. "I should have paid more attention to what they were doing."

"Now, that's just plain nonsense, Sam Duncan," she told him firmly, setting the tray on a nearby coffee table. She put an arm around his shoulders and hugged him fiercely. "None of this is your fault. And it's all going to work out just fine, you'll see. Rex and Lindsay are there, and they'll take good care of the boys. Nothing will happen to any of them."

Her words and her touch were like a balm to his frantic, weary spirit. Sam lowered his face against her soft mass of white curls, battling a sudden embarrassing urge to burst into tears.

THE NEXT DAY was the most horrible that Lindsay had ever spent. She was tired to the bone, deeply exhausted from long hours of struggling through the rain and cold, taking turns carrying Danny's sling as they climbed over downed trees and through cruel masses of brambles that tore at her clothes and her body.

They had no idea if anybody was searching for them, though Allan sometimes claimed to hear airplanes passing above the clouds, far to the south and west of them. But Danny's condition was worsening along with the weather, and they couldn't risk waiting to be found. They had to keep struggling back toward the ranch, hoping to run across a party of hunters or other campers, somebody who could help.

Lindsay and Rex had no time for the talk she'd promised. In fact, they hardly exchanged a word all day. Both of them were busy encouraging the boys and looking after Danny, whose fever rose at intervals, then ebbed with small doses of their precious aspirin supply.

Lindsay had a deep gash on the calf of her leg where a jutting branch had torn though her jeans the day before. The cut was becoming red and sore, obviously infected. It throbbed with pain, making walking difficult. But she kept the injury to herself, reluctant to add to Rex's burdens, knowing she would never use any of the medication that Danny needed to keep his pain and fever at bay.

More than anything she wanted to give way to despair, just sink down in the woods, bury her face against her knees and sob aloud in fear and misery. But that was a luxury she couldn't allow herself. All of them were at the edge of physical collapse. The boys looked to her and Rex to maintain an air of confidence.

In the midst of trauma, the separate personalities of the boys became more evident, and Lindsay was proud of all of them.

Tim Bernstein was the most delicate, and was suffering more than the others. He struggled along, his thin body racked by fits of coughing and labored breathing that his inhaler did little to help. But whenever Lindsay expressed concern, he smiled at her and waved his hand with feigned nonchalance.

"It's nothing," he gasped. "I'll be fine."

Jason was clearly worried about his brother and took over much of Tim's pack to ease his burden. The two friends, Allan Larkin and Lonnie Schneider, marched along together, too weary for once to argue and bicker, but they kept a steady pace and didn't complain. Lindsay was moved almost to tears by the way Lonnie shared his hoard of granola bars without being prompted.

Clint was tireless. He insisted on helping to carry Danny most of the day and shouldered extra packs for those who were bearing the other end of the little boy's makeshift stretcher.

From time to time he glanced at Lindsay, his face strained and unhappy, and she resolved to have a long talk with the youth once they managed to reach safety. Maybe Clint was ready at last to open up. It would be wonderful to have something good come out of all this mess, she thought wearily.

Making camp at nightfall was a chore almost too hard to endure. Lindsay boiled the pots of water and handed out bowls of soup, which the boys gulped down in silence before they retired to the one large shelter Rex and Clint had built. The rain was falling more heavily and they were all cold and shivering. The other boys surrounded Danny's sleeping body in the litter, huddled together like puppies to keep out the cold.

"Come for a walk with me," Rex said to Lindsay as he helped her pack away the cooking equipment. "The kids will look after Danny for a little while."

She looked up at his strained face, then got to her feet, too tired to argue.

They walked to the edge of the camp and into a thicket, along a narrow path made by passing deer.

"At least I hope it's only deer that use this path," Lindsay said aloud. "If we ran across a bear right now, I'd probably just lie down and let it eat me."

Rex grinned with a brief flash of his old humor, but didn't respond. Instead he sank down onto a fallen log in the shelter of branches that arched overhead, then drew her down next to him, putting his arms around her and pulling her close to him.

Lindsay huddled against him gratefully while he unzipped his jacket and wrapped it around her body. She burrowed into his chest, loving the feel and scent of him, the warmth and hardness, wondering how she could ever have thought she didn't love this man more than anything in the world.

"Now tell me what's wrong, Lin," he whispered. "What's been worrying you all this time?"

Lindsay took a deep, ragged breath. After four years of keeping her secret bottled up, never talking about it to anyone, she could hardly force herself to begin. But once she started to tell him, in a low, halting voice, the story came out almost of its own accord.

Rex held her, listening in silence.

"It happened four years ago," she said. "I was in Denver for a conference, staying at a hotel downtown. Somebody knocked on the door and I opened it without thinking. I guess I just assumed it was the chambermaid. A man pushed his way into the room and grabbed me. He had a knife and said he'd kill me if I made a sound."

"God, Lin! I didn't know anything about this! You've never…"

She rolled her head on his chest, and he stopped talking.

"This man was so awful, Rex. He was tense and jittery and filled with rage, practically foaming at the mouth. I don't know why he picked me to attack, but I've learned since that he stalks hotels and preys on young women who are obviously traveling alone.''

"He's the same guy who…''

"Yes, he is.'' Lindsay clutched him while the familiar horror rose in her throat, almost choking her. "Rex, just let me tell the story.''

"Sorry, darling. I won't interrupt again.''

Lindsay went on to tell about the atrocities that had been done to her. In a controlled, expressionless tone, she told of bondage and torment, of ridicule and savagery and hours of paralyzing fear when she was certain she wouldn't survive the night.

"He didn't actually rape me,'' she said. "He did everything else, every cruel and humiliating thing you could imagine, but not that. I've found out afterward that he saves rape for the end, the final act in his little drama. With me I guess he just ran out of time, because he untied me and left about three hours later. I was a total wreck, completely destroyed. Naked and shivering, howling like a baby.''

"Oh, sweetheart,'' Rex whispered.

"When he was gone I lay there for a long time, then got up and started having showers. I had six showers that night, Rex. For about a year I showered two or three times a day, until I finally realized I had to get myself under control.''

"I can't believe this,'' he muttered. "I just can't believe what I'm hearing.''

Lindsay ignored him. "The worst thing wasn't the pain, or even the humiliation of what he did to me,'' she said. "It was the total helplessness. Nobody has ever made me feel like that, Rex. I was so ashamed of the way I just gave in to terror and didn't do anything to fight back. I'm still ashamed.''

"But surely you called the police, Lin? You must have reported this right away.''

"I couldn't. Rex, I'm such a coward. He said he'd kill me if I ever told anybody. Somehow he knew my name and where I live, and he said he'd come after me, no matter how long it took. He said…" Her voice broke. "He said if I ever had a baby, he'd come and kill it. He showed me the knife, and told me in detail how he'd cut my baby to pieces if I ever told anybody about him."

Rex swore fiercely under his breath. "So you didn't ever go to the police?" he asked.

"I never told anybody. Until this minute, I've never talked about what happened. I had half a dozen showers, got dressed and packed up my clothes, then drove home and tried to go on with my life."

"But that guy…"

"He's still doing it," Lindsay said tonelessly. "A few times I've seen a story in the paper about some woman being attacked. It happened around the time of the bachelor auction, and again a couple of weeks ago just before we started planning this trail ride. But he wears a stocking mask now and nobody ever sees what he looks like. The police can't catch him."

"But you saw his face, Lin? Do you think you could identify him?"

She shuddered. "I'll never forget him. That face is engraved on my memory forever. I could pick him out of a lineup of five hundred men."

"Lindsay…"

"He still calls me sometimes," she said tonelessly. "Mostly he just breathes into the phone and hangs up, but a couple of times he's told me to keep quiet if I know what's good for me."

"The filthy bastard," Rex said grimly. "Look, you know we need to go to the police about this."

"But I *can't*," she told him in despair. "I just can't do it, Rex. I'm still so terrified of him. The thought of going to court and testifying against him, and having him in the same room and watching me..."

"I'll help you," he promised, his voice husky. "I'll be there every minute, darling. You need to do this or you'll never be free of him."

"I'm such a miserable coward," she told him, feeling hollow and desolate. "Because of me, other women have been hurt. It's gone on for years, Rex, just because I can't bring myself to deal with this."

"Of course you're afraid," he said. "Who wouldn't be? But we can do this together, Lin. You won't be alone anymore. I'll help you."

"No!" she said. "I can't do it, and I can't involve you in this, either. I'm a pitiful coward, and I don't deserve to have a man like you in my life. So just leave me alone, Rex. We won't ever be together, and we'll never talk about this again."

She struggled to get away from him, too distressed to think about her weariness or the cold, or even the throbbing pain in her leg. While he watched silently, she limped hastily away from him, back toward the camp, where the boys huddled together in the gathering darkness under their makeshift shelter of pine boughs.

CHAPTER SEVENTEEN

DANNY WAS GETTING steadily worse. The little boy spent a restless night in the middle of the shelter where he tossed and turned, his teeth chattering occasionally with chills, though Rex and Clint each gave up one of their blankets to help keep him warm.

Lindsay stayed up with him until after midnight, her face tired and drawn in the fitful glow of the campfire, wiping the child's forehead with damp cloths and trying to make him comfortable.

Rex looked on, his heart breaking with the knowledge of her pain. But she avoided his eyes and resisted automatically when he finally tried to force her toward her sleeping bag.

"Oh, come on, you're dead on your feet, Lin," he muttered. "You can hardly stand up. What good will it do us if we wind up having to carry you, too?"

At the curtness of his words she gave him a brief glance of despair, turned her back and crawled into the sleeping bag without another word.

Rex sat up late into the night with Danny, smoothing the damp curls from the little boy's forehead, cuddling him and telling him long, fanciful stories about Scout the dog and Rex's adventures with his little brother, who had been so much like Danny.

Funny, he mused, how a disaster like this brought all the buried pain to the surface.

Lindsay had finally been driven to confide her dreadful

secret, and even Rex himself was talking aloud about things he hadn't allowed himself to remember for years.

But unlike Lindsay, Rex wasn't tortured by his memories. Telling Danny about that long-dead little brother was actually a relief, a kind of cleansing that washed away decades of pent-up anguish. Rex found himself exhausted, but strangely light and free.

He looked at Lindsay's body in the sleeping bag next to the boys, her matted golden hair spilling onto the pillow, and wondered if there was anything in the world he could do to help her.

Pushing her to call the police wouldn't do any good, and would only make her more miserable. But until she could rid herself of the fear and shame of her experience, take command of her life and do the right thing, she'd never be free to love anyone.

His heart ached with the frustrating irony of finally getting close to her, and then finding this insurmountable obstacle standing between them. At the same time he felt a flood of tenderness and love unlike anything he'd ever imagined.

Rex could hardly bear to think that the force of his great love wasn't able to protect her, but this time he knew it wasn't enough.

Involuntarily he reached to touch her shoulder, then drew his hand back and huddled in the shadows again, looking down at Danny.

The cold penetrated to the core of Rex's being. He looked longingly at the mass of warm sleeping bodies, wishing he could crawl in among them and give way to the yearning for sleep that drugged his mind and made his eyes heavy.

A blanket slipped around his shoulders, and he felt a hard young body press close to him.

"Go to sleep for a while," Clint murmured in the darkness. "I'll watch Danny."

Rex shook his head and savored the warmth of the blanket, clutching it across his chest. "I'll be fine," he whispered back. "Get some rest."

"You're so damn stubborn," Clint said, but there was a rough edge of affection in his voice. "Whoever thought a lawyer would have such guts?"

Rex grinned in spite of himself. "Hey, lawyers are really macho guys, you know."

He held out the blanket and made a brief gesture of invitation. Clint hesitated, then settled down close to him. Rex let the blanket fall around the boy and held him in the crook of his arm, sighing with pleasure at the warmth. They huddled together in silence, listening to the stirring and occasional murmurs from the sleeping boys, and Danny's labored breathing.

"Is he going to be okay?" Clint asked.

"I don't know," Rex said honestly. "He's got some kind of internal infection at the site of that break in his leg. It's swelling and looking more tender every time I check it. If we can't get him to a doctor soon, I'm going to be damned worried."

"I feel like such a jerk." Clint's voice was hoarse with emotion. "What an ignorant stunt, putting those horses up front to pick the trail."

"You were mad at everybody," Rex said quietly. "And being angry like that can make any of us do stupid things."

He felt Clint's body stiffen with surprise. "How do you know what I was feeling?"

"Because I went through pretty much all the same things when I was your age," Rex said. "For a couple of years, I was so mad at the world I could hardly talk to anybody."

"You?" Clint pulled away to stare at him in the darkness.

Rex drew the boy close to him again. "What did you think I was doing at Lost Springs when I was a teenager? Attending summer camp?"

"But you're so..." Clint struggled for words. "You drive such a big car, and wear all those fancy clothes, and..."

"Listen, Clint, and I'll tell you a story." While the boy sat close to him in silence, Rex talked once again about the kind of childhood he'd endured, and the shattering death of his mother and brother.

"That guy *killed* them?" Clint asked in horror. "Right there in front of you?"

"Right before my eyes," Rex said quietly. "For a lot of years I felt guilty because I couldn't stop him from doing it."

"But you were just a little kid," Clint said. "Even younger than the Bernsteins over there, right?"

"That didn't stop me from feeling guilty," Rex said. "And it sure didn't stop me from hating everybody in the world."

"So what did you do?" Clint asked. "After they were killed, I mean."

"Well, mostly I did a whole lot of things I'm not very proud of."

"Like what?" Clint asked tensely.

Rex went on to tell the boy things he'd never confided to anybody in his life, details about the time he'd spent on the streets before he finally arrived at Lost Springs Ranch, and some of the crimes he'd committed in order to survive.

As he talked, he felt the boy's body relax against him in a curiously childlike and trusting fashion. Rex cuddled the youth as if he were no older than little Danny.

"So I know where you're coming from, Clint," he said. "I've been there. I've done worse things than you and still pulled my life together."

"You think I can pull my life together after all the shit I've been involved in?"

"I know you can," Rex said. "We wouldn't have brought you to the ranch if we didn't believe you had all kinds of potential, Clint."

The boy made a brief, choking sound. Rex stared tactfully at the fire while Clint struggled to compose himself.

"But what if we don't get out of this?" the boy said at last, in a low, strained voice. "What if Danny...what if he dies or something?"

Rex leaned over to feel the little boy's neck and forehead. Danny was in one of his brief spells of remission from the fever, sleeping comfortably, his skin cool to the touch.

"Danny isn't going to die," Rex said firmly. "Not while you and I and Lindsay have breath in our bodies. We'll get him out of here somehow."

"Lindsay can't even stand to look at me," the boy muttered, his voice breaking. "She hasn't said a word to me all day. She hates me."

"She doesn't hate you," Rex said. "Don't ever think that."

"Then why won't she talk to me?"

Rex looked again at her slim outline in the sleeping bag. "She isn't talking to anybody right now," he said. "Lindsay has her own problems to deal with, Clint. Believe me, she's not thinking bad things about you."

"What kinds of problems does Lindsay have?" the boy asked.

Rex remembered her whispered confession, her anguish as she told him the story of her torture and her subsequent fear. He thought about the four long years of suffering she'd endured and felt a lump rise in his throat again, almost choking him.

"I can't tell you," he said at last. "It's something she

needs to work out on her own. But believe me when I say she's not mad at you, Clint. She cares a whole lot about you, and wants to help you. We all do.''

"You really love her, don't you."

"Yes," Rex said quietly. "I love her more than anything.''

"So will you be getting married if we…when we ever get out of here?''

"I don't know," Rex said, his heart aching. "That's up to her, and she says it won't happen."

"Why not?"

"Because of these problems she has," Rex told him. "There's a whole lot of stuff Lindsay needs to deal with, and none of it's going to be easy."

"So, what can you do?"

"Nothing, I guess, except keep waiting and help as much as I can.''

"Before this trail ride," Clint whispered, his voice barely audible over the steady pattering of rain, "I was planning to run away. First chance I got, I was heading back to Denver to get into the gang again."

Rex felt a brief chill of alarm. "I see. And what are you planning now?" he asked, trying to keep his voice casual.

"If Lindsay doesn't hate me," Clint muttered, "I guess I'd like to stay at the ranch. I want to help with the smaller kids, and look after the horses, and learn all that stuff from Sam.''

Rex smiled in the darkness and tightened his arm around the boy. "Now, that sounds like a better plan to me."

"And someday…"

"Yes?"

"I'd like to go to college and get some training to be a social worker. It'd be neat," Clint said gruffly, "to help kids like you and me. There are thousands of them out there, you know."

"I know. The ranch can only help a handful of them, but every little bit helps."

"So you think I could do something like that?" Clint asked, clearing his throat.

"I'm sure you could." Rex hugged the boy again in the darkness. "Hey, man, if a smart-ass street fighter like me could become a fancy city lawyer, I guess anybody can do anything."

Clint made a strangled sound, and Rex realized it was the first time he'd ever heard the boy laugh.

"I was wrong when I called you a fancy city lawyer," Clint whispered. "I think you're one of the toughest dudes I ever met."

"And don't you forget it, kid." Rex cuffed the boy's shoulder in playful fashion, then moved reluctantly from the warmth of their shared blanket to check on Danny.

The fever had reappeared as suddenly as it left, and Danny was chilled and shivering again. His teeth chattered as he tossed his head and uttered scraps of incoherent speech.

Rex hurried to mash an aspirin in water and force it between the boy's dry, chapped lips. Behind him Clint moved around with tense efficiency, adding more logs to the fire without being told and boiling a kettle of water for some tea to warm the little boy's stomach.

THE MOOD among the searchers down at Bighorn Ranch was growing increasingly grim as each day passed with no sign of the missing hikers. Their search area was expanded all along the northern and southern base of the foothills in case the Lost Springs riders had somehow strayed off the usual trails.

"But it's useless," Karl Fuller told a wet, weary group assembled in the ranch living room on the evening of the third day. "Farther up the slopes, the tree cover's so thick a plane flying overhead probably couldn't even see riders down below."

"But this is eight people with four horses," one of the ranchers argued. "A group that big should be easy enough to spot."

"If they're all still together," another cowboy contributed, making a few people exchange startled, frightened glances. "And if they really do have those other horses."

"Why wouldn't they still be together?" Sam asked sharply.

"What if somebody fell into a cave? Or maybe a group of boys went off on their own and got lost. After all this time, you tend to start thinking something unusual must have happened."

Sam couldn't bear it. He looked around, craning his neck to see if he could catch a comforting glimpse of Gwen in the kitchen, but there was no sign of her.

Since that first night when Gwen held him while he cried on her shoulder, they'd barely had a word alone. More and more, he ached for just a few minutes with her, if only to sit quietly and feel the comfort of her presence.

"They have no more than four horses," one of the forest rangers was saying. "And they're going to need all of them to pack supplies. That means they're on foot, trying to make their way home in this rain."

"All the more reason they've got to be on a marked trail somewhere." Karl frowned at the big map above the fireplace. "But if they were, dammit, we'd have seen them by now. We've covered practically the whole network of trails."

"So what do you think happened, Karl?" somebody asked. "Did a spaceship come down and carry them off, or what?"

There was a dispirited ripple of laughter, quickly stilled. Jamie Tailfeathers came into the room carrying a steaming mug of coffee and a sandwich. Everybody sat a little straighter in their chairs, turning eagerly to look at him.

The young Sioux artist was slim and handsome, wearing a trendy nylon jogging suit and leather cross-trainers. He had close-cropped hair and an easy, confident manner. Except for the small copper arrowhead dangling from one ear, he looked like a stockbroker or accountant off on a weekend jaunt.

Jamie crossed the room with easy confidence and stood near the fireplace, bending to warm his hands before he faced the group.

"I can't find any tracks from the original party," he said. "They left almost a week ago. It's been raining ever since and the returning horses have come back down over their old trail."

The group digested this in silence.

"But what I did find," Jamie added, "is those horses that came home…they didn't come in from any of Karl's marked trails."

Still holding the coffee, he reached up with a slender, paint-stained finger to indicate a point on the map above the fireplace.

"It's hard for me to tell," he continued while the group listened, mesmerized. "The trail is rocky, there's been a lot of rain and we had to cross a few fast-running streams that hide all tracks. But we took one of the police dog handlers along this afternoon and he pretty much confirms my theory."

Jamie smiled his thanks to Karl Fuller, who handed him a riding crop to use as a pointer.

"It looks like the horses came back down from a point above this trail here." He indicated a thin line at the top of the map, an area that had not yet been searched because it went high into the mountains.

Sam stared up in disbelief, then looked at the handsome young tracker.

"Jamie, that can't be true," he protested. "You're showing a point practically at the summit. Nobody in their right mind would take those kids so high."

"And don't you always let the horses pick the trail?" Karl asked, turning to Sam.

"That's right." Sam frowned. "None of our horses would head up that way. They're trained to make a circle through the foothills, with just a day or two of high climbing to give the kids a thrill."

Jamie looked at him with sympathy. "In my opinion, Sam, your horses got way off track somehow. And," he said gently, "I'm afraid your boys may be getting a lot more thrill than they bargained for."

Sam felt a clammy touch of dread. He settled back on the couch, listening to the rush of conversation around him.

Karl and the forest rangers argued over whether they had enough information to warrant taking helicopters up into the mountain peaks in search of the missing boys. Rob Carter talked grimly about the rain and chill at higher altitudes, and the possible health dangers as a result of exposure.

Because the local residents had such faith in Jamie Tailfeathers, it didn't occur to any of the searchers to argue with his assessment. Many of these men had watched him find a trail across solid rock, searching out scraps of fallen shale, tiny bits of pollen brushed off shoes, traces of nettles dropped by passing animals.

Eventually new rescue plans were made based on Jamie's conclusions.

The horseback forays were immediately disbanded, with the new approach being to fly groups up by helicopter as soon as it was daylight, and drop them on the higher trails after setting prearranged meeting points to fly in supplies and relief personnel.

Sam listened to it all through a blur of fatigue. Embarrassing tears misted briefly in his eyes.

Just tired, he thought, brushing impatiently at the tears with his shirtsleeve.

A man got so worn-out, he didn't know what he was doing.

He got up and left, pulled his jacket from among a stack of them on a table on the back porch, then wandered out onto the ranch veranda and sat on the porch swing, staring up at the darkening mountains while rain drummed on the cedar shakes of the roof overhead.

Somewhere up there in the forbidding expanse of mist-shrouded trees were Rex and his boys. And Lindsay, his darling girl...

He brushed again at his eyes, then felt a gentle hand on his arm. Gwen was sitting on the swing next to him. She took hold of his hand and gripped it firmly in both her own. Sam felt a soothing warmth begin to steal over him, but all he could do was smile and mutter a brief hello.

"Oh, poor Sam," she whispered. "You're just worn-out, aren't you?"

"I looked around for you the past couple of days," he said. "But you're always either busy in the kitchen or I can never find you."

"There's so much work to do, feeding all these people." Gwen leaned back in the swing, sighing. "Every now and then a bunch of us go upstairs and have a communal nap while the other shift is working."

"Have you been here the whole time?" Sam looked at her through eyes gritty with tiredness.

"Twyla and I went home yesterday for a few hours to get fresh supplies and check on Brian. It was pretty hard for me to come back," she confessed, her face turning pink. "But still, not as bad as I'd expected."

"You're finding it hard because of all the work?" he asked in sympathy. "Or the discomfort of living here with so many other people?"

"Oh, goodness, neither of those."

She shook her head so vigorously that the white curls bounced. Then she looked into his face as if searching for something.

"You really don't know, do you Sam? Nobody's ever told you...about me," she concluded awkwardly.

"What about you?"

"I have agoraphobia, Sam. I can't leave the house. When I go out into unfamiliar places, I get terrible panic attacks."

He stared at her. "You mean, like the one you had that day when the owl..."

"Exactly like that."

Gwen still held his hand. Automatically, she began to stroke and caress his fingers, with a touch so comforting that Sam hoped she'd never stop.

"I've been a virtual prisoner in that house for years," she said. "I've been trying to get better, but sometimes it seems impossible."

Sam leaned back and cleared his throat. "What causes something like that?"

"It's usually the result of trauma. Some awful things have happened to me, Sam. But," she added, looking down at their linked hands, "nobody's much interested in hearing about other people's troubles."

"I'm interested in everything about you, Gwen," he said huskily. "Every little thing that ever happened to you in your whole life."

She smiled, her face pink with surprise and pleasure. "You are?" she whispered.

He nodded solemnly. "Every single thing."

She met his eyes, then looked down again. "When I told you I couldn't…go out with you," she whispered, "I know how much it hurt you. But it hurt me even more. Sam, I was dying to go and have a nice dinner with you, and do some dancing, and talk and laugh and feel young. I cried all night after you went away, and hated myself for being such a mess."

"Oh, Gwen…" He freed his hand gently so he could reach out a long arm and draw her close to him.

Gwen snuggled into his embrace. Sam thought he'd never felt anything quite so wonderful.

"Is it getting better?" he asked. "Did it help at all to force yourself to come this far, and stay away from home for days on end?"

"Much better," she said against his shirtfront. "This was kind of a brutal shock therapy, all right. But I'm feeling really optimistic. With all the worry about those poor little boys, I haven't had a single panic attack since I got here."

"When you turned me down," he murmured against her hair, "I thought you just had no time for a clumsy old bald geezer who doesn't even know how to talk to women."

"Well," she said with a touch of asperity, "that just shows how much *you* know, Sam Duncan."

He chuckled and drew her closer.

It would be nice, Sam thought drowsily, to sit like this for the next twenty years, just rocking with her in the porch swing while they watched the world go by.

If only…

"They'll find your boys," she whispered as if reading his mind. "Now that Jamie knows where the horses came from, they have something to go on. You'll see, we'll have them all back safely by morning."

"God, I hope so, Gwen. I just can't…"

Sam's voice broke. Gwen got to her feet and drew him up, steering him toward the door. "I'm going to find you a bed, and see that you lie down on it for at least a couple of hours. You're practically dead on your feet.''

''But I can't...''

''Sam,'' she told him, ''if you and I are going to be friends, you have to learn not to be so damned stubborn. Okay?''

He smiled down at her wearily. ''I sure do want to be friends with you, Gwen.''

''Well, good. Then behave yourself.''

She looked so fierce that he had to suppress a chuckle when she led him into a sleeping room and helped him lower his long body into one of the makeshift beds.

Gwen sat next to him while he drifted off. Sam was sure that just before sleep claimed him, she began to stroke his face with her gentle hand. For a moment he thought maybe she even bent and kissed his cheek.

But he might have been dreaming that part, because he was asleep before he could react.

CHAPTER EIGHTEEN

LINDSAY WAS DREAMING about a room where one wall was all glass, looking out on a tranquil blue ocean. In her dream she lay in a bed shaped like a pair of wings, and her naked body was heaped in flowers.

Rex stood next to her, also naked, holding a silver bowl. He drew a handful of petals from the bowl and sprinkled them over her, letting them fall softly around her like warm flakes of snow.

He was so handsome, and the room was beautiful, and the loving passion in his eyes made her want to cry. She reached for him, drew him closer, began to touch and caress him....

Suddenly she woke amid the group of sleeping boys and looked around, blinking at the rough pine boughs overhead and the cold gray sky beyond the opening of the shelter.

The shift to reality was so abrupt and painful that she couldn't hold back the tears any longer. In her dream they'd been tears of love and happiness, but now they felt bitter, as corrosive as acid.

She remembered telling Rex about her attack, and wondered what he must think of the cowardly way she'd kept the truth to herself all these years.

Fortunately, Rex seemed unaware of her. His attention was wholly fixed on Danny, who still clutched his teddy bear, though by now it looked as ragged and dirty as the rest of the campers.

Lindsay got up, splashed a bit of water on her face and

limped over to stand next to them. Rex glanced up at her, his eyes shadowed with fatigue, his jaw heavily stubbled.

"My God." Lindsay stared at him. "You didn't get a wink of sleep all night, did you?"

"I'll be fine," he said, trying to smile. "Anyhow, most people sleep a whole lot more than they need to. Right, Clint?"

The boy nodded, passing by with a steaming kettle. "I'm making soup for the boys," he told Lindsay. "And there's nothing else to do right now. You can lie down and rest a bit more if you like."

Clint's offer sounded incredibly tempting. All at once she realized how weak she was, even light-headed. In fact, if she hadn't sat quickly on a nearby blanket, she would have fallen.

Rex was at her side instantly, kneeling close to her. "What's wrong?" he asked, putting a hand on her forehead. "Are you feeling sick?"

"Just…it's nothing." Lindsay shook her head, a big mistake because her temples began to ache with a dull throb. "I'm tired and hungry, that's all. How's Danny this morning?"

"He needs a doctor," Rex said grimly. "If we don't get out of here today, I'm going to leave you all with Clint and strike out on my own tonight. Alone, I could move so much faster. Besides, I can walk all night without wasting time to make a camp."

"No!" She clung to him in panic. "We can't split up the group, Rex. We have to stay together. What if you were…"

Rex waved a hand to cut her off. He tore some fabric from her jeans to examine the cut on her leg, then rocked back on his heels, frowning.

"Oh, *hell*," he muttered, looking at the angry red gash. "Dammit to hell."

In her weariness Lindsay felt another wave of familiar shame and guilt, as if she'd done something wrong. But Rex caught her expression and gathered her into his arms, kissing her cheek.

"Sorry, Lin," he murmured. "Pay no attention to me. I'm just a little cranky today."

A little cranky today, she thought, watching bleakly as he turned back to Danny.

Rex sounded as if his newspaper had been delivered half an hour late, or there weren't enough cinnamon sprinkles on his latte.

He was going without food or sleep, carrying a double pack, caring for Danny around the clock while he bore the responsibility for the whole group on his shoulders.

And the man observed that he was feeling "a little cranky."

Through a blur of mist and sorrow, she watched Rex and Clint prepare breakfast, then help the boys break camp and load their gear. They made arrangements for the first shift to carry Danny who was now sleeping deeply, his face pale and still.

"Oh, Rex. Is he..." Lindsay stared at the little boy in alarm, one hand covering her mouth.

"He's okay," Clint said, pausing to drop an arm around her shoulders. "Danny's just sleeping right now. Rex and I have managed to get his fever down again, but we had to use the last of our medicine."

Lindsay nodded and forced a smile. "Clint, you're such a rock," she whispered through her waves of pain. "I don't know how we'd ever be able to manage without you. And I want to...thank you for it."

To her surprise, the boy's face blazed with happiness, and tears glistened in his eyes.

"You look to be in pretty rough shape," he murmured,

gazing down at her in concern. "You want us to rig up one of those hammocks for you, Lindsay?"

"Of course I don't," she said. "I fully intend to walk out of here on my own two feet."

She turned and took her place in the ragged file of boys heading into the trees. They moved steadily downward, all of them speculating how long it would be until they came across some kind of beaten trail that would lead them home.

As they trudged along, hour after grueling hour until the day began to darken once again into night, Lindsay's fevered brain skipped from one image to another in random fashion.

She saw her father, sturdy and happy, working with all the boys at Lost Springs. And Rex at fifteen, hard-edged and handsome, giving her a lazy, meaningful smile that took her breath away.

His beloved face vanished, replaced by that grinning monster in the hotel room, and the way he'd robbed her of every shred of pride and dignity and self-worth, terrorizing her all these years....

"I can't go to the police," she whispered to Rex's distant back. "Don't you see I just *can't*?"

But Rex was carrying Danny all by himself at the moment, slogging through the rain, and he didn't hear a word she said.

Lindsay began to dream of things she'd like to eat, remembering her favorite meals of all time, arguing with herself over which kind of salad would go best with which entré.

And the dessert would have to be...

She stumbled and fell headlong in a morass of swampy soil littered with pine needles. Rex and the others had vanished into the trees ahead, but Lonnie Schneider was soon there beside her, helping her up. Ineffectually, he tried to clean some of the wet muck from her clothes and her hair.

"Never mind, Lonnie," she said, her teeth chattering with the cold. "I'm afraid my personal grooming is beyond repair. It's going to take more than a brushing to get me tidy again."

"Hey, you and me both," the boy said.

Lonnie looked exhausted, and seemed to have lost about ten pounds. His cheeks were thinner, his eyes darkly shadowed. Nevertheless, he dug into his pack and found a granola bar, holding it out with a smile that lit up his dirty face.

"It's my last one," he said. "Here, take it."

Lindsay hesitated, then took the bar, opened its tattered wrappings and split it in half, offering the other part to the boy. They stumbled along side by side, dripping mud and rain as they savored bites of the chocolate-covered bar.

"Food for the gods," Lindsay murmured with her mouth full. "Pure ambrosia."

"If you could have anything in the world right now," Lonnie asked, "what would you want?"

Lindsay considered his question blearily, knowing he was trying to keep her alert and on her feet.

"A hot, hot bath," she said. "With scented bubbles." She sighed, picturing this lovely vision. "And on the counter," she added, warming to her fantasy, "there's a warm fuzzy bathrobe and some clean flannel pyjamas. And just next door there's a big soft bed waiting for me. The covers are all turned back. The sheets are brand-new, and the pillows are huge and fluffy and music is playing somewhere."

She stumbled over an outcropping of rock, making her leg ache fiercely, and would have fallen to her knees if Lonnie hadn't caught her.

"What about you?" she panted, struggling to stand erect again.

"If I could have anything in the world," he said, "I'd start with a big bucket of…"

But at that moment a call came ringing out of the woods ahead of them, announcing Lonnie's turn to carry Danny's litter. The boy yelled back and splashed off through the puddles, his slicker flapping around his legs in ragged tatters.

Lindsay watched him go and pushed herself to keep walking through her fog of pain and weariness, trying to recapture that warm sweet vision of the scented bath and clean bed.

What she hadn't told Lonnie was that her imaginary bed was far from empty.

Rex lay there, waiting for her, and Lindsay smiled at him.

He had the covers turned back over his broad hairy chest, and his hands folded behind his head in leisurely fashion.

"I never knew you had so much hair on your chest, darling," she told him.

She'd spoken aloud again, but it made no difference. The wind caught her words and whipped them away, far into the distant mountains.

"I didn't know anything about you," she went on. "I thought you never cared about anything but money, Rex. I was wrong about everything. And now it's too late, because I've ruined my whole life."

She knew she was crying when the tears that coursed down her cheeks were hotter than the steady drumming of rain on her face.

But now the dream was back. She stood next to the bed, opening her robe and stepping out of the pyjamas. Rex reached out to draw her close, stroking her breasts with a gentle hand.

"It's all right, sweetheart," he whispered. "That whole

nightmare is over and we can be together all the time now.''

''Which nightmare?''

''The man who attacked you. He's gone, sweetheart.''

''But where is he? How can it be over?'' she asked in confusion.

''Because you did the brave thing, darling. You made it right. I'm so proud of you....''

His face faded, along with the music, the inviting bed and the scented bathroom.

Alone with her cold and pain, Lindsay gulped back a sob and stared up at the unforgiving mountains, then down at the muddy trail, wondering how she could go on.

One foot in front of the other.

By now she could hardly bear to put weight on her swollen leg. She used a fallen tree branch as a crutch, dragging herself along, knowing she had to keep moving.

One foot in front of the other, two steps and then a rest. Two steps and a rest...

Rex is just ahead of you. If you keep walking, you'll get to see Rex again. Keep walking. Just a few more steps...

She was alone in a clearing. Some of the boys had vanished into the trees ahead of her, shepherded by Rex, who always supervised Danny's litter. The twins, under Clint's guardianship, were still behind her.

So when she heard the chorus of shouts, it was hard to tell where they were coming from.

Ahead or behind?

Lindsay looked around in confusion, then decided to keep struggling forward, simply because she couldn't bear to retrace the path she'd already come. Every step was such a battle.

The yells increased in volume, accompanied by a noise she couldn't identify. Lindsay floundered into the trees and hauled herself along the trail they'd made just ahead of her.

The undergrowth was thick and she had to climb over boulders in places, an almost impossible task.

She was about to give in and lie down for a rest under the wet trees when Rex arrived, running toward her, his sunken eyes alight above dark-stubbled cheeks. Without a word he swept her into his arms and carried her out of the brush to another clearing, where a wide-bellied rescue helicopter stood waiting for them.

NEXT MORNING, Lindsay woke in a bed by a window. It wasn't the bed of her dreams, shaped like a pair of wings and brimming with flower petals, but it felt almost as heavenly.

The sheets were white and crisp, the pillow was soft, and everything smelled so wonderfully clean.

"Heaven," she whispered aloud. "Wherever I am, this is pure heaven."

Her throat was raspy, her lips chapped and dry. On the bedside table she saw a water glass with a bent straw, picked it up and drank thirstily, then began a cautious exploration of herself.

She wore a soft cotton hospital gown that opened in the back. Her hair had been freshly washed and felt like silk, such an unexpected treat that she couldn't stop fingering it in drowsy satisfaction.

On her left leg she sensed a heavy bandage. But there was no pain, though the infected calf had been incredibly tender by the time they were rescued.

She had a moment of terror, wondering if they'd amputated her leg. When she lifted the covers and peered under, Lindsay saw the outline of her foot and ankle, and sank back with relief against the pillows. After a while she realized the absence of discomfort was mostly related to her dreamy, blissful feelings when she stared out the window.

Obviously they were giving her some potent drugs to kill the infection and ease the pain in her leg.

She closed her eyes, letting herself fall back into a soft billowing mass of pink cotton candy that smelled like rose petals.

When she woke again, Sam Duncan was gazing down at her anxiously. Lindsay blinked and stared, then reached up to touch his craggy cheek.

"Are you real?" she asked. "Because sometimes I can't tell."

"I'm real, all right." Sam gripped her hand, his blue eyes glittering with unshed tears. "And so are you, thank God."

"It was so cold, Sam. For the last few days I couldn't ever seem to get warm, and my leg hurt so much...."

"It's a damned good thing Jamie told us where to look, and we found you when we did. Another night out there wouldn't have been good for anybody."

"Especially not for Sam," a gentle voice said nearby.

Sam moved aside to reveal a small white-haired woman with a sweet face. He put his arm around the woman with a touching air of pride.

"This is Gwen McCabe," he told Lindsay. "It's not real easy for Gwen to keep traveling around to all these strange places, but she wanted to come see you and the others."

"It's easier when I'm with Sam," the woman said, smiling up at him.

Lindsay had met Twyla's mother before, but didn't understand why it was hard for Gwen to travel. However, it was easy to see Gwen meant a whole lot to Sam, and that made Lindsay happy.

"Hi, Gwen," she said, extending the hand that wasn't hooked up to the IV drip. "I'm so happy to see you again."

Gwen moved near the bed and took Lindsay's hand, holding it in both her own and smiling tenderly. For the first time since Karen Duncan's death, Lindsay had a warm sense of being mothered, and realized it felt wonderful.

"Well, well." Sam beamed at the two of them. "Now there's somebody else who wants to talk with you for a while and the nurse said just two at a time, so Gwen and I had better go."

He started to move away, his arm around Gwen in a warm proprietary fashion that made Lindsay smile.

"Bye, Sam," she called.

Her uncle turned and gave her a little wave, then took Gwen's arm and left the room, pausing to speak quietly to somebody waiting in the hallway.

Lindsay held her breath, hoping fiercely that it would be Rex who came through that door to tell her he'd found a way to love her despite her cowardice. Her spirits plummeted when she recognized Clint standing awkwardly just inside the room, wearing pyjamas, cloth slippers and an old dressing gown.

But immediately she forced herself to smile and extend a hand.

"Hello, Clint," she murmured. "It's good to see you. How are you feeling?"

"Fresh as a daisy," the boy said with a shy, radiant grin. Lindsay smiled back, realizing with a little shock that until the trail ride, she'd never seen anything but a cold, surly expression on this boy's face. Now he seemed like a different person.

He straddled a vinyl chair, sitting on it backward with his chin resting on the top, and studied Lindsay gravely.

"You were pretty sick," he said. "Worse than any of us thought. The doctors were afraid you might have gangrene in your leg."

Her eyes widened.

"You don't," he said hastily. "It was a bad infection

but they've got it controlled with drugs. You're going to be fine."

"How about you?" she asked.

Clint shrugged. "I was okay as soon as they gave me a meal and a good long sleep. Most of the other kids are the same, except Tim. He's been having pretty bad asthma attacks. But they've got it all under control now. This is a real good hospital."

"And what about…" She stopped awkwardly.

"Everybody knows what I did," he said, raising his chin bravely, dark eyes full of pain. "Rex told them, then said he didn't want it talked about any more because the whole thing was over. The other four horses got back to Wolf River, about the same time as ours reached the Bighorn, and Sam and Gwen are driving over to pick them up tomorrow. Everybody seems like they've forgotten how it happened."

"And so they should," Lindsay said. "Nobody could have done more to help us and those kids, Clint. You were wonderful."

He looked at her gravely. "You haven't asked about Danny," he said at last.

Her heart stopped beating for a moment. "I'm afraid to," Lindsay whispered.

Again Clint smiled, looking so young and handsome that she thought wryly about all the hearts this boy would set aflutter in years to come.

"Danny's okay," Clint reported. "He and his teddy came through with flying colors. They both have big splints and bandages on their legs now."

Lindsay chuckled, then began plucking nervously at the blanket. "His infection…"

"It took them most of last night, but they finally came up with an antibiotic to kill it. His fever's gone now and he's just resting. They say he'll need to take medicine for about a month, but he's going to be all right.''

"Oh, thank God," Lindsay whispered.

The relief was almost too great to bear. She lay back and stared out the window, struggling to compose herself while grateful tears slid over her cheeks.

Clint got up and patted her shoulder, then tiptoed from her room with the ties on his bathrobe trailing.

Lindsay watched him go through a mist of tears and realized she hadn't asked about Rex.

There was still time to call Clint back. But she didn't say anything, because she was afraid of what he might say.

Her next visitors were the two female reporters from the television newsmagazine. They filed into the room and stood by her bed, looking totally unlike the intimidating, aggressive pair who'd visited her just a few weeks earlier at her ranch office.

"Sorry about all this, Lindsay," the plump blonde said. "When you told us about this trail ride you'd planned, we had no idea you were going to be giving us such a terrific story."

"I'm really glad you're enjoying it," Lindsay said dryly.

"It's great," the dark-haired reporter told her with enthusiasm. "We've got interviews from most of the boys and some of the people on the search team, all kinds of wonderful human interest stuff. We're putting together a minidocumentary."

"It should bring a whole lot more national attention to your ranch," the blonde chimed in. "And that means more money. It's a great operation you've got out there."

"Well, thank you," Lindsay said, touched by their warmth.

"We haven't managed to talk with Rex Trowbridge yet," the tall woman said. "Do you have any idea when he might be available?"

"I haven't seen him at all since we got back."

Lindsay closed her eyes briefly, then opened them to find the two women watching her in concern.

"God, you're brave," the blonde said. "Getting stranded up there with all those kids and bringing them back alive and well.... You're going to be an inspiration to women everywhere."

"You've got to be kidding," Lindsay said bitterly. "Me, an *inspiration?* I'm the biggest coward in all the world."

Tears stung her eyes and began to trickle down her cheeks.

"Hey," one of the reporters said, moving closer to touch her shoulder. "What's the matter?"

Lindsay hesitated, then took a deep, shuddering breath. She was still terrified, but it was time to break free of her painful memories. If she didn't do this now, she was never going to have any kind of life.

"Can I ask you something?" she said. "On a completely different subject?"

"Sure, anything."

Lindsay looked at their tape recorders and clipboards. "Off the record," she said.

"Absolutely," the dark-haired woman assured her.

"If somebody was the...the victim of a crime in this city a few years ago," Lindsay said, "and she finally got up enough courage to go to the police, who would she talk to?"

"Denver has a great police force. And there are a few detectives who deal specifically with assaults." The blonde looked down at her shrewdly. "That's the kind of crime this is, right? A sexual assault."

"How did you know?" Lindsay asked.

The other woman leaned over and patted her shoulder. "We see it all the time," she said gently. "You have to go for it, Lindsay."

"It's so hard to talk about." Lindsay gazed up at them from the bed. "Especially after these years of keeping it to myself."

"But the guy's still out there?"

"Yes, and he's still assaulting women."

"Then go for it," the blonde said, looking fierce. "Nail the son of a bitch. And afterward, if you want somebody to do a good, balanced story, call us. We'll be fair with you."

"Okay, but I don't want anybody to know about this yet," Lindsay warned. "Right now, it's going to be hard enough to talk to the police."

"Count on us. We'll send somebody over this afternoon," the other reporter said. "You can do it, girl," she added, patting Lindsay's shoulder with an encouraging grin. "Hey, you brought six boys down from the mountains. You can do this."

Lindsay tried to smile back, but she was too tired. Fatigue settled in her limbs, making them limp and heavy. Her eyes drifted shut, and this time she slept too deeply for dreams.

When she woke at last, the sunlight was fading and two people stood by her bed. One was a middle-aged man with close-cropped hair, wearing a sport jacket and tie. The other was a slender woman in slacks and a blazer.

Both showed police badges in worn leather folders and identified themselves as Detective Schmidt along with his partner, Detective Simmons.

"A reporter called and said you wanted to talk to us," Detective Simmons said. "But if you're not feeling up to it just now, we could—"

"No!" Lindsay clutched at the woman's arm. "No, please don't go away. I need to get this over with."

The two detectives settled by the bed and got out notebooks while Lindsay lay back against her pillows and stared at the window.

THE POLICE OFFICERS left about an hour later, hurrying out into the hallway, their faces taut with excitement.

Some of the boys stopped by to kiss Lindsay's cheek, pat her arm and talk about how awesome it was to be in the hospital. Clearly their adventure was already assuming mythic proportions, the kind of story that would be told for years, with many embellishments, by the boys at Lost Springs Ranch.

One by one the boys went away, and a meal was delivered. Lindsay ate it mechanically, yearning for Rex. But he hadn't come to see her and she was still reluctant to ask about him, afraid that he wanted nothing to do with her.

After supper she drifted in and out of sleep while darkness gathered in the sky beyond her window, filling the hospital grounds with misty violet light and long fingers of shadow.

Suddenly he was there, smiling at her, his blue eyes sparkling.

Lindsay couldn't tell if he was real or just another of her wistful dreams. Silently she reached up and stroked the hard plane of his freshly shaven cheek and felt his wry, crooked grin.

"It's really you," she whispered. "I thought you didn't want to see me anymore."

"Oh, Lin, how could you ever think that?" He leaned over to brush her forehead with his lips. "I've slept practically around the clock. Couldn't even wake up to eat, so they had me on IV fluids for twenty-four hours, but I had steak and potatoes for dinner just now."

"And you're all right?" Her eyes surveyed him with loving anxiety.

"I'm just fine. How about you?"

"I'm feeling wonderful."

When she said it, Lindsay realized the words were true. She was light as a feather, carefree as a child. And so much in love...

"How's Danny," she asked. "Have you seen him?"

"I just came from there. He's awake and talking with some of the other boys. They have the kids all together in one big room, and it gets pretty noisy in there. I couldn't stand it very long."

"We have to get started on the paperwork right away, don't we?" she murmured. "I want to adopt Danny as soon as I can."

She smiled mistily, then became aware of Rex watching her in astonishment.

"Something's different, Lin. What's happened to you?"

She ignored his question. "I never knew you were so handsome," she murmured dreamily. "Such a rugged, take-charge kind of guy, my big mountain man. I love you, darling."

Tenderly she ran a hand over his shoulders and touched his mouth, then let her fingers trail down his chest again, toward the crotch of his hospital pyjamas.

"My hero," she whispered, fondling him. "The best man in Wyoming."

He caught her hand and held it against him, grinning. "Do you care to explain this shameless behavior, young lady? Last time we talked, you told me you never wanted to have anything more to do with me."

"I talked to the police today, Rex."

His eyes widened in astonishment. "You *what?*"

"Two nice detectives, a man and a woman. I told them the whole story."

"Do they think they'll catch the guy?"

"They're certain of it. They already know who he is, but they need a witness who can give them a positive identification. They plan to arrest him tonight and charge him tomorrow after they get my confirmation.''

"And you can stand to go through with this, Lin?''

She looked directly into his eyes. "If you'll help me, I can.''

"Oh, Lindsay.'' He leaned closer to stroke her forehead and touch her face with a gentle, lingering hand. "Darling, I'll be there every minute. Every step you take, I'll be right beside you.''

Lindsay's heart overflowed with joy. She couldn't find the words to tell him how she felt. "But not...'' She faltered, then went on. "But not so far away, I hope.''

He looked puzzled for a moment, then understood. A light dawned in his face.

Careful not to jar her leg or disturb the IV in her arm, he lifted back the covers to climb onto her narrow bed, stretching out and sighing in pleasure.

Lindsay nestled into his arms with a sense of joyous homecoming unlike anything she'd ever known. Rex drew the covers back over them, stroked her back and hips, touched her hair and murmured words of endearment while she snuggled against him, kissing the warm hollow of his throat.

Hours later they were still wrapped together, sleeping deeply, when they were caught in the beam of a nurse's flashlight. Lindsay woke long enough to give the woman a drowsy, rueful smile.

The nurse smiled back, pulled the covers a little higher on their shoulders and tiptoed from the room, leaving them all alone in the shadowy stillness.